The Other Side of Death

Sarah Bluett

The Other Side of Death

Prologue

Helen loved to run at night. She found comfort in the darkness surrounding her, as she always liked to hide in the shadows. Every evening, dusk brought a flurry of bats rising from their daytime slumber, filling the clear sky with thousands of wings. Helen would mark this event with a quick check of her home to ensure it was clean and enticing before checking herself in her vanity mirror. Derek expected perfection, wrapped in a bow, ready for him to unwrap as he pleased. She often stared at her reflection with a critical gaze. If Derek expected perfection; Helen delivered.

It was about this time she thought about her nightly run. As she brushed her auburn hair, and selected a dress to please him; she appeared diligent in her commitment to him, yet would think about her feet on the pavement, music in her ears, relieved to run—but never far enough away to hide in those shadows permanently.

She tied her laces shortly after nine in the evening, sweat trickling down her hairline towards her lip as she bent to the task. The heat was stifling, but it didn't deter Helen. This evening, Derek sat watching the television, whiskey in hand, the ice clinking against the tumbler. He lifted the glass to his mouth, eyes ever watchful, even when he was doing something else.

She loved the dense air, the river lapping, and the other sounds of silence. It had always been a comfort, something she craved since she was young. Darkness made her feel whole and genuine. She was unsure why but suspected it had to do with the invisibility it offered. Or so she thought.

Her new hometown of Cooinda sat nestled in the northern part of New South Wales at the base of Mount Wollombi, an ancient volcanic mountain that rose from the rim of the Cooinda River over twenty million years ago and now lay dormant. The Cooinda River ran for approximately eighty kilometres, snaking its way from the New South Wales–Queensland border, heading southeast through a handful of towns until it reached the Pacific Ocean.

Cooinda, originally established in 1902, was like other towns found in the state's north. Everyone's business was open for inspection, and some of the families had lived there for generations. Helen began running at night not long after she and Derek moved. The town was full of old cane farmers and their wives, bored drug addicts, and uneducated youth who thought living off welfare was a rewarding way to live — or too stoned to care. Helen quickly learned to avoid town during the day unless she was with Derek or her parents-in-law.

The townsfolk loved it when she ventured in. Everyone wished to be her friend — as she became the wife of the wealthiest cane-farming son in town. Derek, a handsome bachelor, had moved away from Cooinda not long after finishing school, living in Melbourne, leisurely taking much longer than needed to complete a business degree while comfortably living off the allowance his parents afforded him. He was only twenty-six when he met Helen, and they married within a year.

Helen was stunning. All her life, she and her looks battled in a complex relationship. She knew she was beautiful. She hated how it defined her, made her miserable, and shaped her identity.

There was a photo from the turn of the century of a woman in New York City who fell to her death from the top of the Empire State Building, landing so neatly on the sidewalk she looked as though she was taking a nap. Her beauty captivated the world, and Helen thought it sad how the world remembered her beauty but not her name. She knew that after her own demise, people would not remember her other than her thick auburn hair, porcelain skin, and large green eyes—once described as "the gateway to the soul"—and, of course, her supple, shapely figure that men craved and often abused.

She left her home and cut through the cane field that surrounded the front of the property, separating their quaint cottage from the road. The long dirt driveway cut through the middle of the sugarcane that earned her husband's family a fine living. There was another driveway to the left of theirs. This one was wide and inviting, with a regal appearance. It led to her parents-in-law's home.

Theirs was the main homestead and sat self-righteously at the centre of the entire farm. It formed an elegant structure, built at the turn of the century by Derek's great-grandparents, who later added cottages for their growing clan. There were four cottages altogether, all sitting on the river's edge, spaced half a kilometre apart along Cane Road, which housed only these few homes and ran northwest out of the Cooinda town centre.

Helen always avoided the driveways of her own home and her in-laws, preferring the narrow trails that cut paths through the tall cane, allowing the workers to access the farm safely. This is where she headed now, starting with a quick walk and progressing to a jog by the time she reached the road. When she emerged from the cane, Helen was about half a kilometre from her own driveway, yet still on Cane Road. She tucked in her head as she turned right, comforted by the pounding of her sneakers on the asphalt, and the sensation of sweat as it trickled faster down her face and onto her neck.

She had begun running years ago as a teenager, and her lean body now moved fluidly, her feet barely contacting the pavement. Her heart rate quickened, and the humid air clung to her like a cloak, concealing her heart and pushing her further from her home, her life, her existence.

She almost ran into the car a few minutes later. With her head down and her concentration focused, the car loomed from nowhere, parked diagonally across the kerb, blocking her path. She changed her direction slightly so she could stay on the hard surface of the road, rather than the gravel along the sloping gutter. As she passed the driver's door, it opened, and she came face-to-face with a young man

"Shit, sorry," he said. His voice was low and fluid, like melting butter. Helen's heart jolted slightly.

"No worries." She smiled at him, her eyes careful not to meet his directly. As she sidestepped him, he grabbed her elbow.

"Please get in the car." His voice was so low she could barely hear him, and confusion seeped quickly into her consciousness.

"Get in the fucking car." This time his voice was sinister, and her brain caught on. Helen, with her heart thumping, regarded his gaze hesitantly. They were deep brown, like a river, filled with moments like this. His gaze caught hers, his hand still on her arm, and an invisible grip tightened around her heart like a vice.

"I don't want you to scream, or be afraid, but I need you to get in the car right now." As he spoke, he manoeuvred her swiftly into the front passenger seat, and before she even found the words within her, she was sitting in the seat, the door locked by the keys he miraculously held in his hand. He stared at her from the other side of the glass, holding the keys up so she could see them.

"Don't move," he said, and moved to the other side of the car, slid into the driver's seat, and started the engine.

The kidnapper moved east on West End, retracing her steps, onto Cane Road, which became Main Street. Then, he drove through town toward the far side, onto a long, solitary road, one Helen didn't know existed, or where it led. She stole a glance at her captor. He was handsome. Not clean-cut like Derek, but with an unkempt, rough quality. His eyes stayed focused on the road, his demeanour relaxed, unconcerned.

Her thoughts flashed back to earlier in the evening, when Derek stroked her hair as they sat on the lounge watching some menial show on TV, and a pang of resentment flared towards this man for ripping her away from the life she despised. She thought of the phone call she had made to her sister earlier that day that had gone to voicemail, and she wondered if she would ever see her again.

Death didn't scare her, and in her heart, she always expected to die young. How could she not? Everything in her life until this moment pointed to this. Her life was meaningless, and she knew it. The question she asked herself at that moment was, would she die because of her beauty? If it were to be, then it would be; however, she could not help but consider the irony of God's plans. She closed her eyes and focused on calming her rapid heart rate, praying to God, hoping he would reconsider the inevitable, as her captor sped away from her already limited freedom.

{ 1 }

Being a -town cop was a privilege Tom Turner had enjoyed for the last eight years. Tonight was no exception. A fight broke out at one of the two local pubs in Cooinda, which then escalated into two hours of patiently listening to patrons earnestly explain what happened. To Tom's ears, it was all candy and roses; he loved the town, with hardly any crime and warm, welcoming people, unlike when he'd been a cop in Sydney.

He listened to Jenny Newton the waitress explain the social classes of the town and how Henry Lowe had come into the bar with guns blazing after he found out his sister Julia was sleeping with, and now pregnant to Cain Lewis, who double-crossed him in high school ten years ago by stealing his high school sweetheart. Julia pleaded with Henry to make peace with Cain, reminding him that the past should stay in the past.

The response was not what Julia had hoped for, as Henry pursued Cain into the pub, to discover him bragging to anyone who would listen about how good his swimmers were.

Henry threw the first punch moments later, and it was all downhill from there. Before long, the bartender Josh (a sexy loner who had arrived in town a month before and who reminded the girls in town of Tom Cruise in Cocktail) had to call the cops to break up the fight.

Tom and Constable Louise Hunt had arrived shortly after, finding both Henry and Cain sobbing and hugging in the gutter outside the pub. A round of sloppy punches was enough to get ten years of anger out of their blood. Tom heard drunken expressions of "life's too short" and "I love you, man," as he desperately tried to stay abreast of the information Jenny was sharing with him, and he was now feeling weary and agitated.

He started his career in South Sydney and had seen more shit than he liked to talk about. Or think about. In 1990, after a messy divorce, he decided on a sea change and the areas of northern New South Wales needed competent cops. In country towns, it was the law enforcers who either made a community or broke it; Tom jumped at the opportunity to make a positive change.

Once settled, Tom found he loved country life, and he bought a little property in a tiny town south of Cooinda, with a population of around 650 people. Kanya housed a pub, a general store, and a family-owned petrol station, and sat along the old highway, once a popular spot for travellers to stop and have a cup of coffee by the river.

Cooinda's police station was the head of the entire district. He was a rural homicide detective, which meant he oversaw all serious crimes. The northern part of NSW rarely saw murder, yet he was always busy with other offences such as drugs, theft, and assault. It was a large district, and not once in eight years had he worried that he had made a mistake. Cooinda, including the surrounding villages, was home to about twelve thousand people, where rural crimes often depended on the good folks to help solve crimes. Compared to the pressure he dealt with in Sydney; it was a walk in the park.

One thing he loved most about his town was the friendships he'd formed over the last eight years. As he listened to Jenny, he looked at Lou and winked. Grinning, she led her longtime friend Henry over to a seat. She'd gone to school with everyone at the bar that evening. She and Jenny were as close as cousins, and Henry Lowe was her age, with his sister Julia a year behind them. Cain was a year above her and Henry, and he and Lou dated a few times throughout high school. It still astounded Tom just how much he'd grown to love small-town life. Cooinda breathed life into so many people. It's mountains and rainforests, with the rivers that run to the ocean less than an hour away. He knew the young people couldn't wait to get away from Cooinda and its boring nightlife; however, most of the time it drew its people back, enveloping them in warm, safe arms. He watched now as Lou navigated the confusion of Henry and Cain's explanation of their dispute, where Cain exclaimed to Lou, with tears in his eyes, "I'm gonna be an uncle, Lou! A freakin' uncle!" He slapped Henry on the back as Lou glanced up at Tom and sighed wearily.

Tom may have loved the -town vibe, but after growing up in Cooinda, and only ever leaving for a brief time while at the academy, Louise easily felt frustrated and claustrophobic. Now was one of those times. "Boys, I'm happy you have sorted out your personal business, but did it really have to be at the expense of the New South Wales Police Department?" She chastised.

"Sorry, Lou," they chorused, not really sorry at all.

Lou couldn't help but grin and shake her head in exasperation. "Well, if you have no other grievances, Tom and I will be on our way?"

The boys nodded, and Jenny added, "Thanks, Lou, thanks, Tom. Sorry to bother you, but Josh was just being a responsible bartender."

Tom nodded and looked over at Josh, who kept busy behind the bar. As a newcomer to town, it wasn't his place to get involved with the petty quarrels of the local riffraff.

Other than Jenny and Lou, he barely knew any of them. He arrived in town only after his grandmother passed away a few weeks ago, and he wanted to pay his respects to the last of his family he still liked. His aim now was to save money for a few months, then hit the road. In the last couple of weeks, he had befriended his co-worker Jenny, who then introduced him to Lou. Other than that, he kept to himself. He raised his hand in acknowledgement of Tom's thanks. "Just doing my job, Constable," and going back to work.

Tom and Louise left the bar with Jenny calling out, "I'll see you in church, Lou!" It was only ten in the evening, and the warm wind wove through Main Street, stirring up the pollen from the trees. Tom closed his eyes for a moment, feeling the warmth of the night air on his face, feeling blessed to be living in such a beautiful part of the world.

He was a lucky man. All that was about to change.

{ 2 }

The call came into the police station regarding a missing person a few short hours after Lou and Tom finished with the Henry Lowe and Cain Lewis fight. It was three in the morning, and Tom stifled a tired groan. Gathering his keys, wallet, and phone, Tom called out, "Lou, let's go; we've just received a missing person's call."

Lou, already on her feet, adjusting her uniform, nodded distractedly at Tom. "Right behind you, mate." Of all the constables Tom worked with, she was the most career driven. She never complained, never missed a shift, and was always happy to do her job. She had grown up in Cooinda, which sometimes offered a unique perspective on the job that Tom appreciated. Tom learned she was a great constable and a kind friend.

Even at three in the morning, the air hung low and still. Deep into February, the nights were often unbearable. There were many nights, even after years of living in this humid weather, that Tom would lie awake, the ceiling fan on flat out, sheets thrown off, his skin glistening with sweat as he would wait in anticipation for the cool change to come through. On these nights he would swear to himself that he'd have air-conditioning installed ASAP, but then a local would tell him air-conditioning was for outsiders, and he'd forget the idea, desperate to be a local.

Tonight was one of those nights. As he and Lou settled into the Police issued Commodore Sedan, he cranked the air conditioner, impatiently waving his hands in front of the vents as the cool air spilled into the car, vowing that 'enough was enough, I'm calling the air conditioner people tomorrow and getting a unit in my living room', and Lou smiled and nodding. They talked little on the short drive to Cane Road, each lost in their own thoughts and comfortable in the absence of chit-chat, as the local radio station played 'Burning down the house', a remake by Tom Jones and the Cardigans that had come out a couple of years before.

When they slowly turned onto the long, narrow driveway of Derek and Helen's home, Tom suddenly felt heavy with tiredness. As he stepped out of the car, he could hear the hum of the cicadas, an orchestra tuning their instruments in a low and persistent hum. Tom closed his eyes and listened carefully for the rumble of the semi-trailers about a kilometre away, as they broke speed along the highway connecting Northern New South Wales to the border of Queensland, where the sunny Gold Coast beckoned.

A feeling of uneasiness settled over him, and he glanced over his shoulder. The black night swallowed any light, and all he could feel was the warm, low breeze rustling the towering cane that surrounded him on three sides. The cicadas stopped their song simultaneously, and the abrupt silence made the hairs on his arms prickle. "What the fuck?" he whispered to himself. Even as he finished the words, the cicadas restarted their tune again in perfect harmony and unison, and the uneasiness left as fast as it had arrived.

Derek hung up the phone, relieved that the police would be over shortly. At least Tom understood it was a serious matter that his wife had disappeared; he should've known better than to let her go running. He paced angrily around the kitchen, trying to decide if he should wake his intolerable parents, or wait until Tom and dull Lou arrived. Helen had never been gone for her run for longer than an hour, and he knew she wouldn't be stupid enough to run from him, so in his head, the logical solution was that something had happened to her.

Derek was not the type of guy to panic, but he recognised the fluttering in his stomach, making him nauseas. He poured himself the last of his whiskey from the decanter in the dining room and began pacing their farmhouse. The house was meticulous thanks to Derek's insistence. Helen had learned quickly how to keep a home up to his standards, and after they moved back to his hometown of Cooinda, the cosy farmhouse which stood nestled within the cane of his parents' farm was a miniature version of his parents' grand farmhouse. Derek's family was wealthy and powerful in their world. Anyone who met them was quick to recognise their self-acknowledged power. Derek believed you would never meet another couple more arrogant, obnoxious, and wilfully ignorant than Mr and Mrs

Cox. Little did Derek realise; he was the arrogant and obnoxious one. His parents, hardworking and raised with gratitude for their land and their home, had failed to pass on their gentle nature to their only son.

Unfortunately, Derek and Helen's home was the closest to his parents. The other houses had tenants: a couple who worked for his parents as caretakers, and the long-time farm manager with his wife and adult children.

As the only child, Derek was very much welcomed home by his mother and father, who worshipped the ground he walked on and prayed he would become educated and one day capable of running their farming business once they passed. Derek, keen to get his inheritance, kept his parents happy by learning the business, but knew, deep down, there was little chance he would continue the family business after their passing. Cooinda was a hole, and he couldn't wait to get out of there and back to the real world, this time with his money.

Shortly after three o'clock, Derek heard a car making its way towards the house. He finished the last of his whiskey and made his way out to the front porch to greet Tom and Lou. As they parked, he stood on the porch to greet them. He had to admit Tom looked tired. The heat and humidity could be relentless at this time of year, and he almost felt sorry for the man for a moment until he remembered what was going on.

He didn't even bother to shake their hands but muttered, "Thanks for coming, Tom, Lou. Come inside." He spun on his heel and walked through the door, leaving it gaping for Tom and Lou to follow behind.

Tom took his statement, asking the standard questions. When had Helen left for her run? How long was she usually gone, and did she run the same route every night? He wrote everything down in his notebook. Tom finally stopped taking notes and asked Derek the hard question. "Did you and Helen have a fight tonight, Derek? Or any time in the last couple of days?"

Derek looked up sharply at Tom and then glanced at Lou as she stood and walked around the living room before moving into the hallway, heading towards the bedrooms, to ensure nothing was amiss. Derek knew Tom was just doing his job, knew Lou was just doing what she needed to do.

He finally answered, "No, Tom. No fights. Not today, not much at all, to tell you the truth. We're not the fighting type. She is an easy-going woman who enjoys her quiet life." He shrugged and looked up towards the front door, willing Helen to walk through it, smiled at her guests, and apologised for causing all the fuss. But the doorway stood empty.

Lou appeared back in the lounge room and smiled nervously at Derek, unsure of how to behave. They had known each other since they were young, and Lou's mother had worked for Derek's parents as their housekeeper for many years. Lou had only ever been in the main homestead a handful of times as a young child and had certainly never been inside Derek's home. She knew their connection embarrassed him. Her mother; the hired help. Derek had noticed her glancing around the house when she first arrived, curiosity winning over professionalism. Derek was used to being in control, and for the first time he worried life had taken a diving swoop, scooped up everything he held in the *'important, do not let out of your sight'* drawer, and was gleefully swirling it through the air while it laughed wickedly at his vain attempt to control everything. Helen was one aspect he needed to keep a firm hand on. Her beauty left her vulnerable; he had a responsibility to protect her. He loved her. He was jealous of her; she brought out a fierce contempt in him that even surprised him.

His mother, Ruth, always warned him she was too much for him. Dear old Ruth adored Helen and was always trying to keep one arm protectively around her. Protecting her from him. It seemed though she hadn't done a decent job this time. Helen had always needed protection from herself.

Out on the front porch, Tom explained to Derek what would happen next. "If Helen is not home by morning, or you haven't heard from her, I'll write her up as an official missing person," Tom explained. "The fact that she's left all her belongings here concerns me, and I am taking this seriously, Derek. If you need me, just call. Please. It's what I'm here for."

Derek nodded and watched as Tom and Lou walked back to their car. At one point he noticed Tom pause and look towards the cane, as though he was expecting Helen (or not Helen) to come walking out of the cane field. Derek looked towards the cane, a shiver running up his spine. As he watched, the cane parted, and he saw his wife walking toward him, her bloody corpse dressed in her running gear, a shoe missing, blood caked in her hair, her arms outstretched, and she smiled at him. A chip marred her front tooth. "Derek, I'm home..." her voice was low and deep. The image left him quickly, and he shook his head, trying to erase it. Tom and Lou were already reversing, and he could see Tom staring at him from the passenger seat, a bewildered look on his face, as though he had just seen the same image of Helen. Their eyes locked for a moment, scrutinising each other, until Derek blinked, looked away. He turned and walked back inside, shutting the door to the tall cane and darkness outside.

He poured himself a stiff drink. Whiskey was his first choice, but that was gone. Bourbon it was then. Adding ice and then recapping the bottle of Jim Beam, Derek took his drink out onto the back deck and sat in the dark. The river moved quietly in the night. The ripples met gently with the shore, and the soft hum of the insects added a melody that stirred Derek into submission. He closed his eyes and sipped his drink. "Where the fuck are you, Helen?" he whispered into the dark.

The unexpected vocal noise interrupted the churn of the crickets and mosquitoes, and the night was unexpectedly still for a few moments. Derek listened intently, waiting for his wife to appear before him once again, bloody, at the bottom of the porch stairs. He pictured her ascending, gently reaching out her hand to him, and his heartbeat quickened in fear. He opened his eyes and saw only darkness, and he sighed in relief. The river continued to ripple, and the insects returned to their activities. Derek put his drink down, buried his head in his hands, and sobbed.

{ **4** }

Rebecca lit a cigarette, inhaled deeply, and stared in fascination at the young man beside her. The room she lay in had high ceilings, with peeling paint and chips the size of boulders in the hardwood floor. Her low futon was in the middle of the room, and thin white curtains hung on the large, thin double-hung window, which led onto a fire escape.

Outside, the wind howled, causing the window to rattle continuously. To anyone else, it could have driven them mad, but Rebecca found the noise almost musical. As the ferocity of the wind and sleet rose and fell, her one window to the world harmonised itself, keeping her alert to any potential dangers, reminding her the world was not only full of beauty but also full of natural elements which were to be respected in their formidable presence. It was only early in the afternoon for her, but the weather in Brooklyn, New York, had been shocking for the last twenty-four hours, and she, along with millions of others, had played it safe, and stay off the streets. February was usually terrible, as winter dragged on, refusing to soften its ferocity, and in fact, displaying a continuous and horrendous display of snow, sleet, and never-ending darkness, before it would finally quieten down and consider making way for Spring.

Rebecca had spent the afternoon in bed, drinking coffee, smoking, and watching reruns of Seinfeld on cable until the neighbour Antony had knocked on her door for his weekly booty call, just after seven that evening. Now, a little before midnight, as she finished her smoke and admired Antony's sleeping face, she stubbed out her cigarette and leaned over and kissed him softly on his shoulder. 'Hey there,' she said, stirring him from his slumber. Antony rolled over and grabbed her breast. Next to the bed on the floor, her phone rang.

Antony said, "Do you often get midnight phone calls?" "Ignore it," she whispered. She opened her eyes to see Antony glance down at the floor and look at the caller ID, his large hand staying firmly on her breast.

"It's Helen," he told her. She shook her head, ensuring his hands stayed firmly on her breasts as she continued to move atop him.

"Leave it," she whispered. "Fuck me again, please. My sister can wait."

By dawn Antony had left, and Rebecca sat on the edge of her bed, her hair hanging wet around her bare breasts, smelling of lime and coconut after a hot shower. She dialled Helen's number, finally returning her call. As she held the phone to her ear, it rang a few times, then switched to Derek's voice from their message service. She hung up the phone without leaving a message, having learned long ago that Derek always 'accidentally' deleted her messages without passing them on to her sister. It was around dinnertime in Australia, and she assumed her sister was eating dinner or on her run. She placed the phone back onto her bedside table and flung herself back onto her futon, closing her eyes. The weather surely sucked. Hopefully, it would clear up soon, and she could get back to work. Being alone in New York City didn't bother her that often, unless it reminded her of just how alone she really was.

She drifted into a fitful sleep, the howl of the wind and rain rattling her brain into slumber. Her dreams were a confusing mash of images that flashed across her subconscious. She was watching Helen dance. In a slow, sexy sequence, her twin wore a short black satin nightgown that clung to her hips and breasts as she swayed to a melancholy tune.

Helen was watching herself in a large mirror that hung on a timber wall. In the background, Rebecca could see herself in Helen's reflection, watching her from a timber dining chair. The mirror hung on a wall; the only structure in a wooded area, and the timber chair she sat on was in the dirt. She too wore the same satin nightwear, but when she looked down, she noticed her feet were in wet, mud-caked runners. As she watched her sister dance, a feeling of uneasiness settled over her, and she realised they were in danger. Rebecca tried to stand up but felt glued to the chair; her arms and legs were like tar and too heavy to lift. She tried to say her sister's name, but only a frustrated hollow noise escaped her throat.

Rebecca awoke drenched in sweat on her bed in her loft apartment just after lunchtime. Her head was pounding from the wine she'd had the previous evening. She gingerly sat up and looked at her digital clock. It was 12:53 in the afternoon. The weather seemed to have settled into a cold, steady drizzle. The wind and snow had finally stopped. Sighing, she climbed out of bed. Shrugging off the strange dream, attributing it to the large amount of alcohol she'd consumed, she headed into work. She left her apartment just before two in the afternoon and headed to the city. After almost twenty-four hours of most folk being held captive by the weather, it was bedlam. She weaved her way up Broadway, and turning onto Walker Street, striding purposefully towards the design studio, headphones plugged into her Walkman, tuning out the noises of the street, she had forgotten all about her sister's call.

***

Four years previously, Rebecca had been living in Melbourne, sharing an apartment with strangers, working for a decent-sized creative agency.

As twins, she and Helen were extraordinarily close. Their parents were self-involved narcissists, and this further solidified the twins' bond. However, Helen had met Derek the previous year, and within a few months had been married and whisked away to bumfuck nowhere. Rebecca had been furious, although not at Helen. She had always been the 'weak, impressionable one'—which was bullshit. Rebecca understood Helen's longing for love and attention from a man who would provide the care and protection they lacked in their childhood. As soon as she had met Derek, she knew there was something behind his gaze that wasn't right. He'd always seemed pleasant enough, although a little controlling for her taste. However, she had never been too worried about Helen, and had mostly been happy for her, that she had found love and everything she had been looking for in life. However, Derek's announcement that he needed to move back to his hometown to help his family's business devastated her. (Cane Farmers? Seriously?)

Parting with her sister had been horrible. It was all she could do not to cry and beg her twin to stay in Melbourne. Instead, she had supported her, been excited for her, calmed her fears of moving so far away, and told her it would be a fabulous beginning to an incredible life with Derek. The first week after Helen and Derek had left, she had gone to work, smiled, interacted, and acted completely normal, but at night, after hours, when the world was asleep, or making love, or giving birth or dying, she would sit on her balcony, listening to the street noise of Melbourne below, and silently sob at her sisters' departure.

Her boss soon offered her an opportunity she couldn't refuse. Creative director at their company's New York office. A girl's dream, right? When she had rung Helen to discuss it, Helen was unusually exuberant, overenthusiastic at the idea of Rebecca leaving. Rebecca felt flabbergasted. Helen, the quiet, the meek, who thought moving to rural New South Wales was like moving to the other side of the world, was encouraging her sister to *go* to the other side of the world? As she sat on the phone to her twin, inhaling her Marlboro Light, with a glass of tequila and soda by her side, she finally asked, "Helen, are you okay up there?"

"Me?" Helen had exclaimed, with a (mock) expression of surprise in her voice.

"Yeah, honey, something doesn't quite sound right," Rebecca exhaled lazily toward her window.

"No, sis, I'm completely fine. Absolutely thrilled at such an exceptional opportunity for you.... And I get to visit you in New York City!"

Rebecca sighed, deciding to drop it. If her sister wasn't entirely happy, she would tell her when she was ready. That was something she had learned about Helen a long time ago. She processed things inwardly but would always find her path to Rebecca. They were like one soul.

She sighed. "So, how's Derek the Farmer?" she asked, and Helen had giggled.

"He's fine, always busy. Derek doesn't really cane farm, you know; he overseas their entire business, including property and other investments. They're very wealthy, you know." "What about you? Any job prospects?"

Rebecca could almost hear her sister shift uncomfortably in her chair over two thousand kilometres away.

"Well, not really. Cooinda isn't big. I guess I could learn the administrative side of things for the business, but I'm not really into that."

"What about teaching again? Surely there are schools up there too?"

"Yeah, yeah, that's what I'll do, eventually. I've just been really busy settling in since we got here, and I haven't given it much thought."

The conversation moved to other and months later, Rebecca thought it was strange her sister still hadn't started teaching. She loved it so much, and it suited her personality. But she had been so busy at that point, packing and organising to move to New York, she had put it in the back of her mind.

The next minute, two years had passed, and she had just renewed her contract and visa at work to stay another two years, and she never really suspected what Helen's life was really like, and the unimaginable had happened. Her life from her sister had not only become geographically removed but emotionally removed as well. They were worlds apart in every way possible.

It wasn't until ten that evening that Rebecca finally arrived back home and found out that she had three voicemail messages waiting. Slowly, a frigid chill made its way up her spine as she listened to the faraway, strange voice.

"Hi, this is Detective Tom Turner. Could you please call me back at this number? I work for the Cooinda Police Department." What followed was information on how she could contact him. By the time she disconnected, her heart racing, fumbling to dial 5 to listen to the next message. This one was from Derek, short and to the point "Rebecca, call me; it's about Helen, and it's important."

She dropped the phone back into its cradle and scrounged around in her bag for her address book, flicking through to find Helen and Derek's home number As she dialled, her breathing was heavy and laboured.

"What the fuck is going on?" she thought to herself in a panic. "Please, not my Helen, please, God, no."

Derek answered on the first ring. "Helen?"

"Derek?" she almost whispered. "It's Rebecca."

"Jesus, Rebecca, I tried to call you."

"What's going on, Derek? Some detective left a message on my phone. What's wrong with Helen?"

She heard him sigh on the other side of the world. "I don't know, Rebecca. She was out for her usual run last night, and she never came home." …. The silence after this explanation was deafening. Rebecca waited for Derek to elaborate, but obviously there was nothing more for him to say (well, to her anyway).

"What? What do you mean she hasn't come home? Has she left you, or has someone taken her? Is she hurt?"

"I don't know, Rebecca." She could hear an edge in his voice; the type of voice that wasn't accustomed to being spoken to in such a way.

"The police are doing all they can, and my folks and I are out helping and cooperating as much as possible."

There was a sudden change in his tone. The texture of his voice had turned to gravel, and a controlled, businesslike manner had replaced the depth, the emotion. Rebecca tried to keep her cool. If he had hurt her sister, he'd regret the day he was ever born; but right now, she needed to keep her cool so she could get herself across the world to the middle of nowhere and find out exactly what was going on and where her sweet Helen was.

"I'll be on the next available flight out," she said calmly.

"Look, Rebecca, that's probably not nec…"

Rebecca slammed the phone into its cradle, stuffed her address book back into her bag, and began planning. By midnight, she had talked to her boss, who understood the situation and promised to do their best without her. She called the airline and booked a flight from JFK to LAX for early the next morning and would be on a plane to Brisbane the following evening. She spent the rest of the night pacing frantically, packing, and chain-smoking. Just past four in the morning, she slipped a note under Antony's door. They weren't an 'item', however; their sexual interludes were regular enough that he would notice was gone for more than a couple of days.

The weather was picking up again, and the snow swirled around her face as she pulled her luggage from the car and thanked her driver. She turned away from the weather, from New York, from her life, and headed into the terminal, all the while begging the universe to keep the weather at bay until they were safely in the air.

The weather delayed her Qantas flight by two hours, and she deplaned in Los Angeles for an hour layover at six that evening. She was back in the sky by ten o'clock and realised she could not remember the last time she had slept. She had spent the five-hour flight from New York to Los Angeles drinking and flicking through a magazine. As she settled in for the long-haul flight, she tried to get some sleep, worried she'd be stone-cold crazy by the time she reached Brisbane. She arranged her pillow, pulled the blanket tightly around her, and drank whiskey neat, waiting for the booze to make its way to her brain and numb her mind, her soul. As she drifted into a fitful sleep, a sob caught in her throat, alerting a passing flight attendant who flicked a worrisome look toward to the pale, dishevelled woman in seat 36B who seemed to have the weight of the world sitting squarely on her petite shoulders.

She dreamed of Helen. They sat together on the banks of a river, in a place that Rebecca did not recognise, yet knew it was home. Their feet splashed in the water, and Rebecca noticed Helen wore jeans and had not rolled them up. She watched the water and mud make its way up her sister's legs, although Helen seemed not to notice. She was looking across the river, laughing and pointing. Rebecca looked to where she pointed, but all she saw was fog.

A tightness enveloped her, and she had trouble finding air. She turned to Helen. They needed to leave. But Helen was gone. Rebecca turned around frantically, searching, but all she could see was the thick fog. She tried to call for her sister, but her words were meaningless, and her mouth heavy, as though filled with dirt. She tried to move and struggled to stand, and realised she now wore the jeans Helen had been wearing, and the mud was seeping up to her thighs. Frantically, she tried to brush it off, yet in kept creeping towards her waist. Rebecca was terrified and looked for Helen, for anybody, but the fog was now so thick it brushed against her face. Or was that something else? Panic seized her, and she tried to scream, but no sound came out.

She awoke in a cold sweat, a flight attendant standing beside her, a concerned look on her face. Behind her stood Helen, her hair wet, plastered to her face, one eye swollen shut. She grinned at Rebecca, and a tooth fell out of her mouth. Rebecca screamed. A tortured sound that escaped as a croak. The flight attendant gently touched her shoulder, bringing Rebecca firmly back to reality.

"Are you okay, Miss? You were having a nightmare."

Rebecca nodded, grateful to be awake. "I'm okay, thanks. Sorry for the bother." She whispered weakly.

"Oh, nonsense," said the kind woman, named Kelly. "I'll get you a stiff drink. Another whiskey?"

"Actually, could I please have a vodka soda?"

"Coming right up." She smiled and gave Rebecca's shoulder an affectionate squeeze. Rebecca put her head back and stared at the ceiling of the plane, afraid to close her eyes again. She sighed, waiting for her drink, the dream slowly fading, and she realised it was going to be a long flight.

{ 5 }

Rebecca's flight landed at Brisbane International Airport thirty hours after her brief conversation with Derek. She had travelled from New York to Brisbane in approximately twenty hours, and she was wound so tightly that she worried she'd snap in half. Thirty hours of too much coffee, no food, no sleep, and the occasional shot of vodka was a recipe for disaster.

It was now Monday morning, Queensland time, and she had skipped a day while flying over the Pacific. Helen had been missing since the previous Thursday evening. As she made it through customs, collected her luggage, and finally emerged into the arrivals lounge, the first thing she did was to find a pay phone and place a call to Detective Tom Turner, who had left her the original message regarding Helen. She had been halfway across the Pacific when she realised in horror that she had never returned his call after talking to Derek and began making her frantic plans.

She dialled the number and waited to be connected, silently praying Helen was already back home, and this long trip would cause a well-needed holiday to see her sister. Finally, the Cooinda police station connected her to Tom's phone within a few minutes, and he answered on the second ring. Rebecca noticed that the detective's voice sounded weary. "Rebecca Thorn?" he asked politely. "Yes, hi Detective. This is Rebecca Thorn. I'm so sorry I didn't get back to you sooner. I've just landed in Brisbane."

"Oh, well, that explained that." Tom sounded surprised but not displeased. "When I spoke to Derek regarding getting in contact with you, he implied you and your sister were not close, and with you being in the States, you would have little inclining to come here or have any idea about your sisters' whereabouts."

Rebecca almost dropped the phone, and she stood silently with her mouth agape until she heard; "Hello.... are you still there, Ms. Thorn?"

"Um, yes, sorry. Still here." She cleared her throat, trying to keep her cool. "Not sure where Derek got the notion that my sister and I are not close; however, I don't have a clue about her whereabouts. I need to be here. I need to find my sister. Something's not right."

"Why do you say that?"

"I don't know, Twin-ition I guess."

Tom chuckled. "Twin-ition - I like that. Well, I'm keen to meet with you. The police officially listed Helen as a missing person, and I am the lead detective on her case. There is a lot going on down here in Cooinda. Have you ever been here before, Ms. Thorn?"

"No, I can't say that I have, Detective. I'm about to hire a car and hope to be there by lunchtime."

Tom glanced at his watch. It was almost eight in the morning. "Okay, let's meet up this afternoon. Unless you need to get some sleep. Do you know where you are staying?"

"No idea, but I'll figure something out. I would prefer not to wait to see you, though. Can I come straight to the police station?" Rebecca asked.

"Absolutely. It's a couple of hours' drive from the airport to Cooinda. We are on Main Street and easy to find. I look forward to seeing you this afternoon." Tom smiled into the phone.

Rebecca sighed gratefully, trying not to burst into tears. "Thank you so much; I appreciate you seeing me today. I'm so worried I wouldn't be able to sleep, anyway."

"No worries at all, Miss Thorn, and please call me Tom."

The Toyota hatchback Rebecca rented from the airport was ready and waiting, and a brief time after getting off the phone to Tom, she was driving away from the airport, heading south, over the Queensland border into New South Wales, and towards Cooinda. The rental car's road map book was on the passenger seat, and luckily, getting out of Brisbane and onto the highway heading south was signed well. It wasn't until she was close to the NSW border she had to pull over and figure out where she needed to go. The trip took her about two and a half hours, and she cruised along with the window down, chain-smoking, with the stifling humidity smacking her in the face and the radio playing a mix of current songs repeatedly. She had never visited Helen in Cooinda, as her job in New York had taken her so soon after Helen had moved there with Derek. She was keen to get there now, though not for the scenery.

Her exhaustion was at its peak, and she knew she should not be driving. On the flight, visions of her sister suffering — crying out her name for help from a dark, unknown place, but receiving only silence — haunted her restless sleep.

Rebecca didn't know what physically being in Cooinda would do to help find her sister, however she knew, once she came face to face with her brother-in-law, her senses would clear, and she would have a better understanding of his involvement (if any). Much to her dismay, she had realised she knew little about her sister and Derek's life, other than what Helen allowed her to know, and the gut feeling that had settled in the pit of her stomach was far from comforting. She knew she shouldn't be jumping to conclusions before talking to the police and even Derek himself, and finding out all the facts, but this early in the game, Rebecca's suspicion lay squarely on Derek.

Feeling nauseous and exhausted, she tried as best as possible to concentrate on the road, finally seeing the exit for Cooinda. Shortly after, she took the exit with a sigh of relief and within minutes drove along a long, straight road, hugging a river that ran amongst some of the most beautiful landscape she had ever seen. Sugarcane stretched as far as her eye could see on both sides of the river, and the road dotted with farmhouses set back from the road as she followed her map closer to the township. Beyond the cane were masses of national parks that butted into each other down the coastline of New South Wales. Cooinda sat only about forty kilometres inland from the Pacific and seemed to rise out of nowhere.

As described, the Cooinda police station sat in a prime position on the main street. Next to the building stood the courthouse, and across the road, someone had transformed a beautiful old Queenslander-style home into a pub. She found parking further up Main Street and walked the short distance back to the station, eager to meet with the detective and find out what had happened to her twin.

{ 6 }

Tom's days were busy, and his nights restless. In the four days since Helen went missing, there had been no traction on finding her, either dead or alive. Every night when he climbed into bed, he closed his eyes, and images of Helen would float across the darkness, resulting in a sleepless night.

The townsfolk were out in droves helping in coordinated search parties along Helen's running route, and so far; nothing. The police staffed a tip line in shifts. He had spent most of the last three days following up on these tips and checking in with officers who were out leading the search teams. Monday morning, after a quick cup of coffee, Tom headed into the station, settling into his desk chair with the tips from the night before. Tom was disappointed to discover the tips were dwindling fast after only three days. Three calls had come into the tip line overnight, and none of them seemed to be anything solid. One woman had claimed Helen had turned into a cat and was currently prowling in her backyard, scaring her pet cockatoo, Charlie.

Shortly after this, he received the call from Rebecca Thorn. It was now a little after two in the afternoon, and he was expecting her to arrive shortly. He had a mountain of paperwork he decided to do to fill in time, and before he knew it, the police receptionist Lily announced Rebecca's arrival. Tom made his way over to the conference room, where he discovered another one of his constables was standing outside. Ava Hart had been with Tom longer than Lou had been. But unlike Lou, had only been living in Cooinda since her promotion and transfer six years ago. She was a few years older than Lou and had a diverse set of skills compared to his other senior constable. While Lou was fanatical about the intricate details and diligent in documenting and recording these details, Ava's skills lay in her ability to see into people, to communicate in a way that Tom always admired. She treated people with the utmost kindness and respect and was an asset to the team. Now they settled in and waited until Lily showed Rebecca into the room.

Tom had obviously seen Helen in and around town, and someone had introduced him to her once at the Annual Cane Festival two or three years ago. He was not, however, prepared to meet Rebecca. He knew they were twins, but it honestly took his breath away to see her walk into the room. Their looks were truly identical; however, his reaction to Rebecca took him by surprise. Her bright auburn hair, porcelain skin and clear emerald eyes were mesmerising. Her cheekbones and nose were narrow and symmetrical. Rebecca's face was...art, and it was not something he'd seen in Helen. He pondered physical attraction and how it worked and realised his heart was aflutter.

Lily introduced both Tom and Ava to Rebecca, who smiled politely. There were dark rings under her eyes, and her auburn hair was pulled back into a loose bun. Tom saw trickles of sweat in her hairline and saw her bare arms glisten. She must have been uncomfortable after leaving New York's climate. To Tom, she was still stunning; her exhaustion adding an authentic element to her beauty. After settling down and getting Rebecca some cold water, they began their discussion. Rebecca thought Derek was involved in her sister's disappearance.

"Have you been to see Derek yet?" Tom asked, glancing at Ava, who had a notebook and pen at the ready.

"No," sighed Rebecca. "I know it may seem like I'm jumping the gun, but Derek has never struck me as the honest, caring type, if you get what I mean."

Tom looked sharply at her. "Can you expand on that, Miss Thorn?"

"Please call me Rebecca, and no, I can't really explain what I feel. I don't really know Derek. He made a point of dragging my sister away from me as soon as he could. Helen and I have unfortunately grown apart since we both moved. However, it is not for lack of love on either of our parts. The more time she spent here, the more withdrawn she became. Something was wrong, but I never pushed it. I was so far away from her, it was easier to believe her when she told me she was okay..." Rebecca's voice had softened to a whisper, and Tom saw tears well in her eyes. She shook her head and wiped her eyes, glancing at them both. "Sorry," she said, "I'm just tired."

Ava shook her head, reaching out and placing a hand on Rebecca's. "Never say sorry. We want you to be as honest with us as possible. It's the best way for us to understand and see a clear picture of Helen's life, which will help in finding her."

Tom was impressed as usual. It was difficult to make people comfortable, to draw them out of their shells, especially in these circumstances. Ava's sensitive nature made her excellent at this aspect of her job, and he was grateful she could put Rebecca at ease.

Tom sighed and ran his hand through his hair. "Rebecca, other than a bad feeling, and not really knowing Derek very well, is there anything that has given you a clue where Helen might be? Is there a possibility that there is a boyfriend she's run off with, or if she is in an abusive relationship, she's escaped, and left her belongings behind?" Rebecca sighed. Everything was finally getting to her, and tears began sliding down her cheeks. "God, I hope she has just run off. But honestly, I just don't know." She clutched her hand to her heart, pressing her hand flat against her breast, her sob catching in her throat. "It's just like, in here," she tapped her heart, "that there is something going on. I just sense it."

Tom nodded, glancing at Ava, whose eyes filled with sympathy. He sighed, the weight of the world crushing him.

They wrapped up their conversation with Tom asking Rebecca for her contact information.

Rebecca smiled at his question. "I don't have a cell phone, sorry. And don't know where I'm staying yet."

"There are two or three motels in and around town," Ava said. She stood up. "Let me speak to Lily, our receptionist. She should be able to get you booked into something in no time." With a quick smile and assertive nod, Ava left the room.

Rebecca glanced at Tom. "Wow, that's small-town accommodation for you. Thank you so much."

Tom laughed. "Not everyone is that friendly. Ava has a knack of making anyone and everyone comfortable, like they are all part of a big family."

Ava was back within moments. "Lily is organising a room for you now."

Rebecca nodded gratefully. "Wonderful. Although I'm not sure what I'm supposed to do now, I'm here. I'd be useless and go crazy if I just checked into a motel and sat there twiddling my thumbs. I could have done that in New York."

Ava nodded sympathetically. "Well, how about you help with the search efforts? There are two or three parties of volunteers out every day."

Tom nodded in agreement. "Derek's parents have been out helping. In fact, his father, Fred, has been the main coordinator."

Rebecca agreed, feeling a little more in control for the first time in days. She left the police station shortly after, having organised with Ava to join the search the following morning and collected her motel booking information from the friendly receptionist Lily.

She stepped into the oppressing sun and wandered around town aimlessly, not ready to drive to her motel. It was not even four in the afternoon, and she wanted to keep herself awake for a while longer so she could try to adjust to the time difference.

Cooinda's town centre had six streets in a simple grid pattern, with a shaded park at one end, sitting alongside the river which ran through the town, separating and defining the north and south ends of town by a sturdy yet quaint bridge.

Each street had shops including of chemists, cafes, gift shops, dress shops, and two supermarkets, one at each end of the town. She saw a pub that stood at the end of the main street, a short walk from the station. Its grand wrap-around veran-dah with wrought-iron railings, and old timber siding oozed charm, and she stopped to have something to eat and a couple of drinks. She was craving a vodka and briefly wondered if she was becoming an alcoholic.

The pub was quiet, typical for a country town in Australia on a Monday afternoon. She ordered a drink from the nice and friendly bartender named Jenny, who stared at her, eyes wide. "You're back," she said, a smile on her face. "Apparently, Derek was worried sick." Puzzled for a moment, but realising quickly, Rebecca sighed and shook her head. "Um, no, I'm Re-becca, Helen's twin sister." She held her hand out politely, and Jenny shook it, looking embarrassed. "I'm so sorry. Lou told me you were coming into town. I should have realised."
"Lou?" asked Rebecca.

"Oh, she's a constable. And my best friend. She has been working hard looking for your sister," she smiled sadly. "It's just so awful. I've been praying for you all."

Rebecca smiled politely, reminded herself that a town like this must not have secrets and that news like this would spread quickly. She accepted her drink from Jenny and, once in hand, made her way to the outdoor garden dining section at the back of the pub, which was currently empty. The bistro menu would not begin service for another hour. She sat down heavily and lit a cigarette. She closed her eyes and inhaled her Marl-boro Light deeply.

Helen was sitting across from her when she opened her eyes, her hand stretched out, and her green eyes wide. Pale-faced, with a trickle of blood meandering down her forehead and into her left eye. Her mouth was open, as though she were saying something, but no sound emerged.

Rebecca cried out in fright, standing abruptly, her chair clattering over. She stumbled backwards, away from her sister. Her heart was pounding in her ears, and she wanted to close her eyes, but had the conflicting feeling that the image would disappear if she took her eyes from it for even a moment. Helen's eyes were sad, angry, and she was mouthing something now, looking directly at Rebecca with an outstretched arm.

Rebecca tried to control her fear and study any part of her sister's presence. She then took a hesitant step closer to Helen, noticing her ripped blue leggings and a Nike T-shirt. Helen's feet were bare, and her hair hung limply around her shoulders. Dirt had replaced its auburn shine and lustre. Helen kept mouthing something as though she were trying to talk; but no words would come out. Rebecca studied her sister, her head pounding against her skull. She took another step towards her sister, stretching her hand to her twin. As she did this, Helen faded.

"No!" Rebecca gasped, lunging toward her sister. But it was no use. Helen had faded as quickly as she had arrived. And she was alone at her table, her chair knocked over, her vodka sitting on the table, the liquid rippling from the supernatural disturbance. A sob caught in her throat, and she grabbed her chair, pulling it upright. She sat, took a gulp of her vodka, lit a fresh cigarette and stared at the spot her sister had just stood in, willing her to return.

From inside the bar, Jenny watched the scene take place in the courtyard. It was empty other than Rebecca, and when she saw her jump backwards knocking her chair over, she assumed she'd spilled her drink. She grabbed a cloth and began walking around the bar, at the ready to help. She stopped and looked with a hesitant expression on her face as she watched Rebecca stare in fear at the plant across from her table. Allergic maybe? Better grab the antihistamine too, just in case.

Jenny didn't mean to startle Rebecca, but it was almost impossible not to. She was so mesmerised by the plant that Jenny became concerned there was a snake hiding in the pot, like one had done a few months previously. "Um, are you okay? Is there another snake?"

For a moment, Rebecca forgot Helen and stared at Jenny as though she were from another planet. "Snake?" She glanced around nervously.

"Oh, no, sorry, I just thought, with the way you jumped up, that there may have been a snake in the garden. The little buggers sometimes try to come in for a drink." She smiled, a wide, carefree grin, and Rebecca remembered how friendly Australian people were.

She shook her head. "No snake. I'm fine, thanks. Just jet-lagged and seeing things. I'll be okay." She smiled weakly and collected her things. "Sorry, I have to go." She left the courtyard, leaving Jenny staring at her with a concerned and curious expression on her face. She would have to call Lou and tell her all about her encounter with Helen's sister. The poor girl probably just needed a friend.

{ 7 }

Rebecca didn't know what made her walk toward the police station rather than heading to the motel to check in, but she was standing in front of it before she even realised. Her brief encounter with Tom only an hour before had left an impression of a kind and caring man. She would be a fool not to admit he was also attractive. His tall, muscular build, thick dark hair that was slightly greying and chiselled features had reminded her of a Hollywood actor.

She had no one to talk to and, in her own mind, justified coming to him with information he should know to help the investigation. She shook her head, already embarrassed for her future self, as she climbed the front steps, and pulled the heavy timber door that led into the reception of the police station.

Tom was surprised that Rebecca had arrived at the police station again within the hour. Ava was out having a quick break when Lily called through to announce Rebecca's arrival once again, so he decided to meet her at the reception desk.

Rebecca looked upset. The bun had come out, and her hair cascaded around her shoulders, and her eyes were red, as though she had been crying, and Tom instantly thought an altercation might have occurred between her and Derek.

"Rebecca?" Tom walked quickly towards her. He was touched that she had come to him for support. As he reached her, the tears finally appeared, spilling down her cheeks.

"Shhh, it's okay...." he soothed her for a few more moments, and when the sobs subsided, Tom steered Rebecca out the front door. He had a junior constable there now to man the station. Shane was new to the force, keen to learn, and eager to help. Helen had disappeared, search and rescue teams deployed, and he needed more staff than usual. The station was chaotic with coordinators checking in, and Shane's job was keeping track of the checkpoints and participants of the search.

They moved away from the chaos of the station and began walking east towards the river and the local park that sat on the river's embankment, a popular spot for picnickers and parents whose children wanted to play in the playground. They didn't talk at first, and Rebecca had her head down as they walked. Tom's heart was breaking for this woman, who was alone in the town, with no family, and who must be frantic about her sister's whereabouts.

As they sat on a park bench facing the river, he finally asked, "Is it Derek?"

Rebecca's head dropped, hair hanging down. Even in the situation, Tom couldn't help his heart beating a little faster as his arm pressed against hers. He berated himself silently for his reaction.

With a shaky voice, Rebecca told Tom about what had happened at the pub. Even as she said the words aloud, she knew how stupid they sounded, yet somehow, she knew he wouldn't ridicule her or laugh at her. She told him everything, and he only nodded, listening, his eyes looking into the distance as his thoughts battled within him.

For a while, neither of them spoke. Finally, Tom whispered, "Do you think Helen is trying to get a message to you?"

Rebecca was relieved she had come to Tom to confide in. Her instincts had told her he would understand and be a trustworthy confidant. Her personality was the sort that needed conversation, needed connection and trust. Thrust into a strange new world, away from New York, a thriving city that never slept, made her feel isolated when she had seen Helen. There was no one from work, no Antony, no parents. There was only Tom, and she hoped she could trust him. As she sat next to him, their arms touched, and she quivered. A yearning that lay dormant, now stirred in her belly.

Tom spoke again. "When Derek called me the night Helen didn't come home from her run, I drove out to the house. When I was getting out of the car, the strangest thing happened..." He paused. Feeling awkward and suddenly unsure of himself. He looked at Rebecca, who stared at him with large expectant eyes that glistened with grief.

He continued; "Everything was so still, not even the crickets made a sound. I sensed someone was watching me."

He paused, shook his head. "It was uncanny; I haven't mentioned it to anyone," he shrugged, slightly embarrassed. He wanted her to understand, though. Now that she was in town, he worried about her. Townsfolk would not take kindly to a woman's ranting about ghosts or apparitions. The heavily Protestant and Catholic populations in the town were traditionalist in their faith and would have little patience for an outsider who talked such nonsense. There was a Hari Krishna community on the outskirts of the town, who owned property and a church, who were called a cult by the townsfolk. Every Saturday morning the "Hari's" would come to town in their hippy clothes, smelling of weed, and chant through the streets, "disturbing the peace, and making a racket." Tom would always listen to the complaints of the people, and then gently reminded them that people had the right to practice their religion and gather and sing in the streets. It was freedom of speech.

Tom quite liked the Hari Krishna community. He would often go out to their property for a delicious vegan meal and mingle with the people, who mostly wanted to keep to themselves, and be self-sufficient. They were always welcoming and friendly. He knew they grew weed amongst their other fruits and vegetables, but to be honest, he found their religious and ethical behaviour far more authentic than most of the Christians he'd ever met and always pretended not to notice their weed-growing habits.

Once, a couple of years ago, one of the young children from the community had been hit by a car and killed. Tom had been the first to arrive at the scene, and he had sat with the child, her blood-soaked, matted hair stuck to her head, which he cradled in his lap. She had died quietly, while the drunk mother who had slammed into her as the girl had happily skipped across the road, sobbed from the driver's seat of her car. The ambulance had arrived minutes later, minutes too late.

A few months after the child's funeral, Tom was walking through Main Street on a Saturday morning as the Hari's did their weekly chant around town. As he came out of the chemist, clutching his medications in a paper bag, he looked up, and saw her. She was walking alongside her mother, whose eyes focused on the heavens, as she banged her Tamborine, and sang to her God. The little girl's image was clear for only a moment and faded as quickly as it came. Tom never spoke of it; yet never doubted it. He had never affiliated with a church (his parents were agnostic), but he always had an inclination toward life after death. It was something he pondered often yet rarely spoke of.

As he and Rebecca sat on the bench, the river rippled quietly along, with the odd fisher occasionally idling by in a boat, causing the water to ripple against the shore.

"I don't doubt you, Rebecca, but we need to keep this information low-key. -town folk like Cooinda are traditional in their thinking and may not take kindly to what you're saying. Especially Derek."

Rebecca nodded and sighed. "It was just so real. If I had reached out, I would have been able to grab hold of her and not let her go." The image of Helen was as fresh in her mind as it was when it happened.

Tom nodded, his eyes looking out over the water, silent. Then suddenly he stood, grabbed her hand, as naturally as he'd take hold of a lover's hand and said, "Come on, it's about time I introduced you to Derek's parents."

{ 8 }

Tom hoped that taking Rebecca to the Cox's; and giving Derek the opportunity to see his sister-in-law in his town would provoke some sort of reaction, giving him the opportunity to see Derek, and follow his gut on whether Derek was involved in his wife's disappearance. Until that point, he was undecided about Derek and his involvement; however, he was leaning towards Derek telling the truth. Rebecca's intense dislike for her brother-in-law showed she saw a side of him that was not trustworthy.

He radioed the station and asked Lily to phone Ruth and Fred to tell them he would come by and to see if Derek was also free to meet him at his parents' house. He then left a message for Ava, who had planned to follow up on other work and leads for the afternoon. Life had to go on, and there were other things that needed to be done, aside from working Helen's case, and he needed his officers to hold the fort. As the head detective of the Homicide Squad in their police district, it was his job to delegate the tasks between the few people who worked beneath him.

As Rebecca and he settled into his car, he admired her profile, marvelling again at her beauty, and wondering to himself if his growing infatuation was purely a physical one. It had been a long time since he had been in any kind of meaningful relationship, and after his marriage had broken down, it had taken him many years to build any kind of trust, with anyone, for a long time. He had also seen so many of his friends' marriages also come apart at the seams, and he often concluded he had a fine life, with his quaint cottage, and his government job that he loved. He had mates in Cooinda and always told himself he was perfectly content.

As he sat next to this woman now though, he remembered the feelings at the beginning of relationships, the excitement of getting to know someone, the constant lovesick feeling that stirs in the stomach, making anything such as eating or sleeping, mundane. He knew getting involved with someone in these circumstances was not ideal; or even allowed; however, meeting Rebecca had sparked buried feelings he might not want to control, and he had the uncanny feeling it was important. Like whatever brought them together was a sign. And however, they interpreted the signs, would either be the beginning of something new, or the beginning of the end.

They drove in silence to Derek's parents' house, which sat majestically on the riverfront — a sprawling brick and timber homestead with wrap-around verandas, and large bay windows. Their driveway was long, stretching from Cane Road for a kilometre until it became circular, allowing people to manoeuvre their cars and turn around. A large spotted gum tree stood in the middle of the circular driveway, shadowing it from the scorching sun. Rebecca stepped out of the car and marvelled at the old homestead, remembering Helen describing it as "farm snobbery." She understood what she was talking about now that she was standing in front of Derek's parents' home. Growing up in Melbourne, and then moving to New York, Rebecca had always identified as a city girl. They had never been on holiday as children and had certainly never experienced the type of country lifestyle that Helen had become accustomed to over the last few years. Their parents were both functioning alcoholics who could hold down steady jobs, but never actually offer any financial security. When the girls were children, their parents paid minimal attention to them, their time and money always going towards other more important things. It was not until they were young adults and had their own jobs that they earned their own money.

Rebecca had only been in town for a few hours, and she was already noticing the different levels of class. And like so many places, could be associated property. And the Coxs' was certainly impressive. Tom looked at Rebecca as she stared at the homestead and thought to himself that she reminded him of a little girl seeing a cinema screen for the first time. She stared ahead, appearing cool, yet quietly impressed.

Rebecca knew that Derek and Helen's house was close to the main homestead, and she glanced around hoping to catch a glimpse (she couldn't see it through the cane) and simultaneously looking for anything amiss. On either side of the house and running parallel to the long driveway was the sugarcane. It was not currently burning season, so the cane was long, in some places, well over six feet tall. Rebecca knew about the cane fields but hadn't given them too much thought over the years. It was dense and dark, with the occasional pathway through it, allowing easy access. She stared at it and noticed the psithurism coming from within, and it stirred a feeling of uneasiness in her. Goosebumps broke through on her slender pale arms, and she hugged herself as though cold. She glanced at Tom, who was standing on the other side of the car, studying her quietly.

"Are you okay?" he asked gently.

Rebecca nodded, taking a deep breath, shutting the car door. "Let's do this."

Derek and his parents sat inside the elegant living room, which was to the left of the front door through a high archway framed by ornate woodwork. The home had a wide hallway that ran the depth of the house from the front door to the back door, with grand rooms off each doorway in the hallway.

A flustered woman dressed in a grey and white maid's outfit answered the door. Rebecca was surprised Derek's parents had a housekeeper. Helen had never mentioned one, and the idea of a housekeeper who wore a uniform and answered the door for her employer seemed outdated, and amusing. Rebecca wondered if she had stepped into an old movie.

Derek's father, Frederick Cox, was a tall, distinguished-looking man, with a narrow frame, silvery-grey hair, and a weathered face. He had a mix of money and farming to his look, with trouser pants and an expensive plaid shirt tucked neatly into them, held up by a belt. His thinning hair was neatly combed, his pale grey eyes looked worn and tired; hardened somehow. He stood from his wooden and upholstered armchair, stretching out his hand to Tom. "Thanks for coming again, Tom." His voice was soft yet commanded.

When he glanced towards Rebecca, his eyes widened with shock, and his words stammered, "Good afternoon, Miss Thorn; it's lovely to meet you."

When she and Helen had spoken over the years, she often spoke of her father-in-law, Frederick. He was from old farming money, and even though Rebecca had never met him, she knew from the way Helen spoke of him that he was charming, hardworking, and very much a gentleman. She knew that both Derek's parents were devastated when he and Helen had eloped in Melbourne, with only Rebecca in attendance (much to Derek's annoyance, as he wanted it to be 'romantic, you know, just the two of us'). Derek was their only child, and even though Helen would never say it, Rebecca always got the impression they expected more from him — as a son, a business, as a human. However, in meeting Fredrick and Ruth now, she saw a side to them that made her feel sorry for them. Unfortunately, they had raised a spoilt and obnoxious son. And they knew it.

Derek stood next to his mother in front of the lounge opposite a regal brick fireplace with a timber mantel. He had changed little since Rebecca had last seen him, nodded politely, and much to Rebecca's surprise; tears welled up in his eyes. He sat down shakily, while his mother, Ruth Cox, stretched out her hand and shook Rebecca's. Her handshake was firm, her hands petite and brown with the sun, like her husband's. Her hair was blonde, with grey hairs peeking through. And she guessed she had originally been a blonde and noted that Derek had inherited his mother's good looks. Her eyes were bright blue, and even though she must have been in her late fifties or early sixties, she looked much younger.

Rebecca knew Ruth adored her sister, and she instantly warmed to her. Ruth smiled sadly at her. "My goodness, you'll have to forgive Fred and me. We have seen photos of the two of you, but it's still a bit of a shock to see you standing here." The tears fell freely, and Rebecca instinctively reached over the coffee table between them and gave her a warm hug.

"I'm so sorry," she whispered. Her voice wavered as she pulled away and sat next to Tom on a two-seater sofa. It was quiet. She could almost hear his heart beating, so close to hers.

Tom cleared his throat. "Thanks for meeting with us. This is not a formal meeting. We appreciate your inviting us into your home. Rebecca only arrived yesterday, and I thought it was time for us to reconnect."

Tom had to play his cards right with this family. The family had been interviewed, and he had spoken to Fred and Ruth Cox separately, taking their statements after Helen had gone missing. Their accounts of when they last saw their daughter-in-law seemed genuine, and their housekeeper had confirmed their alibi. They had been at home watching television at the time Helen left for her run and then showering and getting ready for bed. Derek was the main person of interest until Tom cleared him, or the investigation moved in a different direction, or until he had to refer it to the coroner. Unfortunate or not, spouses were always the first under suspicion in these types of cases, until cleared. And so far, Tom could not clear Derek. He was at home alone when Helen left for her run, and to that fact, Tom could not confirm if Helen had even gone for a run. In the last few days, their home and surrounding property had been searched, and nothing suspicious or out of the ordinary reported. So far, this was a missing person's case. Hopefully, it would not progress to a murder investigation. The case was going cold, and fast. If Helen didn't turn up, dead or alive, soon, Tom dreaded passing the investigation to the missing persons unit. He had seen families torn apart after loved ones stayed missing for long periods of time.

"So, Derek, do you mind going over once again what happened the night Helen left for her run? I know I've taken your statement, but it would be ready over the entire day, leading up to her run. As much as you can remember, anyway. And remember, this is just a casual conversation, more for Rebecca's sake. She may know where Helen may be based on something you say...you know, being sisters and all." Tom sat back comfortably on the sofa, giving the impression he was relaxed, even though Rebecca sensed the tension in his body.

Derek leaned forward with a sigh and ran his hand through his dirty blond hair. "I'm really not sure how much help you'll be, Rebecca. I mean, you guys hardly ever spoke." He shrugged his shoulders as though he were apologetic, but of course Rebecca knew he was not. Helen said nothing directly to her, but she knew Derek did everything in his power to stop the two sisters from talking on the phone too often. Little did he know.

On the lounge next to Derek, his mother cleared her throat, looking guiltily at Rebecca, and then at Derek. "Well, sweetie, Helen used to call Rebecca quite a lot from our phone when she would pop over here to visit me."

"Did you not know this?" Rebecca said sweetly. She couldn't help herself. Derek's cheeks flushed, and he cleared his throat. "Well, of course, she would tell me sometimes, but I'm a busy man. I certainly wasn't interested in the drivel you ladies indulged in over the phone."

Rebecca could see him actively trying to project a particular persona. She could see he had excellent control of his dark side when in public, but suspected he was different around his wife. Her heart ached at the thought of Helen being subjected to his control and manipulation. She berated herself for not recognising the signs. She did not know... or it was too difficult for her to face, given she was fifteen thousand kilometres away... and, well, she was a terrible person.

Derek continued in a soft, controlled voice, now addressing Tom, "I never stopped Helen from calling her sister. Ever. She could have talked to her as much as she wanted to from our home. I've no idea why she would choose to make those phone calls from here."

Ruth cut in, "Well, I think, dear, that she just wanted a little more privacy when chatting with her sister. I think it must be a twin thing," she trailed off.

Rebecca could see that Ruth was used to treating Derek delicately to avoid his temper.

Rebecca glanced at Frederick, who was sighing in frustration. "This is no time to be tiptoeing around him, Ruth. Derek, Helen came over here to call her sister because she knew you watched every damn thing she did. Now I suspect you've had nothing to do with her disappearance, but I also damn well suspect that she has left you and has gone as far away from you as possible. If I were her, I certainly would."

Frederick's words hung in the air. Everyone sat silently. Rebecca was gaping slightly at Fred, but Tom was watching Derek's every move, and his reaction to his father's words closely. Now we were getting somewhere.

"Derek, can you tell me truthfully? How was your marriage to Helen?"

Derek was rigid, his face crimson red. Rebecca could see the veins in his neck protrude as she saw his visceral response. "For one, my father has no idea what he's talking about. My marriage to Helen is perfectly normal. She is happy. I have never hurt her. And two, it's none of anyone's fucking business what my marriage is like." He stood, pointing his finger at everyone in the room.

Frederick stood calmly facing his son. "Derek, sit down." His voice was commanding, unquestionable, final.

Derek looked around the room, a nasty expression settling over his face. He was a bully. He was not weak. Unless he was in the presence of his father. He sat almost sulking now.

Tom sighed and stood up. "This was supposed to be an informal meeting; however, a woman is missing. Derek, I will find out what your marriage was like whether it comes from you or the people around you...it's a small town, people talk."

He looked at Frederick and Ruth. "Thank you for having us. Please stay close to town over the coming days, I need you all to be available at any moment, depending on where the investigation is going," Tom turned again to Derek, "if you have anything you need to say to me Derek, something that you think will help me in finding your wife, then you need to tell me. I'm saying this straight up; you are the first person of interest in this case. The spouse always is. So, if you want to clear yourself, I'd think long and hard about what, if anything, you must tell me about Helen."

Tom gestured to Rebecca, who stood, staring hard at Derek. She hated him with every fibre of her being, but she knew there was nothing left to say that hadn't already been said to Tom in their original statements. However, she couldn't help herself. "Derek?"

He glanced at her hesitantly, full of animosity. "Yes, Rebecca?" he was keeping his cool.

"If you have hurt Helen, I will find out." She stared at the arrogant, good-looking man she had let take her sister out of her life, and he stared back. After a minute, his stare wavered, and he glanced away, shaking his head.

He waved his hand at her, dismissing her. "Get the fuck out of my house," he said casually, as he stood and sauntered out of his parents' lounge-room and into the family room at the rear of the house.

The housekeeper, who had shown Tom and Rebecca in, kindly showed them onto the front verandah, leaving Frederick and Ruth alone in their grand living room. The sun was not as hot now, and it hung low in the sky. Rebecca noticed that the humidity had increased.

She looked over the cane fields towards the north and noticed dark storm clouds gathering. The cane rustled softly around them as they walked back to Tom's car, parked in the driveway. They had only been at the Cox's for a little more than half an hour, but Rebecca knew her entire world had changed. Coming face to face with Derek was what she expected; however, meeting Ruth and Frederick had given her some hope back. She knew in her heart that they both loved Helen and would do nothing to hurt her. She suspected Frederick and Ruth could never believe their son could hurt his wife, and she was guessing only time would tell.

They both quietly got into Tom's car, and as she sat in the passenger seat, she noticed an envelope sitting on the dashboard. The white shine of the paper caused a reflection on the windscreen that made her wince. She grabbed it from the dashboard as Tom climbed in and closed his door.

"Tom, was this envelope here earlier?" Surely, she would have noticed it.

"What envelope?" he asked, glancing her way. She held it up to him, and he shook his head.

"Nope," he shrugged with a puzzled look on his face as she handed the envelope to him. He casually opened it, and she saw his eyes widen as he pulled out the contents. It was a stack of about seven or eight photos.

"Oh, my god Rebecca." He paused, flicking through them quickly and then handing her back the envelope. He quickly buckled his seatbelt. "Let's get out of here and go back to the station."

As he manoeuvred the car and took off down the long driveway through the cane fields, Rebecca scanned the photos. They were of Helen, but the photos were all taken discreetly. One was of her walking out of the chemist in town, her hair blowing across her face, another of her climbing into her car, a smile on her face as she looked across at someone out of shot of the camera, getting into the passenger side of the car, and a few more random photos of her going about her business in town. In each of these photos, she was dressed differently, showing they were taken over time. And finally, of Helen, leaving her home, the photo was dark, obviously taken in the evening, as she left for her nightly run. Helen was on the porch by her front door, the outside lamp next to the door capturing her beauty. Her hair was tied high in a ponytail, and she was wearing jogging gear. The photo captured her closing the front door as she turned towards the stairs of the porch.

A sob caught in Rebecca's throat as she gazed at her sister. She touched the photo, wishing she could cross the divide, reach through the glossy photo paper, and take hold of Helen's hand. Stop her from going on her run. She moved her finger over the yellow print at the bottom right corner of the photo where it was time-stamped: 4.2.99.

"Tom," Rebecca whispered, instinctively grabbing his arm as he clutched the steering wheel. "This photo. It was taken the day she disappeared."

$$\{\,9\,\}$$

It was about seven in the evening when Derek drove the short ride home from his folks' house. After Tom and Rebecca had left, he had stayed at his folks' place while Fred berated him, talking to him as though he was still a child, and his mother chastised him gently. He knew they were all worried about Helen, but she was his wife, goddammit, and his parents now seemed more concerned with the bloody sister. Now he was just angry and exhausted. His parents had betrayed him.

He was also feeling irrationally furious that Rebecca had shown up. Logically, he knew she'd want to help find her sister. Yet, he had spent the last few years ensuring Helen had little to do with Rebecca. When he had first met Helen, he had found the stronghold Rebecca had over her irritating. His beautiful, meek Helen had always needed a firm hand to guide her, and until he had come along, Rebecca had done so with an air of ownership reserved only for a husband. It was his duty to Helen to protect her from the world.

Rebecca had shown little regard for Derek, and he knew he could only ever be the centre of Helen's world if he separated the twins. He had no siblings and little understanding of the strong connection between them; and often found himself infuriated by it. Now, seeing her in his parents' home, looking like Helen, yet nothing like his precious wife, he was beyond annoyed, and berating himself for even letting the woman know that Helen was missing.

Sighing wearily, he tried to dismiss his thoughts of Rebecca. What's done was done. The disastrous afternoon had made his thirst for a stiff drink insatiable, and all he wanted to do was sit by the river, drink in hand, and forget about the day. He turned the corner through the thick cane, away from his parents' homestead, and his car approached their cottage. He glanced up towards the front porch and noticed the living room light was on. While he pondered whether he had left a light when he had rushed out of the house earlier in the day, the room suddenly turned opaque. Derek inhaled sharply and eased his foot off the accelerator. Was someone in his home?

"Helen?" he whispered quietly to himself. He stared intently, inching slowly towards the house. He stopped short of the spot he usually parked and got out of his car as quietly as possible, wishing now that he had walked the half a kilometre to his parent's house earlier in the day, so he could have an element of surprise to whoever was in his home.

The house remained silent, but he was sure he had seen the light go off. Was she home? Had she come home to him? He quietly shut his car door and began walking towards his home. As he reached the steps, the light on the front porch flickered. Derek stopped. He realised he was clutching the timber railing and breathing heavily. He was afraid. Unfamiliar with the feelings stirring inside him, he hesitantly climbed the steps of the porch and reached the front door. As he reached for the doorknob, the light flicked off again, plunging the porch into darkness.

"Derek." The voice was a whisper and came from behind him. He spun around, expecting to see his Helen standing there, but there was no one. Frantically he looked around, his heart pounding, and sweat building in his hairline. The night air hung moist, and the northerly breeze was warm and uncomfortable. Once again, the cane rustled in the dark, and he moved towards the edge of the porch, looking around the front of the property for any movement. The voice had been right behind him. Had it been Helen's? He worried he was losing his mind. Suddenly afraid to turn his back to the cane, he walked backwards to his front door, praying that he had left it unlocked so he wouldn't have to turn his back to whatever was out there beyond the cane. He grabbed the doorknob, and thankfully it turned, the heavy old door creaking as it opened inwards. He fumbled for the light just inside the door to the left and flicked the porch light back on. Once again, the porch was lit up, and the uncanniness left Derek as quickly as it had snuck up on him. He was losing it. He shook his head, bewildered. Had he even heard a voice? He'd barely slept since Helen had gone missing, and logically speaking, it made sense that he would want to hear her voice.

He quietly moved inside and shut the door to the world. From the window next to the front door, he parted the curtain and stared outside, and as he reached towards the light switch to flick off the front porch light, he saw it flicker again and then go out, and if he had turned at that moment, he would have seen the shadowing figure standing behind him, retreat slowly into the Master bedroom off the hallway. Once again, the porch was dark, leaving Derek's hand shaking, an inch from the light switch, terrified to turn around.

Tom and Rebecca arrived at the station to find Ava still there. Lou had already begun her night shift, and the two ladies sat, Lou behind her desk, and Ava perched on the edge as they discussed the handover details. Lou looked shocked when she saw Rebecca trailing Tom into the bullpen and had to recover her expression before Rebecca noticed. She had spoken to Jenny before coming to work and knew Helen's twin had arrived in town. It still didn't remove the awe of just how identical the sisters were.

Lou quickly covered her reaction by standing and holding out her hand. "Constable Louise Hunt. It's a pleasure," she said warmly, shaking Rebecca's hand firmly with a smile.

Rebecca nodded. "It's nice to meet you, Louise."

"Oh, please, everyone calls me Lou," she said casually, sitting back down at her desk.

"Anything exciting happen while I was out?" Tom looked at Ava, who informed him that nothing interesting had happened and that the town had not fallen into despair in his absence. His position in the Northern District covered a vast area of northern New South Wales with only a couple of senior inspectors trained in the homicide squad to cover the entire region. Not only was major crime his first responsibility, but all crime. In the initial stages of a missing persons case, it was his job to collect and collate information to turn over to the Missing Persons Unit. He knew someone would assign a case manager to the case if they didn't find Helen soon. And if the case turned into a homicide case, then it would automatically be his job to investigate.

In rural towns, police often relied on the help of the community and outsourced search and rescue and collection of DNA, which had taken place over the last few days. Because Helen ran the same route every evening, sniffer dogs had picked up her scent and followed it along her normal route. They had lost her scent not far along Cane Road. The dogs had lost her scent abruptly, and Tom suspected she had gotten into a car.

Investigators had collected her DNA from her toothbrush and hairbrush, and they also took swabs from Derek and his parents in the first twenty-four hours of the investigation while Rebecca was in transit. If they found any evidence, they would at least have DNA to compare it against. In the meantime, apart from gathering information through interviews and searching, other work had to be done.

Rebecca followed Tom into his office, and she sat on the other side of his desk, slowly looking through the photos once again. She couldn't seem to take her eyes off Helen. A few times she clutched her fist to her chest, astounded that her heart could physically ache. Her emotions were so raw, and she was so helpless.

Tom leaned back in his chair, studying Rebecca quietly as she looked through the photos. As a cop, he was concerned about her. These photos turning up implied something sinister at work, and now she was seeing her sister. Did that mean Helen was dead? As a hot-blooded bloke, he was concerned for her because she was just so darn lovely. Not just in looks but in everything about her was appealing. She was warm, caring, honest, and strong. He decided she needed a distraction.

"So, what do you do for a living?" he asked.

Rebecca glanced up at him, still distracted, but politely answered, "Um, I'm in advertising. I'm a creative account manager for an international firm."

"Wow," he paused, "impressive." He looked at her as her head bent forward, back to looking at the photos. "I think I should enter these photos into evidence," he suggested quietly.

"Oh yeah, of course, sorry."

"No problem." He reached over and gently took them from her and worked through the motions of entering them into evidence.

As he worked, he asked her casually, "So, what does a creative account manager actually do?"

Rebecca stared at him. His question seemed irrelevant. Annoying. But she didn't want to be rude. So, she explained her job to him. The more she told him, the more follow-up questions he asked, the more she enjoyed a relaxed normal conversation about work. She was an enthusiastic artist, and she loved graphic design.

Tom discovered she loved to sketch and paint, and that surrealism was her favourite form of art. Her biggest desire was to see Paris and go to the Louvre, but she had yet to do so.

"I've been to Paris," Tom said casually.

She stared at him, her green eyes wide with interest. "You'll have to spill every detail."

"I'd love to. I developed a love of travelling in my twenties. Give me a map, and a million bucks, and I'd happily retire." Tom grinned a melancholy grin.

She smiled and put her head down, suddenly sad again. She had trouble comprehending life beyond each day now; the idea of Helen not being found was incomprehensible, and moving on with normal life, impossible. Until they found her. Suddenly Tom moved next to her on the two-seater lounge in his office. He sat down and took her hand. She looked up into his soft grey eyes. Tears welled in her own, and she was sorry the brief and lovely moment of normality had ended.

"We'll find her, Rebecca. I promise you; we are doing all we can to find her."

****

Outside Tom's office, Ava worked diligently on spying on Tom and Rebecca. Tom's office was only partially visible, and she couldn't stop herself from looking through the window that ran vertically the length of his door. She could partially see his desk and the lounge that flanked the wall separating his office and the 'bullpen.' She could see them sitting together, and she wondered what they were talking about. Rebecca was a nice girl, and Tom was a sweetheart. Ava was engaged to Mark, her long-time boyfriend, and she was happy, but she was still human. Tom was gorgeous, kind-hearted, and had a quality that made women giggle and blush when he walked into a room. It was a great tactic when questioning people, and she'd seen him in action, using it to his advantage. It would be nice to see him with a nice girl, but she worried that if he had developing feelings for Rebecca, it would make him even more invested in the case, and that could be detrimental to everyone involved.

She glanced at the clock and sighed. She technically should have clocked off already, but since Helen, she couldn't ignore the urgency in the air. Shane was also still there, completing the reports from the day's search

Ava sighed and turned her attention back to the computer and continued to complete the report she had been working on, looking forward to seeing Mark, kicking her shoes off and settling in with a glass of wine. Just after seven, Mark arrived. She saw him stop and talk to Lou at her desk and could see them smiling and chatting. A moment later he continued to Ava, and she smiled at him. "What are you two gas bagging about?" she asked.

"Your Hen's night," replied Mark and winked.

Ava clapped her hands with glee. "Oh, my goodness, I can't wait!"

Mark laughed, came around to her side of the desk as she stood, and they embraced. "Tom still here?" he asked.

"Yeah, he and Rebecca have been in there for ages," Ava replied, nodding towards Tom's office.

Mark raised his eyebrows. "Should I know who that is?"

"That would be Helen's twin," Lou spoke from behind Mark, startling him.

The women laughed as he turned to Lou, chastising her for sneaking up on him before walking over and knocking on Tom's office door.

He waited until he heard his friend call out, "Come in!" before he opened it and popped his head in.

"Hey mate. Are you off soon?" He glanced at Rebecca and smiled politely, trying not to stare at her. The resemblance to Helen was uncanny.

"Yep, off at six."

Mark grinned. "Oh really? How's that working out for you?"

Tom shrugged. "Well, six in the morning is still six," he said, as Mark laughed.

"Dinner?" Mark asked and glanced back at Ava, who nodded.

"I'm bloody starving." She said.

***

That was how Rebecca found herself having dinner with strangers on her first night in town.

Tom made the executive decision for them to go to the local Chinese restaurant within walking distance from the station. As the four of them bade Lou goodnight, who smiled and waved wistfully as they departed, leaving her to start her long shift.

Rebecca still marvelled at the warm air that engulfed her as she made her way outside. It was not yet dark, but the sky was projecting a twilight glow, and she could hear the rhythm of the insects as the four of them walked further into town.

Tom walked alongside Mark, who had become a friend since he had moved to town. Mark grew up in Cooinda, as did Lou, and they had met at Lou's birthday party a few years back, hitting it off instantly. Mark was easy going, affectionate to Ava, and loved animals. He was a veterinarian and had opened his own clinic before he was thirty. At thirty-three, he was a remarkably successful vet and known and loved by almost everyone. Ava and Rebecca walked a few feet behind the men. Rebecca pushed down the twinge of nerves as they set out. It seemed wrong to be doing something so mundane as having dinner. She wanted to be out looking for Helen. She couldn't wait to join in first thing in the morning. Hopefully, after catching up on much-needed sleep.

The Chinese restaurant sat among a cluster of shops that ran along Main Street. Directly across from it was a church. It looked familiar to Rebecca as she made her way inside the restaurant. She glanced back at it nervously before closing the door to the restaurant, following the others inside.

Surprisingly, the conversation between the four of them was much smoother than she expected. Tom ordered a bottle of wine for her and Ava to share, while he and Mark ordered beer. The food was good, the company delightful. Mark was a natural entertainer and naturally made Rebecca feel at ease. He didn't dodge the subject of Helen but began talking about her almost instantly, telling her a story of the time he had met her at a party that Derek had taken her to not long after they had moved home. Rebecca listened, enthralled. The details Mark was offering of Helen's life were something that Helen had never offered. He explained how Helen had offered a story of herself in her teaching days.

"I tell you, her eyes lit up when she spoke of it. I was surprised when she said she wouldn't go back to it. When I asked her why she was, she shrugged it off and said she'd rather concentrate on having kids of her own." Mark shrugged easily.

Rebecca instinctively leaned over and touched his arm. "Thank you, Mark," she said. "Talking about Helen like this — well, it's been great." She smiled. "And thanks for dinner, everyone. It's been great getting to know you all, but I'm exhausted and really need to head back to my motel. I still haven't even checked in. And I desperately need to get some sleep." She stood, putting some cash on the table.

"Do you know where you're going?" Tom asked.

"I'll figure it out." She replied with a smile.

"Nonsense. I'll drop you off." Tom glanced at the others. "Is that okay, guys?"

"What about my rental car?"

"I can pick you up from the motel in the morning," said Ava. "Your car will be fine where it is." She and Mark stood up, and they all made their way outside onto the street. A light drizzle was falling, creating a new level of humidity Rebecca didn't think possible. Ava and Mark said goodnight and began walking to their car.

Tom turned to Rebecca. "You okay to stay here out of the rain? I'll run back to the station and grab my car." Before she could say anything, she was standing alone in the night.

The streetlights glistened in the rain, creating an abstract effect on the road. The church across the street stood regally, and Rebecca had the sudden urge to paint the image before her.

She smiled to herself until she saw Helen. She stood to the left of the church, in front of a sign that read, *"When life isn't a bed of roses, remember who wore the thorns"* Her heart rate quickened, and exhilaration seized control of her.

Helen still had on her running gear. Her appearance was identical to when she had seen her earlier that day. But this time was different. This time, Helen was not looking at Rebecca., she was gazing at the entrance to the church, her finger pointing to some invisible thing. The church was closed, its doors locked. It was a beautiful old church, built most likely in the early 1900s when the town boomed.

Rebecca's gaze quickly drifted back to her sister. She was still there, her arm stretched out, looking at something that Rebecca was not privy to see. Rebecca walked closer, closing the gap between herself and Helen. She was terrified of her disappearing again, and for a minute wondered if it was a hallucination, or if Helen had returned to her. As that thought processed, Helen faded. Rebecca's step quickened, desperate to reach her sister before losing her again. Not caring who was near to hear her, she called out, "Helen!"

Her sister's head slowly turned toward Rebecca, but her eyes stared through her. Rebecca saw the tears wet on her sister's face, saw a trickle of blood down her jawline.

And this time, as her sister faded, Helen spoke, yet no sound emerged. "Derek," she mouthed, as she looked straight through Rebecca, as though she was calling her husband's name because he was standing behind her.

Alone in the night once more, Rebecca shivered and wrapped her arms around herself. Suddenly she was freezing.

Tom noticed a significant difference in Rebecca's mood as soon as he returned. She was visibly shaking; her face was white and staring at the Church. As soon as she saw him, tears welled up in her eyes, and she shook her head, as though she were denying something to herself. She climbed into the car and looked at him directly. "I could really use a drink," she said, her voice soft and shaky.

Without thinking twice, he drove south into Karinya, and within ten minutes they pulled into his driveway. Neither of them spoke as they climbed out of the car, and Tom studied Rebecca as she climbed the front steps of his quaint front porch and sank into a comfortable cane chair. Only then did the tears come. He followed her, squeezed her shoulder, and said softly, "I'll get us a drink," before moving into the house.

When he returned, he held two shot glasses. "All I have is vodka. Is that okay?"

Rebecca grabbed the glass, glancing at him gratefully, and swallowed the smooth liquid in one gulp.

"Do you want to talk?"

"I saw Helen again," was her reply. She was looking out over his front lawn into the night, and she spoke so quietly Tom could barely hear her. Abruptly, she stood up and began pacing his porch. "What the fuck is happening, Tom?" her voice had become frantic. "Am I going mad, or am I seeing her? And if I am, then I must consider the possibility that she is dead and I *am* seeing her ghost" A sob caught in her throat, and rather than start crying again she let out a frustrated growl. She stopped pacing, took a deep breath, and steadied herself. "I think I need to assume she is dead." She said this in a whisper, and almost to herself. She brought her glass up to her lips, realised it was empty, sighed and put the glass down again.

Tom stood up. "No, Rebecca," he objected. "You need to assume nothing. It may not be her ghost you are seeing. What if she is alive and trapped somewhere, desperately trying to get a message to you? Her twin sister? Researchers have found that twins sometimes have a psychic connection."

Rebecca stared at him. "But what if I get my hopes up, and she's really dead?"

Tom sighed, "Look, how about you do whatever you need to do to get through each day, and I'll do my job… which is to treat Helen like a missing person and try to find her. Using any clues that come my way. Including your visions."

Tom fetched a second drink for Rebecca and while she quietly drank, he spoke, "the fact that you describe Helen wearing her jogging leggings, Nikes and t-shirt, down to the exact colours makes me inclined to think Derek was telling the truth about when and why she left the house."

"I was thinking the same thing," answered Rebecca, weary now.

Tom continued, "The tracker dogs found no scent of her past Cane Road, so I have a feeling someone may have picked her up around that point… I wonder if the pub where she first appeared to you is meaningful…" his voice trailed off.

"Well, if the pub is significant, maybe the church is too." Rebecca's voice was quiet. Her eyes were closed, as though she were remembering. "Earlier today, at the pub, Helen was looking directly at me. She was sitting across from me. But tonight, she was looking through me, past me, looking at the church next to her, and pointing towards it. It looked like she was say-ing Derek's name."

Tom looked at her. "Derek's family goes to that church. I might speak to Duncan, their Minister tomorrow. The Cox's wealth contributes to the Church's finances."

"Helen isn't deeply religious, but I know she went with Ruth to church services. I wonder why she did that?" The question was more rhetorical. Rebecca was staring off now, in a haze of vodka and grief.

"Maybe she had become religious?" Tom speculated.

"Or maybe she liked the break from Derek?" Rebecca of-fered. "Either way, the church is important."

After a few minutes, Tom drove Rebecca to the motel, stop-ping along the way at her rental car to collect her belongs. "I can just drive myself from here if it's easier for you?" she sug-gested without conviction.

Tom shook his head. "I'll take you. You've been drinking," he said, glad to find an excuse. All life seemed to have left her eyes, and she was quiet; withdrawn. Her face was still pale, with dark rings forming again under her eyes. Tom was des-perately worried about her. He knew she believed Helen was dead, and deep down he suspected it too. He needed to work this case as hard as he could to bring some closure to the poor woman.

After parking in the motel carpark, he began gathering her things from the backseat while Rebecca walked into the recep-tion to check into her room. She was back shortly after, a key in her hand, along with a breakfast menu and some long-life milk to put in the fridge.

"Room thirteen; of course it is," she sighed dramatically, and Tom couldn't help but laugh at her fatalistic tone.

He carried her suitcase while she carried her duffel bag and other things, and they walked to her room. The motel was a u-shape, set back from the highway that connected Cooinda to the civilisation of the Gold Coast. Room thirteen was tucked away in the corner, and Tom suspected it would be a quiet place for her to get some sleep. Rebecca unlocked the door and flicked the lights on as she walked in. The entire room included a queen bed, a dresser, an armchair, and a round table with a couple of chairs. The television hung on the wall by brackets, and the bathroom was at the back of the room. While bland in style, the room appeared comfortable with the air conditioner spilling its cool air into the room.

He gently placed her suitcase on the stool at the end of the bed and turned to Rebecca. "Try to get some sleep, okay?"

Rebecca nodded, "sure" she replied. She gave him a weak smile. "Sorry. I'm just not really with it."

Tom shook his head. "Don't be sorry, just look after yourself. Your sister needs you too," he paused, "and so do I," he added.

Rebecca grabbed his shoulders and kissed him fiercely. Her lips were soft, yet firm, and her tongue probed gently as he responded to her kiss instinctively. His hand moved up to the back of her head, and he drew her in passionately, exploring her mouth with his own. His low, intense growl broke them apart, and Rebecca pulled away, her eyes shining with grief and lust.

"I'm so sorry." A sob caught in her throat, and she turned away from him.

"No, I'm sorry," he replied softly, berating himself for his lack of self-control. "I'll see you soon, okay?"

Rebecca nodded, her back still to him. He quietly left the room, closing the door behind him, and walked back to his car. The rain was heavier now, and he sat in the dark and waited until he saw the lights in her room switch off, praying she would get some rest. Knowing she was safe, he started the engine. He thought about his home, about the emptiness of his life. Before he could stop himself, Tom lowered his head and sobbed.

{ 11 }

Lou typed slowly, recapping in dot points for the report after her long evening. While Tom and Ava had gone to dinner, she had suffered through a long shift. Now, it was almost six the following morning, and she was expecting Tom to arrive for work any moment. He arrived promptly and greeted her tiredly until he saw her expression. "Everything okay, Lou?" he asked gently.

She sighed and looked up at him. She looked tired and dishevelled. "It's been a long shift, is all. The pub reported a break-in after it closed. Someone stole cash out of the till, and one of their new workers; Josh, did not show up for his shift last night. Do you know that guy, Josh? Well, not only did he not show up for work, but Ang from the Youth Hostel where he is staying has not seen him in a few days... I'm sure he's just out gallivanting, but five days seems like a long time to gallivant."

"Have you sent Jerry out to fingerprint the pub? If Josh has taken off with the cash, he's a missing thief," said Tom.

"He's become a friend over the last few weeks, with both Jenny and me. I couldn't imagine him doing anything like this," her voice trailed off, "anyway, it's just one of those pains in the arse jobs, and reports," she paused, "but to answer your question, yeah Jerry has been out there."

Jerry was their area forensics guy, who served the entire district, along with his entire team of himself and his assistant. He was a busy man and had spent two days in and around Derek's place collecting any potential forensic evidence.

"Well, go home and get some sleep. Night shifts are always the worst," he said sympathetically.

"How was your night?"

"Good," he replied. "I ended up having dinner with Ava, Mark and Rebecca."

"Rebecca?" Lou raised her eyebrows with a mischievous look on her face.

Tom grinned. "Just dinner. She doesn't know anyone in the town."

Lou left shortly after six, waving to Tom, and greeting Shane as he arrived for his shift. It was going to be another warm one, with low cloud cover making it incredibly humid again, indicating afternoon storms might come. The worst part about the night shift in summer was trying to sleep during the day. Her little fibro cottage didn't have luxury items such as air conditioners and dishwashers, and on days like today she wished she'd just bitten the bullet and upgraded her home. As she drove home, she couldn't help but think about Josh. When Jenny had reported the theft, she seemed concerned about Josh. She would call Jen tonight and pop in to see her before she started back on shift and hoped that by the time she awoke that afternoon, all would be back to normal.

Tom was feeling depressed. Last night he had tossed and turned, thinking about Rebecca, his life, and the reasons he had been alone. In less than twenty-four hours, she had him questioning his universe, as he wondered if he was happy by himself, or was he just deluding himself? He sighed as he climbed the steps to the church, and as he walked over the threshold, he hoped God wasn't paying attention to Tom's heart and would concentrate on the matter at hand. That made two of them.

The church was cool and dark. Pews lined each side of the Church and above them, Tom could hear the organ being played softly. He walked further into the church, and Tom craned his neck, looking up towards the organ alcove. Duncan Smith, the minister, played a popular hymn. Tom recognised it yet did not know its name. He raised his hand in the air, trying to get the minister's attention. The music softly ended when Duncan realised, he had a guest. He nodded at Tom and stood slowly, moving towards the stairs that would carry him to the lower level.

Duncan was a distinguished-looking man in his late sixties. He moved slowly and purposefully. He was balding and wore glasses perched on the edge of his nose, often looking at people above them, tilting his head downward, making it appear that he viewed people with raised eyebrows and a surprised expression. Tom had always been friendly with him, although he didn't attend church. He was a friendly man dedicated to his parish.

Lou and Mark had both grown up in the church and had known Duncan all their lives. Tom believed Duncan had even baptised Lou when she was a baby. Tom, however, didn't know him so well. He grinned at him as he approached. "Hi Duncan." They shook hands naturally. "Sorry I called on such short notice. I hope I haven't interrupted you?"

Shaking his head, Duncan asked, "How are you, Tom?" He noticed fatigue in Tom's eyes and silently prayed the man would make it through this awful time with the strength of Jesus.

"Let's take a seat, shall we?" he asked softly as he guided them into a pew halfway down the right-hand side of the church.

"How are Derek, Fred and Ruth holding up?"

"About as well as expected, I guess," said Tom.

"Well, of course I'm happy to help in any way I can, yet I'm honestly not sure how much help that will be," his voice was quiet yet authoritative.

"Duncan, I'm just wanting to find out some information about Helen and her Church activities," Tom paused. "I know she came to church a lot with Ruth and Fred. I just want your opinion of her."

"Well, I see her every Sunday. She started coming only about a year ago. I honestly don't think she was overly religious; however, over the course of the year I noticed a change in her. She started to take communion regularly, whereas at the beginning she only observed, listened, and sometimes prayed. Then, about six months ago, she began coming to the Bible study Ruth attended on a Wednesday morning, as well as the services on Sunday morning and evening." He paused. "In saying that, I didn't get the sense that she had become overly religious. She liked the comfort of the church, as well as Ruth's company. She rarely left Ruth's side, almost seemed scared." His voice trailed off as he looked into the distance, thinking.

Tom's head tilted to the side as he thought for a minute. "Have you noticed anyone new coming to church lately?"

Duncan answered, "No, I don't believe so." Tom sighed. "Is there anything else you can think of that is important? Or not important? Anything about Helen and Derek that you can offer?"

Duncan stared at his hands for a moment. "Well. A few months ago, Helen came to me in confidence about a personal matter. I'm not sure I should share it with you; however, it may be important to your investigation. And I'm not a priest." He shrugged with a mildly humorous expression on his aging face.

"Anything you say will be held in the strictest confidence as part of the investigation." Tom replied, feeling a little breathless.

Duncan nodded. "Well, she and I discussed her desire to have a child. She was conflicted."

"How so?"

"She desperately wanted to get pregnant but was worried about Derek and their relationship. She was fearful for her and any potential child's safety."

"Did Helen ever disclose information regarding abuse to you?"

Duncan sighed. Paused for a moment, as though trying to organise his thoughts. "She said nothing outright. But once she mentioned it, he had lost his temper and knocked her down.

She had hit the side of the dresser in their room, and she had required stitches. She told me; and everyone else; that it was an accident...it very well could have been."

"And what do you think, Duncan?"

"Derek is narcissistic. I think that even if he was not physically abusive towards Helen, he was verbally and psychologically abusive. The poor girl is afraid of her own shadow," he sighed heavily. "I've been praying for her everyday Tom. I hope our Lord is by her side. Wherever she is."

Tom left the church, thanking Duncan for his time. The sun hit him as he opened the heavy doors, and he squinted, reaching for sunglasses that perched on his head.

The pub was only a few minutes on foot, so he left the car at the church car park and walked briskly, caught up in his thoughts. It was midday when he entered the bar and waved to Jenny when he saw her. He knew her only through Lou, and she seemed like a nice enough lady. Tom suspected she revelled in the town gossip a little too much. "Hey, Jenny, how are you?"

"Oh, my goodness, are you here about Josh? He still hasn't turned up, and I'm freaking out!" Jenny was always freaking out, so Tom nodded sympathetically.

"I can imagine you must be worried. Do you know whether his family is in the area?" Tom knew Lou had taken the report, and it was technically her case, but it wouldn't hurt to ask a few questions while he was there.

"As far as I know, his mum lives up in Bundy, and his dad is somewhere in the NT, I think."

"Well, I'll meet with Lou about it this evening, and we will come up with a game plan. Try not to worry, okay? he sounds like he's the sort of guy who moves around a lot." He said this gently, not wanting her to think he wasn't taking her concerns seriously, but he had seen this before with young people who were travelling around the country, working random jobs until they'd saved enough cash to move onto the next gig.

Jenny nodded reluctantly. "That's exactly what Lou said last night."

"I was also here to talk to Dave. Is he around?"

"Yeah, he's here somewhere. I'll check his office, just a sec."

While Jenny was getting her boss, Tom looked around the pub. The place was pretty busy, and he suspected many people were out helping with the search, stirring up extra business for Dave. He'd known Dave since his first day in Cooinda, and like Mark, had become another mate. Dave was older than Tom and Mark, but the three men often met up for a beer whenever their schedules allowed. Dave had only moved to Cooinda when he had bought the pub in the late eighties. He loved his country life and rarely left town.

"Tom, my friend!"

Tom turned to see Dave stride out of the 'employees only' doorway to the right of the bar. Dave had a grin on his face, pleased to see his old friend.

"So much going on for you at the moment. How's everything going?" he asked as he and Tom shook hands.

"Yeah, it's pretty hectic, mate. I'm sorry to have popped in unannounced. I just wanted to chat with you about Helen Cox. And I guess this new man of yours, Josh?"

Dave nodded. "Of course. Let's go take a seat somewhere. Can I get you a drink?"

"Actually, I'm dying of thirst. I'd love some cold water if it's not too much trouble."

Dave nodded and turned to Jen, who had been standing just within earshot, pretending to wipe down the bar, yet only concentrating on the section where she could eavesdrop. "Jenny, could you please bring us a couple of waters? We'll be in the dining room."

Jenny nodded with a smile. "No probs, Dave."

Tom and Dave settled into a corner table in the old dining room section of the pub, which was only open in the evenings and on weekends. The room had high ornate ceilings with beautiful woodworking detail in the archways and window frames. There was a fireplace along the centre of the wall with an old timber mantel, and it was a popular spot for people to come for dinner in winter. Once Jenny had brought in two tall glasses of iced water with a wedge of lemon in each, Tom gulped down the cold liquid for a minute before putting his glass down.

"Okay, I know this may seem strange, but have you ever seen Helen in the pub before?" Dave thought for a moment before shaking his head slowly. "I think I've only ever seen her with Ruth and Fred, or on the odd occasion, with Derek. But Derek was usually here by himself." Dave raised his eyebrows in disapproval.

"Anything I should know about?"

Dave sighed, "Well, the guy is popular, you know? He is always here with mates from school. Mostly Henry and Julia. Sometimes Mark, Ava, Jenny, Lou," he shrugged. "They were all in school together."

"So, he's often here with mates, but he never brought Helen with him?"

"Not that I can remember. Jenny always says that Derek said she was shy, but I think the girls think she's a bit of a snob. You know, from the big city, and thinks she's better than everyone."

Tom silently thought, "If only they knew the truth."

"Okay," Tom said. "And what about this Josh fellow? I have only met him once, the other night when Henry and Cain had beef. He seemed like an all-right fellow."

"Yes, I was surprised he didn't show up for his shift on Saturday. I wasn't overly concerned at that point, though. By yesterday, when he still hadn't appeared, Jenny said she'd called the hostel where he's staying, and Ang said he hadn't been back to his room in a couple of days. Thought I'd better call it in."

"When did you notice the missing cash?"

"That was after. Jenny was setting up for the evening shift yesterday afternoon and realised the cash was missing from the safe. I was planning to take it to the bank on Monday afternoon before it closed. After the weekend is when it has the most cash in it, with the banks being closed on the weekends. By the time Lou arrived last night, I had told her everything at once. Don't suppose the fingerprints have come back yet?"

"Not yet, sorry." Tom finished writing up everything in his notebook and made a note to call Angela out at the hostel later. He finished his water and stood up. Dave stood too, and the friends shook hands. "Call me if you need anything else, okay, Tom?"

Tom nodded. "I will, thanks, mate." He headed out of the pub a moment later, waving to Jenny, who waved back distractedly as she served patrons at the bar.

A light drizzle had started by the time he stepped outside. Tom sighed and bent his head and dashed back to his car at the church. He needed to head over to the search and rescue meeting point and get out and do a few hours of solid searching. Shane was happy to stay back at the station, and he knew Ava was out on her day off, searching for Helen along with Rebecca. He tried not to concentrate on Rebecca for too long, tried not to think of their kiss the night before. However, he thought of her lips, and the noises she made as they embraced, and by the time he got back to his car, he was relieved to sit down to hide his arousal. He sat for a moment with the engine running, waiting for the air conditioner to work its way through the car and cool him down. By the time he arrived at the checkpoint, he was back to business.

The main checkpoint was on Cane Road near Ruth and Fred's home. Fred was there, directing people where to go, handing out maps and water, and keeping himself busy. Tom approached Fred, waiting patiently as he took maps from two young women and a man who had come back from searching. He watched Fred as he thanked the group for helping and bade them farewell as they headed back to their car. When he saw Tom, Fred broke out into a tired grin. The two men shook hands. "How's it all going, Fred?"

"Still nothing. It's like the poor girl has vanished. I just don't understand," he said sadly.

All Tom could do was nod sympathetically. "Well, I'm here to help. Where do you need me?"

"We need more people along the riverbank. The tide is out at the moment, but it'll be back within a few hours. It would be good to get some extra people looking while it's nice and low."

"You got it. I'm on my radio if you need anything, okay? Oh, and is Derek around? How's he doing?"

"Well, he's not here. I suspect he's drowning his sorrows in a bottle of whiskey, feeling sorry for himself."

Tom stared at Fred in surprise. "You mean he's not out searching?"

"Not unless he's planning to find her at the bottom of a bottle." Fred shrugged. His weathered face barely concealed the shame and disappointment. Tom dropped the subject but made a mental note of it. He couldn't imagine a man not out searching for his missing wife. He said goodbye to Fred and made his way down to the section of river Fred had directed him to. There were a couple of search and rescue personnel making their way along the muddy riverbank, carefully combing the mud. There were also divers in the middle of the river. They had been making their way up the river for the last two days, diligently shining their torches into the murky weeds beneath the surface. Tom joined the men on the muddy bank and, before long, was knee-deep in water as he searched for something he prayed not to find.

It was almost dark before he heard the chirp of his walkie-talkie buzzing on his belt. "Tom, it's Lily, are you there? Over."

He grabbed it with ease and answered, "Yep, what's up?"

"You need to get over to Hank Thompson's property. ASAP."

{ **12** }

Visions filled Rebecca's first night in Cooinda. When she awoke, her memories were fragmented. Her sister reaching out a cold hand, face drained of blood as she screamed in silence. When she finally blinked into semi-consciousness, she could feel Helen in the room with her. Keeping her eyes closed, she listened for movement in her room, but there was only silence. Her heart was racing as she opened her eyes, and in her periphery saw the bathroom door swinging closed. Fumbling for the lamp next to the bed, Rebecca bolted upright, alert and trembling. The room stood silent, only the soft hum of the air conditioning unit straining under the oppressive heat. The bathroom door stood open as she had left it the night before, and light from the bathroom window penetrated the room, creating shadows that made Rebecca feel uneasy. Helen was trying to get a message to her; she was sure of it. Yet now she was feeling afraid. And she knew, deep down, that her sister was dead.

She glanced at the digital clock next to her bed, and it glowed red, telling her it was 6:48 in the morning. "Shit," she mumbled, swinging her tired legs out and heaving her body into the shower. Mark and Ava would be there at seven to collect her. Ten minutes later, Rebecca had showered and dressed in comfortable running shorts and a T-shirt that barely reached her belly button. She discovered how poorly she'd packed as she rummaged through her suitcase, most of her items ending up over her shoulder and on the floor at her heels.

Ava knocked on the door a little after the hour and handed Rebecca a cappuccino as she opened her motel room door to greet her. Stepping into the tropical sun, Rebecca felt like the walking dead, still not recovered from jetlag. Ava looked perfect in comfortable shorts and a singlet top, her shaggy brown hair pulled into a ponytail. Her olive skin glowed, and her large brown eyes were sparkling in the sunlight. Rebecca couldn't help but grin as she sipped her coffee, thanking her new friend for the consideration.

By eight that morning, they were deep within the cane fields, walking meticulously in a grid, yelling Helen's name. The day was long and tiring, yet everyone searched without complaint. The number of people who were taking part in the searches moved Rebecca. Almost one hundred people were there, fewer than the previous morning, but still a decent turnout. Once organised into groups, they were sent out to different sections of the town, starting at the location from where the dogs lost Helen's scent, slowly fanning out.

It was almost six in the afternoon when Rebecca stopped for a drink at the pub with Ava and Mark. She was nervous, as it was the same one, she had seen Helen at the day before. It didn't take her long to relax when she saw how busy the pub was. Many of the patrons at the pub had been out on the search, and she recognised many of them. As she passed the dining room section, she spotted Fred with a few older men.

They had been at the checkpoints handing out water, taking names, and handing out maps. Fred raised his hand to her with a smile before continuing his conversation with the one man who shared the table with him.

Ava and Mark settled at a table in the courtyard, in a different section from where Rebecca had sat the previous day. Hidden around the corner and sheltered from the noise. Mark took the women's drink orders and made his way back to the bar.

"I'm so sorry, Rebecca. This must have been an awful day for you. I'm in awe of your resilience," Ava said sadly, reaching out and taking Rebecca's hand. "You must be buggered too. I can't imagine you've slept well."

"No, I've been in a perpetual state of anxiety since I arrived. I was hoping today would be a turning point. I was hoping she'd be found today," Rebecca smiled sadly at Ava. "I'm not sure how much longer I can hold out, to be honest."

Ava nodded sympathetically. "Look, I know we don't really know each other, but I am here for you."

Rebecca nodded; grateful she had made a friend. "Thanks" was all she could muster before Mark arrived back with the drinks. The three drank quietly, chatting about the mundane, yet comfortable in each other's company.

An hour later, when they dropped her back at her rental car, Ava had reached out and grasped her hand. "Please call me whenever you need to talk, okay?"

Rebecca had promised her she would before waving them goodbye and driving back to the motel and the cool dark motel room.

She was just out of the shower when the door to her motel room rattled with a knock. Other than Ava, Mark and Tom, she knew of no one who knew her whereabouts. She suspected it was Tom and was horrified at the thought of him seeing her in her current pathetic state. She stayed quiet, hoping he would think she was not there.

There was a second knock, and she heard a timid, "Hello?"

She didn't recognise the voice. "Um, hello" she answered, just as meekly.

"It's Ruth... Helen's mother-in-law," she added.

Rebecca wrapped her robe tightly around her and pulled her hair back, tying it with the hair tie from around her wrist. She opened the door, enough to see Ruth's face peering at her. It was late afternoon, and still warm. Sweat was lining Ruth's hairline. Rebecca opened the door wider, allowing Ruth to step into her room, escaping the heat.

"I'm sorry; I wasn't expecting anyone. My room's a mess," she apologised as Ruth stood just inside the doorway looking around cautiously.

Rebecca shut the door and led Ruth to the breakfast table, removing her belongings and placing them on the bed. They both sat.

"I've been thinking about you since you came to see us," Ruth whispered. "You are so much like Helen, and it shocked me. I needed to see you."

Rebecca nodded slowly. "I can understand the shock. It made me feel so guilty that I had not been a part of Helen's life for so long. I mean, we talk, but..." she trailed off, and shrugged.

Ruth smiled softly. "To be honest, even if you didn't live in the States, Derek would have made sure you had limited contact with Helen. He even hated that I was close to her."

Rebecca studied her closely. "Do you think he has something to do with her disappearance?"

Ruth looked sharply at her before glancing away. She slowly shrugged. "He's my only son. I love him. But the man has problems. The way he treated Helen was like a piece of property. I'm so ashamed." Tears welled up in her eyes, and her shoulders sagged under the significant weight of parenthood that never ends.

"Treated?" Rebecca asked. "You think she's dead, don't you?"

Ruth paused, but only for a moment. "Yes, I do."

Rebecca nodded. "I do too," she whispered. She reached out her hands, and Ruth clasped them with her own. They both sobbed quietly.

After a few moments, Ruth wiped her eyes and spoke, "There was another reason I came to see you. I should have spoken about this when you and Tom came to see me, but with Derek there, I didn't want to."

"Go on," Rebecca urged.

"I believe Derek may have hired a private investigator or some type of security to watch over Helen secretly. Sometimes when I was with her, out in town or at church, it was like we were being watched. I never mentioned it to Helen, yet a few times I noticed her look over her shoulder, as though she thought someone was behind her. Of course, I saw no one," Ruth shrugged.

Rebecca thought of the photos from the day before, deciding not to mention them to Ruth just yet. "How about I talk to Tom about this when I see him? If it is true, and Derek was having Helen followed, this person could have knowledge of her whereabouts, or even if she were in contact with others. Derek needs to be questioned again about this. He may have information that applies to the investigation."

Ruth nodded. "I know, if possible, though, can you and Tom please not let Fred or Derek know I came to see you about this?"

"Of course," Rebecca answered.

The two women made plans to meet for breakfast the following morning. She said goodbye to her newfound friend, dressed in a nightshirt, and climbed into bed. Within minutes she fell into a deep and dreamless sleep.

The phone in her room jarred her out of her slumber. The loud shrill penetrated her brain, and her eyes flew open, trying to process the sound. She fumbled for the receiver, finally pulling it towards her. "Hello?"

"Rebecca, it's Tom."

"Hi Tom. Thanks again for last night." Her voice was groggy. She glanced at the digital clock that glowed in the darkened room. It read 11:48 pm. She'd been asleep for four hours. She smiled into the phone, pleased he had called her. Even if it was the middle of the night.

"You're welcome," he answered softly. "Are you able to meet me at the hospital now?"

Her heart raced. "You've found her, haven't you?" Her voice was a mere whisper.

"We have found a body, Rebecca. A woman. They took her to the hospital morgue. Derek is on his way there now."

"I'll be there in fifteen minutes" she hung up the phone, not even letting him speak further. She threw on an old shirt and shorts, threw water on her face and slipped out of the motel room within minutes. Her brain was in a fog. She knew this day would most likely come. She prayed it was not Helen. However, this town saw a murder only once a decade; if that, and she knew in her soul that the body would be that of her sister.

{ 13 }

Hank Thompson, a local man who enjoyed fishing along the riverbank down the back of his property, had seen the body on his late afternoon fish and had called the station to report it. It was almost dark by the time Tom, and his team were notified, and they arrived. Hank sat, his head bowed in his hands, waiting for them to arrive. He was on the grass, a few feet back from the water, white as a ghost. His eyes were red from crying, and as he spoke to Tom, he constantly wiped his nose with the back of his hand.

"I knew Helen, you see," he said, his voice shaking slightly. "I would sit behind her and Ruth in church most Sundays."

Tom's voice was soft. "We don't even know if it's her, Hank."

Lou and Shane were on the scene before Tom had arrived, securing the area until the coroner could get there from a town about half an hour away. The area was dark, but they had brought large lamps to set up around the taped perimeter. The crime scene shone in artificial brightness, attracting scores of bugs, flapping, and buzzing around the fluorescent light. Tom had not gone down to the river yet. Hank nodded. "I know it's her, Tom."

Tom sighed, patted him on the shoulder and asked him to stay put. With a deep breath, he headed down to the riverbank.

On the edge of the water, lying across some jagged rocks, was Helen. Her body had floated into the rocks as the tide rose and become stuck on the rocks as the tide receded. She was dressed in her running gear, her hair plastered wet against her face. Her eyes were open as she stared past Tom towards a future that would never come. Tom noticed her shoes were missing, as well as one of her socks, Walkman and headphones. Tears welled up in his eyes as he carefully looked over her body. In Sydney he had rarely known the victims he investigated, and since moving to Cooinda, few people had died violently that he knew. This one was ripping his heart out.

There were many signs of violence on her body, bruising on her swollen, grey face and a deep gash in her hairline. Ligature bruising showed around her neck, indicating strangulation was the cause of death. Her body showed signs of having been in the water for at least two or three days. It had stripped her beauty away, leaving behind an empty shell. The signs pointed to something nefarious. The abuse she had endured was too extensive to have been caused by a fall onto the rocks. The bruising around her neck was manmade, and she wore no shoes. A Walkman could easily slip off her body once in the water, but running shoes? As much as he had been hoping her death was accidental, he now knew it was murder.

Up on the embankment, Tom heard the coroner arrive. He looked up but couldn't see much because of the lighting that shone directly onto Helen. He squinted and called out, "Viraj?"

"Yeah, it's me, mate. Don't get your panties all twisted."

Tom shook his head with a grin, refocusing on Helen, waiting until the coroner reached him at the rocks. The two men exchanged nods as Viraj Hassen examined his surroundings.

"What a fucking shame," he said sadly.

Tom had known Viraj as long as he'd been in Cooinda. The forty-something Australian - Indian man had been born and raised in Brisbane. His father was a doctor, his mother a biologist, so Viraj came from an extensive line of over-achievers. The man was incredibly intelligent, and more 'Aussie' than any white bloke Tom knew.

Viraj carefully pulled on surgical gloves and knelt down next to Helen. His knees scraped on the solid surface of the rock, but he didn't flinch as he studied her body. There was some tearing on her clothes that he inspected, and he reached into his medical bag a couple of feet from him and pulled a handful of baggies out. He passed them to Tom. "Here, make yourself useful for a change."

Dutiful and diligent, Tom passed Viraj the zip-lock bags whenever he held up his hand, meticulously bagging evidence as he worked his way around Helen's body. There were rocks, insects, and hair that became evidence, as well as her watch and bracelet. Viraj held Helen's right hand in his own, examining her palm, long delicate fingers, and fingernails before placing a bag around her hand, securing the bag with a zip tie around the wrist. He moved to the left.

Tom watched Viraj work silently, paying attention to every move. When he paused at Helen's left hand, he waited patiently for the doctor to speak, unwilling to compromise the man's thought process.

Viraj glanced at Tom. "No wedding or engagement ring." He said before he continued with his work. Tom made a note in his notebook. He glanced up around to see what his constables were doing and saw Shane talking to Hank's wife, and Lou was standing by the coroner's van looking towards where Tom and Viraj were. There were a couple of crime scene technicians still on site, taking photos and collecting potential evidence. He assumed Lou was worried about getting in their way or contaminating the crime scene. He made eye contact with her and smiled. She smiled back, her face worn with sadness.

Finally, Viraj was done. "Okay, mate, I need your help to move her, please."

Tom nodded, sliding into a position where he could pick up Helen's shoulders without losing balance on the rocks. The tide was coming in, so they needed to get her moved and check for evidence underneath her body.

The two men heaved Helen up, each carefully manoeuvring themselves off the rocks and onto the embankment. As Tom helped Viraj carry Helen's body to the body bag that lay open on the grass, he had to look away from her vacant eyes that stared up at him as held her by the shoulders. She no longer resembled her twin, her face distorted by death and destruction. Tom's chest constricted with sorrow.

It was another hour before Viraj and the CSI team finished at Hank's place. Tom sent Lou and Shane home, ordering them to get some rest, and reminding them to keep the information about Helen quiet until he had the chance to talk to her family.

Lou and Shane were grateful to head home. It was the first time they had both seen a murder victim in the flesh, and their professionalism impressed Tom.

After Viraj had left, telling Tom he would see him shortly at the morgue, Tom stood looking out over the rippling water towards the cane fields and properties that lined the other side of the embankment. It was dark now, almost ten in the evening, and in the distance, a back porch light shone from the old guesthouse on the other side of the river. It was often bustling with movement of guests, and the grounds were often lit up in the evening, with many guests barbecuing and congregating on the back lawn in the evenings.

He saw a figure there now; more of a bright shadow, standing on the banks of the river. Tom studied it and realised it was a woman. She raised her arm and waved at him. Tom's heart raced, and he moved a few feet closer to the edge of the water, squinting in the darkness. He let his eyes focus on the evening ambiance and stared at the woman as she continued to wave at him. The woman was Rebecca. He was about to wave back to her but hesitated. Was that running gear she had on? Chills crept up Tom's spine, and he was about to move even closer to the water's edge when Hank called out. Startled, Tom turned around to find him standing behind the yellow crime-scene tape. "We all good here, Tom?" he asked softly.

"Yeah, sorry, Hank, I'll be just a second" he turned back towards the river, only to find the waving woman gone.

$$\{\,14\,\}$$

Rebecca found herself at the hospital and realised she didn't remember getting there.

The morgue was a room in the basement area of the hospital. It was a standard square room. There were no drawers to keep bodies in, but a freezer room tucked into the corner. Derrek, Ruth and Fred were also in the waiting area next to the morgue. A man Rebecca didn't recognise was also there. He stood quietly next to Ruth, with his hand placed gently on her back as she sobbed. As she stepped into the room, Derek looked up. Their eyes met, and Rebecca knew instantly that he had nothing to do with her sister's death. His eyes grieved, his hair, dishevelled, and he was visibly shaking. Rebecca automatically reached out her arms, and he strode over, folding himself into her embrace. They momentarily forgot their mutual dislike, holding each other while each longed to hold Helen.

As they moved out of their embrace, Tom quietly came into the room. His presence was necessary in these circumstances, and Rebecca was relieved he was there. Determined not to cry again, she nodded at him. He reached over, placed his hand on her shoulder briefly, then moved further into the room.

"Hi folks, before we go in, I just want to say how sorry I am. Obviously this is the worst outcome, and I am devastated, and so sorry for your loss. There will be an autopsy to determine the cause of death, and until then, the police department is treating the death as suspicious."

"Well, of course it's fucking suspicious," growled Derek.

Rebecca sighed; the brief, heartfelt moment they shared only moments ago, lost already.

Tom cleared his throat. "Derek, this is protocol. I'm not trying to add to your grief or anger. I'm just telling you how these things go."

Derek's face softened, and he seemed to deflate. He nodded, putting his head down.

Tom knocked gently on the door that led into the morgue, and the door opened. A clean-cut, handsome Indian man with a friendly face stood holding the door, and past him, Rebecca could feel death.

"Hello." His voice was kind. "Only immediate family needs to identify the victim." He glanced at Ruth and Fred apologetically.

Fred nodded. "We are here to support and grieve together," he stated.

Derek and Rebecca stepped forward. As they walked into the room, Rebecca glanced back at Tom. "Please come in with us?" she whispered.

He nodded and stepped alongside her as they made their way over to the table that had a sheet covering the body. Rebecca shook, and she felt Tom's hand on her back, firm and warm. She glanced at him with appreciation.

Derek stood on the far side, next to the solemn, nice-looking medical guy. (Was he a coroner, Rebecca wondered?) She and Tom stood on the side closest to the door. The room was cool and sterile. Everything was clean and metal, with white tile covering the floor and most of the walls. The room was much brighter than Rebecca thought it would be, and she squinted involuntarily.

The morgue guy spoke: "So, now I will pull the sheet back to her neck only. I will give you a moment. As soon as you indicate to me with a look, I will cover her up again." He spoke softly, methodically. Derek nodded; his eyes fixed on the sheet. His face was white and his eyes wide, unblinking.

Rebecca stared across at Derek, afraid to look down as the man pulled the sheet back. Derek inhaled sharply as Viraj revealed Helen's face. Terrified, Rebecca closed her eyes. When she opened them, she finally looked down.

Helen lay staring at her, pale blue, distorted and swollen, her eyes were wide open, head turned slightly towards her. Her once beautiful green eyes were now muddy and soulless. Viraj had cleaned her to prepare for their viewing, and her hair was now shiny and soft, fanning around the sides of her face, and was the most human thing about her.

Rebecca reached out and stroked it. Her head lolled slightly as she moved her hand through the auburn hair that matched her own. A sob caught in her throat as she bent down to kiss her sister's forehead. She held her lips to her twin's face, afraid to leave her behind. Finally, she straightened up and looked over at Derek. He seemed afraid to touch her, but his eyes revealed his pain and shock. "I'm so sorry, Derek," she whispered. He tore his eyes away from his wife and looked at her sister.

He nodded, a tear finally escaping and rolling down his cheek. "Yeah, me too."

Out in the waiting room, Fred and Ruth waited patiently. Duncan was still with them and sat next to Ruth. His head hung, eyes downcast. As Rebecca, Tom and Derek walked back into the room, she saw the man's lips moving softly, as though in prayer, and Rebecca realised he must be the Coxs' minister from their church. The one Helen also attended.

Ruth knew as soon as she saw Derek that her daughter-in-law was dead. Panic rose in her like bile, and she swallowed hard, pushing down all the fear and grief that was bubbling on the surface. Fred, whose hardened face suddenly had so many more lines, grasped Ruth's hand and squeezed. She realised that he'd aged ten years in the last four days; his usual tough and weathered persona suddenly seemed withered, frail. They both stood, and she held her arms out to her son.

As he reached them, he whispered. "She's actually fucking dead, mum..." She held him, and, finally, he let himself be held.

Rebecca needed air. As she looked at Derek, Ruth and Fred, who all stood so close to each other, she realised she was an intruder. Tears blurred her vision, and she turned to Tom, seeking his comfort. He was there, standing right beside her, and his hand gently reached for hers, guiding her towards the row of chairs. He looked at Ruth, who broke away from Derek and sat with Rebecca. She pulled her in close, and finally Rebecca cried.

Viraj and Tom moved away from the family. Viraj handed Tom a yellow envelope. Inside it, there was Helen's jewellery that he needed to enter as evidence. Viraj had already processed the bracelet and watch for any particles, DNA and fingerprints. "Thanks for everything, Viraj. Keep me updated on her autopsy, please, mate."

Viraj nodded. "Of course, you'll be the first to know." He moved over to Rebecca and the Cox family, a solemn expression on his face. "I'm so sorry for your loss." He said this quietly before gliding out of the room and disappearing through another door Rebecca had not noticed until that moment.

Tom moved over to where Derek stood with Fred and Duncan. His face was void of expression, and Tom hated to ask questions, yet it was important to do so. "Derek?" he asked, bringing Derek out of his almost trance-like state.

"Yeah?" Derek looked up, almost confused about where he was. Everything was surreal, and he was struggling not to sink to the floor.

"I'm sorry to ask you this now, but I need to for Helen's sake," he began.

Derek's eyes changed to a cautious, weary look, but he said nothing, just waited for Tom to continue.

"Do you know if Helen's wedding and or engagement rings are at home? She didn't have them on."

Derek's eyes changed to a look of confusion as he thought about Tom's question. "She usually had them on. Sometimes in the heat she would get eczema around her fingers though and take them off until it cleared. So, I'm not sure. I'll check at home and let you know?"

"Thanks, I'd appreciate it." He touched Derek's arm briefly before turning to look at Rebecca and Ruth on the chairs. Rebecca's tears had dried up, and she sat shaking uncontrollably, staring into space.

"I think I need to get her out of here," he whispered. Ruth nodded; her eyes filled with empathy.

Outside in the hospital parking lot, the warm breeze rose from the river and sprinkled its relief through the trees. The night was dark, with only a sliver of the moon revealing itself. Rebecca looked up towards the sky and studied the stars as they shone above the earth. She saw a lone shooting star flash through the sky, and she quickly closed her eyes, wishing her sister to roam free. She walked away from the hospital. Tom walked beside her, his hand firmly on her elbow, and within a minute realised she did not know where she had parked her rental car. They wandered around the parking lot until Tom spotted it; parked terribly, taking up two spaces as she had flown into the spots at a forty-five-degree angle. When she saw the car, she felt like such an idiot that she burst into a short laugh. "Holy crap, hope I don't have a ticket."

Tom chuckled quietly. "If you do, I think I can get it sorted."

They stood by her car door, and she leaned against him. He stroked her hair and allowed her to cling to him.

"I don't know how I'm going to get through this," she whispered.

Rather than words, Tom tightened his hold on her. He moved his hand from her hair down to her chin and guided her face to look at him. Their stares held for a full minute before he spoke. "I'll be here." He said simply, and she nodded.

At the other end of the carpark, Duncan watched silently as the streetlamps dimly lit up Rebecca and Tom embracing. He sighed in grief, thinking just how hard it was for the poor girl to lose her twin. He was certainly glad she had found a friend in the detective, yet he noticed their connection might be a little more than that, and he said a silent prayer for them both.

{ **15** }

Wednesday morning, after no sleep, Rebecca drove over to the homestead. There were funeral arrangements to be made, and even though they could not put Helen to rest until the coroner released her body, Ruth and Rebecca began making the arrangements.

Derek also hadn't slept and instead lost himself in the bottle. He refused to leave his house, and Rebecca watched Ruth call him on Wednesday afternoon to ask him about funeral arrangements. She could hear him yelling at his mother. His temper was so quick to flare, his behaviour so unpredictable, she reverted to her original feelings about him, recognising his personality type could not manage grief any more than he could handle love. His narcissism only really allowed him to grieve over what had happened to him. Rebecca would stay away from him as much as possible.

Over the next few days, she did, however, slip straight into Ruth's life. As girls, Rebecca and Helen had never known supportive or even loving parents. Their childhood was irregular amounts of interest, congealed with much larger amounts of disdain. Her parents were lazy, complaining, and self-centred. As functioning alcoholics, their plan to have one trophy child had backfired, giving them two stunning-looking daughters that 'sucked them dry: mentally, emotionally and financially' (her mother's words). By the age of eight or nine, Helen and Rebecca had to fend for themselves. Their parents were always out socialising with friends or working, and when at home, drinking. Until the girls had left home at eighteen, Helen had constantly sought her parents' approval. She was so deprived of love and acceptance that her behaviour had often reminded Rebecca of an abandoned puppy begging for attention. It made her hate her parents even more.

Rebecca and Helen had not spoken to them since they were eighteen years old. Helen had fallen for Derek when they were only twenty-four years old, married by twenty-five, dead by twenty-nine. What had been in between? Had she even been happy? The last few days in Cooinda had given Rebecca the impression that Helen had been deeply unhappy with her life with Derek, and she was seeking fulfilment but unsure how to. It broke her heart that she had lived the first eighteen years of her life trying to please her parents, only to move onto a man who would also prove impossible to please.

On Wednesday afternoon, Rebecca sat and discussed her parents with Ruth. Should she call them? Ruth had more insight into Helen's state of mind about their parents. "She was still so heartbroken, even after all these years," Ruth admitted. "They made her feel so unworthy that her self-esteem was non-existent. I spent so long trying to build her up, but it seems Derek spent just as much time knocking her down." She shook her head, tears in her eyes. "I should have encouraged her to leave. I knew what their marriage was, but I loved her so much.

It was so selfish of me." Her voice dropped to a whisper. "I didn't want to lose her ..."

They sat together on the lounge in the grand living room, where Rebecca had first met them. The curtains were closed, blocking out the inappropriateness of the beautiful, warm day. Rebecca reached out and took Ruth's hand in her own.

"You were the one that kept her going. I can see that now, clear as day. It wasn't Derek that she loved. It was you and Fred. You were the parents she never had, and I think her relationship with Derek was something she tolerated so she could stay with you."

With this, Ruth finally broke. She hung her head and sobbed. Rebecca moved closer and put her arms around her, pulling her close, and stroked her hair. "I won't be contacting our parents, at least until after the funeral. All Helen ever loved is right here in Cooinda."

Later that evening, Ruth decided Rebecca should move her things out of the motel and into the grand homestead. She put up little resistance, desperate to be out of the motel and into a comfortable bed. By the Thursday morning, she had checked out of the motel and settled in the guest room, a large regal room, with heavy dark furniture and a four posted bed. There was an attached guest bath, and the Cox's had even put a framed photo of her with Helen when they were about eighteen next to the bed.

Fred had found the photo amongst Helen's things when he'd been over to see Derek about collecting some of her things to take back to Ruth and Rebecca. He had a fight on his hands, though. Derek insisted it was a breach of his privacy, but his father, stoic as always, had ignored his son's words, strode into the house, and began placing Helen's things into a box he carried with him. "I'm only taking some of her personal items, Derek, things her dear sister will want to hold on to. They never got to say goodbye to each other. Surely you can part with two or three of Helen's things that Rebecca would cherish?"

Derek sat deflated at the kitchen table and lit a cigarette. He watched his father through a whiskey haze as Fred collected two of Helen's favourite books, her makeup, a photo album, items of her clothes, and last, a couple of pieces of jewellery.

"Did you look for her wedding and engagement rings during your drinking?"

Derek nodded, choosing to ignore his father's comment about the drinking. "I looked last night when I got home. I found only her wedding ring. It's in the jewellery box you are looking in now."

Fred sighed and carefully looked through Helen's pieces of jewellery. There were only three or four things in the velvet box, including two pairs of earrings. He studied Helen's wedding ring but left it in place.

"Her engagement ring must have come off in the water," he commented, almost to himself. He heard Derek choke back a sob and instantly felt like a bastard.

He turned to his son sadly. "I know you loved Helen, son, and I am so sorry you have lost her. Please just remember you're not the only one who has lost. There are people around you to grieve with...."

Derek snorted and took another long gulp of his whiskey.

Fred sighed and began walking to the front door. He stopped with his hand on the handle. "I've asked Rebecca to do the eulogy at the funeral. I expect you are okay with this?"

Derek only nodded. He ran his hand through his hair, silently wishing his pompous father would fuck off so he could continue to drink in peace. What the fuck did he know? The man was so drunk on power and money; he thought he controlled the world. Well, that may be the case, but he certainly did not control Derek Cox. Rebecca could read the fucking eulogy for all he cared. Helen would always be his wife. And everyone in town would come to pay respects to him, not her fucking sister or his fucking parents.

* * *

In the homestead guestroom, Rebecca sat at the antique dresser after having unpacked her meagre belongings and showered in the large cream and burgundy tiled ensuite. She washed her hair and shaved her legs for the first time since arriving in Cooinda, and by the time she came out of the steam-filled bathroom she was more human than she had in a week.

The framed dresser and mirror were antique, and Rebecca admired the furniture as she brushed her long auburn hair, staring into space. Before her shower, she had called her boss in New York to let her know about Helen's death. The managing director, Yolanda, was devastated to hear the news, and gave Rebecca her blessing to stay until after the funeral. Connecting with her boss reminded her of just how disconnected she was from her life in the States, and she wondered where her home would be now that Helen was dead.

She swivelled on the stool and slowly looked at her surroundings. The bedroom she had been in for an hour felt more like home to her than her apartment in Brooklyn had in four years, and it made her ponder her own happiness. She sighed, and swung back to the mirror, picking up the hairdryer to style her clean hair. She turned on the dryer and glanced up at her reflection.

Helen stood behind her, watching her. Rebecca cried out, her voice drowned out by the hairdryer, which fell from her hand and clattered onto the stool next to her. Without taking her eyes off Helen, she fumbled for the dryer and switched it off. Helen was not looking at her twin but was looking at something Rebecca was not privy to. For the first time since her sister had appeared to her, she wore something other than her death clothes. This time she wore a pale pink singlet top with a matching cardigan. The knitted ensemble had white embroidered flowers on it that complemented the white jeans she wore. Her hair sat around her shoulders, and her face glowed with a touch of makeup on. Helen was relaxed and appeared to be talking to someone.

Mesmerised, Rebecca watched as Helen talked. Her hands would occasionally move in animated spirit, and it was there Rebecca saw the diamond of her engagement ring sparkle brightly. Helen appeared happy until her eyes changed. Her smile shifted from genuine to nervous, and her attention was drawn to another person Rebecca could not see. It was like watching a home movie reel with no sound. In her reflection, Rebecca continued to watch Helen turn and walk towards the bedroom door, as though being chaperoned out by someone.

She saw her glance back towards the person she had been talking to, an apology written over her gentle face.

Rebecca called Helen's name softly, afraid she was about to disappear.

Helen turned again, this time not to an invisible person in the past, but to directly look at Rebecca. Helen's eyes widened when she saw Rebecca.

Rebecca spun around, away from the reflection, towards the bedroom door, and said her sister's name once more, "Helen!"

The room was empty. Spinning back towards the mirror, praying the connection remained open, but the window into the world beyond was gone, and Rebecca was alone, staring at herself, with wet hair, and an aching heart.

{ **16** }

Five days after Hank found Helen in the river, on a bright Sunday morning, Viraj announced that Helen's post-mortem was complete, her manner was homicide, and the cause was ligaturing strangulation. An official police investigation opened. Helen was released into the care of the funeral home. The funeral would be the following Tuesday at eleven.

Tom sat at his desk, staring at the report from Viraj, grateful the man had worked through his weekend to complete the report.

Both Lou and Ava sat across from him. They looked tired, as did Tom. It had been a rough five days. Not only was Helen found, but Josh, the bartender, along with the stolen money from the safe, remained missing. Lou suspected he might have stolen the money and run, but Ava discovered Josh's wallet in his locker at the pub, minus its cash. Jenny thought Josh was innocent, and so the investigation was ongoing until Josh or the money surfaced. Preferably both.

The heat was refusing to dissipate, and the whole town was on edge since finding Helen. There were more phone calls coming in with citizen's concerns of break-ins, people with their ideas of what had happened and phone calls of people just calling to see if there was anything they could do to help.

Tom had heard that Rebecca had moved out of the motel and into Ruth and Fred's guest room. Ava had seen Rebecca every day for the last few days, and the women quickly became close friends. Tom couldn't be happier with this development. He knew that the night before even Lou and Jenny had met with them, and they had all had dinner together at the pub after Jenny finished her shift. Ava had informed him that Ruth and Rebecca were busy planning the funeral and were leaning on each other in their shared grief. Tom was relieved Ruth and Fred had welcomed Rebecca into their home, but he worried about Rebecca being so close to Derek. He still hadn't been able to rule out Derek as a suspect because he had no alibi. Fingerprints and DNA from Helen's body had not returned and sometimes it could take quite a while to get the results.

Until then, he was at a standstill. Reading the report told them how Helen had died. There were several hematomas on her arms and legs. She had been hit across her head with a blunt object, and several of her nails were broken, indicating she had struggled. A lot. And finally, there was bruising around her neck, and no water in her lungs, confirming someone had strangled her, with a rope of some sort. There were fibres pulled from her skin currently being analysed; however, Tom knew how difficult it was to get clean results after being in the river. The water had bloated and discoloured her body, and he wondered if the mortician could offer an open casket. He glanced up at his two constables, who sat opposite him, looking at him as he read the report. They had both already read it, and each was feeling heavy and exhausted.

"So, Tom. What do you think?"

Tom sighed, "well, it is giving us a clue to motive. But until they finish analysing the evidence, the only thing we can really do is some old-fashioned police work. We need to talk to the town's folk again; we need to watch everyone closely; find out as much as we can about Helen's last few days, and most important... attend her funeral next Tuesday."

Lou nodded. "Hold up, what's the clue to motive. Have I missed something obvious?"

"I was just about to ask the same question." Ava agreed.

Tom shook his head. "No, nothing obvious. I was waiting for the autopsy report to prove my suspicion that Helen was not sexually assaulted. When she was found fully dressed, I suspected the crime was not sexually motivated."

Ava sighed in frustration, and Lou sagged and pursed her lips together. "If not rape, then what?

"Well, we can't exclude the possibility of the crime being sexually motivated, all the report is telling us is that she wasn't. It doesn't rule out that her killer had every intention on assaulting her. She could have fought him off, and he killed her faster than intended."

Lou nodded, understanding the significance and Ava scribbled some notes.

"So, maybe we just go about our normal day, keep our heads down and our ears open. Be there for the people. Hopefully, they will tell us things that they don't realise are important, but it will be?"

"Good idea, Lou. Why don't you do road patrol, and Ava, can you man the station? Shane is also out on road patrol today, and I'm going to go out and talk to the Cox family about the report."

"You sure you don't need me to come?" Lou asked.

"I think we still need to divide and conquer," he answered with a wry grin.

Ava nodded, "Fine with me, as long as I'm out of here in time for my Valentine's dinner with Mark." She winked when she said this, and it made Tom laugh.

"I'll do my best. I certainly don't want Mark on my back. I completely forgot about Valentine's Day, actually, so I'm glad you reminded me."

"It's nice for those of us who have someone," Lou said dramatically before standing and leaving Tom's office, slightly annoyed she got stuck with parking tickets and speeding fines for her shift. Ava grinned in agreement and waved goodbye to Lou and moved back to her desk.

When Tom stepped out into the sunlight, he noticed the hustle and bustle of the town signified Church had just finished. He would often see substantial numbers of people around town on a Sunday lunchtime. Everyone was nicely dressed and more relaxed than usual, and it always warmed his heart. He held Helen's file in his hands, which now held the autopsy report from Viraj, including post-mortem photos, along with the photos that he and Rebecca found on his windshield, witness statements, and photos of the crime scene.

The post-mortem photos of Helen were mostly close-ups of the wounds she'd endured, the bruises around her neck, her dirty feet. He had no intention of showing the family those photos; however, he wanted them close to him. He had been on alert since Helen died. Everyone was now a suspect.

As he walked to his car, parked behind the station, he stayed alert. The day Helen was found next to the river was still so fresh in his mind. Remembering her dead on the riverbank and then seeing her ghost across the river made him so helpless and frustrated. He had not talked to Rebecca about it yet. He was trying to give her time with Ruth and Fred, to make female connections, and to grieve. But he missed her, more than he knew he should. In the short time that she had been in Cooinda, a bond had formed. It was inappropriate and annoying. Tom considered his life settled and happy. He had not craved companionship since his divorce years ago and had never dreamed of getting married again. The only time he had committed to a meaningful relationship with a woman — all those years ago — had left him devastated and bitter when he was twenty-seven.

Rebecca was different somehow. She was more independent than other women he had met, especially since arriving in Cooinda eight years ago. She was career-driven, smart, beautiful, but also had a vulnerability that exposed her gentle nature. He knew it was incredibly unprofessional to be thinking about her in this way while he was investigating her sister's murder, but he was having trouble switching off his feelings. He could see Lou looking at him over the last week, especially in the few days with Rebecca leading up to finding Helen. She had shared something private and scary with him, and he had not only taken her seriously, but had believed her.

Tom thought about Helen standing across the river looking at him, as he looked at her glowing on the riverbank. Had he seen her? Or was his mind playing tricks on him? He had been exhausted and had been listening to Rebecca's stories for the couple of days before that, living what she had been living, as she had continually seen her sister. It had only been a moment that he'd seen her, like when you're waking from a dream, and it lingers, desperate to climb its way into the world.

As he pulled out of the carpark and turned east towards the homestead, he wondered what he would say to Rebecca when he saw her. It had only been five days since he had seen her, but it felt like five years. He was not looking forward to discussing the report, but it had to be done. Any insight any of them could give him would help the investigation. At present, there were no viable suspects. He was at a complete standstill and was so afraid that the investigation was going cold fast. He knew from experience that the longer a crime remained unsolved, the more difficult it was to solve. Not only could he not stand the idea of letting down Rebecca and the Cox's, but he also despised the idea of a killer roaming through his town, thinking they had gotten away with murder.

The drive to the homestead only took a matter of minutes, and as he turned onto the long regal driveway, and began the journey through the cane, his heart raced. Would his professionalism go out the window? As he gently pulled up behind Rebecca's rental car, he told himself to get a grip.

Derek's car was parked in front of Rebecca's rental. Tom had instructed the family; it would be a clever idea if they could all come together for this meeting. He worried for a minute that he had made a mistake in assigning Ava to another job, as she was always a natural at dealing with highly emotional people, but the department was stretched thin at the moment. He also sought safety in numbers when he saw Rebecca again.

Tom stepped out of the car and glanced toward the cane. The day was still and hot; the blue sky was cloudless. He stood listening, waiting for what? He wasn't sure. The last couple of times he had been out to the homestead, he had the feeling of being watched. Today, however, was just a regular day. The birds sang, the crickets chirped, and in the distance, he could even hear the river lapping against the shore behind the homestead. He walked to the door, and with his arm out ready to knock, the door opened. Rebecca stood in the doorway. Her auburn hair was piled on top of her head, and she wore a pink T-shirt and denim shorts, which revealed her long legs and bare feet. He looked into her eyes, saw the sadness, saw the heavy weight of grief, and he wanted to reach out and hold her.

Instead, he said, "Hi Rebecca."

She stepped out onto the porch and pulled the door shut behind her. Without a thought or hesitation, she put her arms around him, pulling him towards her. They stood and hugged, like two old friends. She had missed him in the last five days but had needed time. Ruth and Fred had taken her into their home, and she was so thankful that they were taking control of the funeral arrangements. She wasn't sure she could manage it on her own, or if it had just been herself and Derek.

She stepped back and looked up at him. "A part of me is gone. I'm hollow. It's like someone has ripped off my arm or leg. I'm so used to knowing she's there... somewhere. Now, she's nowhere."

Her eyes were tearless; her heart, broken. Tom worried whether it was beyond repair.

"I'm sorry I haven't called. I heard you had moved into the homestead temporarily, and I thought I should give you space."

She nodded. "Yeah, it's been..." Her voice lowered, and quivered. "It's been hard." She looked at him again. "Ava told you I'd left the motel?"

He nodded. "I hope that's okay?"

She nodded. Took his hand and led him inside.

The house was cool, with the lofty ceilings drawing the heat to the roof and beyond. Tom's home certainly seemed to hold on to the heat compared to this place. The breeze from the river blew through the back of the house, and Rebecca led him through the grand hallway and into the large family kitchen. Ruth stood at the kitchen counter, preparing scones and tea. The recently renovated kitchen offered open plan living, with a large comfortable family room on the other side of the island workbench.

It had a more casual vibe compared to the formal living room at the front of the house and was decorated with comfortable cane furniture and large soft sofas, light airy curtains, and large slate tile on the floor. Ferns hung from the ceiling, and the kitchen island had timber stools under it, enticing guests to sit as the host prepared food.

There were enormous sliding doors in the family room that led out onto a wide verandah and ran lengthwise along the riverfront, and Tom suspected the family spent the majority of their time in this part of the house.

He also noticed just how at home Rebecca was. She walked into the kitchen, opened the fridge, and removed the milk. On the island, she poured it into a jug and added it to the tray of afternoon tea that Ruth was preparing.

"I'll take this outside," she said.

From another room in the house, Tom heard Fred's deep voice.

"Nonsense, let me make myself useful. Good morning, Tom." Fred strode into the kitchen from the front of the house, having changed out of his church clothes into comfortable slacks and a collared shirt. He shook Tom's hand and then strolled over to his wife, who was still in her Sunday best, and kissed her cheek, reached out and squeezed Rebecca's shoulder before picking up the tray. With steady hands, he carried the large tray ladened with scones, jam and cream, tea and coffee, over to the coffee table. Tom admired the aging man's strength and resilience as his eyes followed him as he moved through the living room. It was only then that he noticed Derek standing on the verandah outside the sliding doors. His back was to the house, and he stood facing the river. A cigarette was in one hand, a glass of whiskey in his other hand. His only movement was the steady rise and fall of his cigarette and drink, as he smoked and drank his emotions to oblivion.

Rebecca motioned for Tom to follow her and Ruth, and the three of them converged in the family room with Fred calling for Derek to join them. Ruth waved her hand towards a comfortable armchair for Tom to sit down. He glanced at Rebecca, who sat between Ruth and Fred. She seemed to feel more secure with them both cocooning her. He sat and put the file on the floor at his feet. Derek remained standing just inside the open doors.

Tom sighed. Discussing post-mortem information with family members was always difficult. This, however, was another level. He knew Rebecca and the Cox's well now, and he still had absolutely no suspects, or even leads. He hoped that the information he revealed today might move the investigation further. If only the pieces could finally be knit together so they could see the complete picture.

"So, thanks for meeting with me today. I can only imagine how difficult this is for you all. I am so sorry for your loss... all I can say is that we are doing everything we can to find out what happened to Helen... and who hurt her."

Derek finally walked over and took a seat. Tom noticed his slight glance at Rebecca, the fury hiding behind the grief. Tom realised just how much he loathed Rebecca coming into his family's life. It would be like seeing Helen every day yet having no control. It would kill him.

"What did the coroner find, Tom?" Derek's controlled voice was curt, no nonsense. Tom's condolences fell on deaf ears.

Ruth's sharp voice interrupts, "Derek, all in good time. Let Tom start where he needs to start. You are not in control of this investigation," her warning to her son was a side of Ruth that Tom had not seen the last few times he had met with them. She always seemed to be a soft-hearted woman, always keen to hide her son's personality. Now, she seemed to have lost that motivation and gained an unfamiliar edge that Tom appreciated.

Fred spoke. "Tom, please continue."

Derek sighed in frustration, stood up and walked to the edge of the veranda again. He lit another cigarette.

"Well," started Tom. "I'm really hoping to share as much of the investigation with you all so you can see something that one of us has missed. If you are up for it, I would like to show you the crime scene photos first." This was not always standard procedure. An investigation could take on a life of its own and not always need to involve family members to help gather information. Often, though, when an investigation came to a standstill, detectives used all the resources available to them, even the family, even if some were suspects.

Derek exploded. He had obviously still been listening, even after moving outside again. "What the fuck, Tom!" He threw his cigarette over the verandah, and it landed in the grass, still lit, the haze of smoke drifting towards the river. He moved back towards the family room. "There is no fucking way I am subjecting my parents to something like that! Are you crazy?"

"Derek, calm down, son," Fred was tired suddenly. Tired of dealing with his petulant child. "I'm sure Tom will be discreet in what he reveals, and I'm sure he is doing it hoping it helps him catch Helen's killer. You want that, don't you, Derek?" He swivelled slightly in his chair and stared at his son.

"Of course, I want that, I just...it doesn't seem necessary is all. What about Mum?"

"What about her?" asked Ruth, her eyebrows raised. "I'm a big girl, Derek. And I have your father and Rebecca right here for support." She glanced at Rebecca and squeezed her hand.

Tom noticed the intentional exclusion of her only son.

"Fred's right. I really need to show you the crime scene. It's always complicated when victims are left outdoors, and even more difficult when victims have been in the water. Evidence gets washed away, and there was a lot of debris at the scene. We don't really know what is significant. And what means nothing? The first thing I need to tell you is that Helen's death has been determined a homicide." He fell silent, letting the information settle over the family.

Rebecca let out a long breath that she didn't even realise she was holding. "Was she drowned?"

"No... someone strangled her before putting her into the river. I'm so sorry."

All three of them nodded. Rebecca put her head down and let out a sob.

"Wait, what?" Derek turned and looked at Tom. "What? Tom, did someone murder her?

"Yes, Derek, I'm so sorry."

"No, I mean, I thought someone had accidentally hurt her..." Derek sat down on the steps that led down to the soft green lawn. "Who would want to hurt my Helen?" His head fell into his hands, weeping.

Rebecca stood up and walked to him quickly. She sat beside him on the step, put her arms around him, and hugged him while he cried for the woman he had lost. Tom marvelled at how Rebecca reached out to comfort him, even though he displayed obvious discomfort, and mostly disdain at her presence. She didn't care, though. The common denominator that brought them all together was Helen. Derek may have been a terrible husband — controlling, narcissistic, an arsehole. But he loved Helen. Even if it was an unhealthy, even dangerous love. But he was still hurting, and he was still human. And Rebecca still felt sorry for him.

After a minute, Derek shrugged Rebecca away, stood up and walked inside.

Rebecca sat on the step, left high and dry by herself. She stared at the river, watching the water lap against the rocks. Derek's dismissal made her feel inadequate, unimportant. He had kept her from her sister for so long, but it wasn't just his fault. She had left. Moved her life to New York, leaving her sister behind with a lousy husband. Helen's only solution had been to turn to the closest people she could. And that had been Ruth and Fred. Suddenly, she realised just how much she had fucked up. Just how alone her sister had been, trapped here. Helen would never have complained to Rebecca that she was unhappy. She would have been too ashamed. Her personality type was always submissive. She wasn't a leader. Unless she had been in the classroom. And since moving to Cooinda, she had not worked, so her self-esteem would have taken even more of a beating. All that hard work after leaving their parents to build her self-esteem up, to get her degree, to teach, and to know she was making a difference in people's lives. Now that was all gone. Snuffed out in an instant.

Rebecca shook and tried to relax but couldn't draw air into her lungs. It was as though someone had just sat on her chest.

The more she tried to breathe, the more she was sure she was suffocating. Built-up sweat in her hairline began its descent to her jawline. She stood, and ran to the side of the riverbank, where she doubled over. It was all too much. There was a mass in her stomach, tight, and on fire. She sank to her knees, put her head in her hands, and screamed.

Tom watched the panic attack unfold before his eyes, and by the time he reached the riverbank, Rebecca's scream had turned to wild sobs. Her hands shredded the grass, and she shook her head, as though in denial. Ruth had reached her at the same time as Tom, and they each gently knelt on either side of her. Neither of them touched her, afraid it would cause even further turmoil. After a moment or two, the sobbing subsided, and she leaned back, sagging against Tom's side. Ruth reached out and ran her hand gently through her hair. Soft murmurs escaped her, as though she were soothing a young child.

Eventually, Rebecca lifted her head, rubbing her face with her hands. She was embarrassed. She was the calm and collected twin, who knew how to control her emotions. Now she felt drained, exhausted. She stared into the river that rippled a few feet from her.

"Thank you," she said to them both. She was about to stand up when she saw movement in the river. Her heart rate quickened again, and she shook loose of Tom and Ruth, shuffling forward on her knees to peer over the bank of the river.

Helen stared up at her. This was no reflection. Rebecca could see her sister as clear as day, floating beneath the surface of the water. Her eyes were open, her gaze firmly on her sister.

"Helen!" Rebecca lunged towards the rocks; all common sense forgotten. "She's there, Tom, I see her!" Before either Tom or Ruth could stop her, Rebecca flung herself onto her stomach; half her body hung precariously over the rocks submerged in the murkiness. Rebecca reached into the cold water, her hands grasping for her sister. She could only feel bits of grass and dirt as she opened and closed her fists trying to grab onto Helen. But she was gone.

Rebecca retracted her arms from the water, looking down for her sister frantically. She turned back to Tom. "She was here!" she sobbed.

Tom grabbed hold of her waist and pulled her up to him, enveloping her in his embrace. "I know, babe. But she's gone again. It's okay," he soothed, holding her, refusing to let go until he was sure she was calm. Rebecca felt his firm and warm embrace and finally stopped resisting. She leaned against him, weeping.

On the verandah, Fred was standing, holding a shot of whiskey ready to give to Rebecca. He had watched her raw display of grief, and his heart was breaking.

Derek sat staring at Rebecca as though an alien had invaded her body. Did the woman have any decorum?

Ruth sobbed quietly as she stood beside Rebecca and Tom, rubbing her back, refusing to leave her side.

Within a few minutes, Rebecca was calmer. She knew she'd seen Helen but also knew her grief was making her crazy. She looked up at Tom. He smiled down at her and wiped the tears from her cheeks. "Thank you," she whispered, looking from Tom to Ruth. She then turned and walked up the few stairs, past Derek, refusing to make eye contact with him, took the drink Fred offered to her, and threw it back. It burned her throat as she swallowed it, but the liquid worked its charm and warmed her insides, working its way through the knots in her body, loosening them. Bit by bit, she began to relax.

"I'm so sorry," she said, as she took her place again between Ruth and Fred.

"Don't be," Tom said simply. "Maybe we should leave this until another time?"

"No," Rebecca said sharply, "we need to do this now. For Helen's sake."

After watching Rebecca's mishap, Tom was hesitant to proceed but could tell she was more determined than ever for him to continue. He sighed and nodded.

He had covered up Helen's body on the crime scene photos before he came to the homestead. All that was visible was the scenery surrounding her body. He laid the photos out on the coffee table in the middle of them, silently watching the four of them slowly lean in to get a closer look.

"The crime scene photographer took photos of the surrounding area. Since someone placed Helen in the water at a location different from where she died, we call this a 'secondary' crime scene. Obviously, we don't know where she was killed yet. I'm not expecting anything to stand out to any of you, but we need to cover all our bases. As this is where the current took her, there is most likely nothing of significance. But still..." His voice trailed off.

All four of them took time studying the pictures. Rebecca was the first to speak. "Nothing looks familiar to me. I'm sorry." She shrugged. "Obviously, none of this landscape is familiar to me."

"The landscape is familiar, yet nothing is jumping out at me, I'm afraid," spoke Fred apologetically.

"Yeah, ditto," said a sullen Derek. "Although, it that near Hank Thompson's property?"

"Yeah, how did you know?" asked Tom.

"I used to go fishing with Hank's son Connor when we were in our late teens. Almost at that exact spot. I recognise the enormous old tree across the river." He paused. "Weird…"

Tom looked at the picture Derek was referring to. The image captured a wide shot of Helen's body, with the river behind her. Across the river was the tree Derek referred to, and Tom realised it was the exact spot he thought he'd seen Helen's ghost wave to him as he had examined her body.

He nodded at the photo. "Did you ever go over to that side of the river to fish?"

"I doubt it," Derek said after thinking for a moment. "It's Angela Parker's land, the old chick that owns the youth hostel. She doesn't like people hanging around on her land that aren't guests."

Tom nodded while he made a couple of notes in his notebook, then gathered up the photos and put them back in the file. The next lot of photos he pulled out were the ones that he and Rebecca had found on his car. If any of the Cox's had been having Helen followed, he was hoping an obvious reactive sign might show as he laid them out on the coffee table. Instead, only curious looks ensued.

"Feels like a lifetime ago we found these," whispered Rebecca.

"We?" questioned Ruth.

Rebecca nodded and explained how they had found the photos the day she and Tom had visited the homestead shortly after she had arrived from the States.

Ruth appeared shocked and appalled as she leaned over and began looking at them in earnest. Her suspicions were confirmed about being followed, so she was less surprised than Fred, who shook his head. "I can't believe someone was following her, and we didn't even notice." He took one photo, staring at it. "You know what this means, Tom? It means her murder was not a random act."

"That's if the two things are connected, Fred."

"Of course, they're connected!" Fred responded, and Tom realised where his son might have gotten his short temper.

"I am treating everything in this file as though it is connected, but I cannot find any evidence of anything at the moment. Someone was obviously following Helen, yet I am at a complete dead end. None of the chemists in town developed them, and there are no fingerprints on them. I've studied them inside and out. Now it's your turn. I need you all to look at these photos as closely as possible. If there is anything you recognise, anything at all, I need you to tell me."

As he looked at a photo of Helen leaving home for her run, Derek said, "Someone took some of these photos on our property. I'll kill the fucking bastard."

"Wait," said Ruth. "Someone took this one from the back of the church." I can see my head, Fred's, and Helen's up towards the front."

"That's right," said Tom.

"Well, often, Janice, Duncan's wife, takes photos of the congregation to put in the newsletter. She could have caught this person on her own film, without realising."

"It's worth a shot," said Tom, taking down a note to call Janice.

Tom stayed another hour, going over everything with them. Rebecca held herself together for the rest of the time, but he could tell she was overwhelmed and verging on depressed. Derek behaved himself, which was as much as he could ask for.

As Tom was about to leave, he mentioned the funeral. "If it's okay with you, I'd like some of the local police officers to attend. To pay their respects of course, but also to blend in, and keep an eye out for anything or anyone suspicious."

Ruth nodded, "Of course, Tom. Whatever you think is best. Everyone is welcome."

"Thank you all so much for your time. I can only imagine how hard today has been for you. And please, if you have questions, or think of anything. Please call me at the station."

They stood, and Ruth reached out to hug him. "God bless you," she whispered, her voice wavering.

Tom only nodded.

Rebecca walked with him out to his car. They didn't speak until they reached his car door.

"Thank you for today. Thank you for being there for me. I was not expecting that to happen. It's just…" Rebecca's voice trailed off as she looked out to the cane.

"I'm just glad you didn't dive headfirst into the shallow end," he grinned.

She looked at him and broke into laughter. He watched her and realised he had never heard her laugh. The poor woman had arrived in the country and had barely smiled, let alone had the inclination or opportunity to laugh. Spontaneously, he reached out and wrapped his arms around her, pulling her in. She sighed into him and put her head on his shoulder. "I'm so…lost," she said, the laughter gone. "My boss contacted me yesterday. She told me she understands what I'm going through, but she needs me back straight after the funeral…"

Tom closed his eyes and nodded, knowing this day would come. He had only known her for a couple of weeks but knew they had shared a connection. He wished he had had the chance to know her in different circumstances.

"I don't know what to do," she whispered. "Leaving with no closure will be horrendous."

"Let's just take it day by day, eh?"

She nodded, pulled away and smiled at him. "How about dinner tonight?"

"I'd love that," he answered simply.

"Great, let's meet in town. Around Seven?"

"Lovely. I'll see you then."

Derek watched from the formal dining room, the exchange between Rebecca and Tom. His emotions were all over the place, and it was not something he enjoyed. When he looked at

Rebecca, he still sometimes saw his wife. This was frustrating as hell, considering she acted nothing like Helen. Helen had been obedient, submissive, mouse-like. Rebecca was none of these things. He watched her smile at Tom, and Derek turned away, the anger building in him like lava pushing its way to the surface. His mother stood quietly in the doorway from the living room into the dining room. She watched him closely as he got his emotions under control. "Yes, Mum?" he asked in his typical authoritative voice.

"I think it's time you headed home, son" she stared at him, her eyes boring into his. He shifted uncomfortably, and nodded, the first one to break eye contact.

"Yeah, I think you may be right." He strode past her, leaving her alone, thinking about how much she had failed as a mother. Suddenly, she was exhausted.

{ 17 }

Tom returned to the station shortly after four in the afternoon. The sun was still high in the sky, even though summer had officially just ended. In this part of the world, seasons held little clout. Often it stayed warm right through till the end of May. Tom sometimes missed the Sydney weather. He missed wearing warm coats and beanies in the winter. He sighed heavily as he stepped out of his car into the blazing sun. His plan was to make a few phone calls and set up times to meet with Duncan and his wife, Janice, and Angela Parker. He was hoping Janice could give some insight into anyone in the congregation who might have been taking photos. Angela was purely for his own curiosity. Lou had already been out to see Angela. He knew it might lead to nothing, but he wanted to look around the area he had seen Helen wave at him. The image of her had stayed fresh in his mind and he thought about it often.

His shift ended at six, so he spent the next few hours finishing paperwork and making phone calls. Duncan and Janice could see him the following afternoon, and Angela was happy to accommodate his visit first thing in the morning. It was Lou's day off the next day, so he didn't mention it to her, wanting her to enjoy her day off. He noticed how hard she had been working, and how much she tried to impress him. He knew she was keen to move up in her career, and he was hoping to put in his recommendation to the department for a promotion for her when one became available. Of all the officers under him at the station, Lou was definitely one of the most resolute and career driven. He would miss working with her when her time to shine finally arrived.

Ava's shift had ended at midday, and at six o'clock Tom and Lou both happily clocked off. Sometimes a call would come in an hour before shift change, forcing overtime to be clocked. Today, fortunately, was not one of those days. He and Lou stepped out of the station at ten past the hour, smiled and bade each other goodnight. Tom had a quick workout at the gym, a shower and a meet Rebecca on Main Street outside the pub. On impulse, he stopped at the Drakes Supermarket and bought a bunch of wildflowers wrapped in brown paper and tied with string.

By the time he strode up to her a little after seven, he was refreshed, clean, and starving.

Rebecca looked stunning. Her long auburn hair hung past her shoulders, and she had put a touch of makeup on. Her green eyes now looked emerald, emphasised by the green dress she wore. The halter top fit snug, embracing her figure, with a long flowing skirt, brown belt and brown sandals to complete her look. She hadn't felt this human since arriving in Cooinda. The guilt crept in while she was getting ready to come out, but Ruth had encouraged her to let herself unwind and enjoy Tom's company. "Make tonight about you," she had said as she watched Rebecca apply her lipstick. "You deserve a night to yourself... Helen would want this."

Rebecca had looked at Ruth in the reflection of her mirror, had seen Ruth's sad smile, and nodded. "Okay, for Helen."

Now as she stood in the street, guilty yet happy, her life in New York was a million miles away, both physically and emotionally. Living in New York was a constant array of work, parties, conferences, pub crawls, and long nights without sleeping. Now she was standing in an unfamiliar town, wondering what else would be open for dinner other than the pub and Chinese restaurant on a Friday evening. Then she saw Tom walking towards her. He wore a casual tee shirt that fit snugly, revealing muscular arms and toned abs, and chino shorts. His hair was slightly damp, and he was clean-shaven. His scruffiness was gone, although the usual alertness remained. He carried a bunch of flowers and broke into a grin as he approached her, and she instantly relaxed. He handed her the flowers, and they hugged briefly. She could tell he was nervous, and it made her smile.

"What's this?" she asked, smelling the bouquet.

Tom shrugged, embarrassed. "Happy Valentine's Day."

Rebecca was silent for a moment and then said, "Bugger. I didn't know what the date was." She then laughed. "Thank you so much. They are beautiful."

"So, happy with a pub feed?"

"Sure."

They made their way into the pub and found a seat in the beer garden. Rebecca had been to the pub a few times since seeing Helen on her first day in town. Every time she glanced at the table, she expected to see her. However, there was nothing ominous about the space. She sighed and looked away.

Tom was studying her closely. Her eyes were serious as she looked across the courtyard.

"I'll get some wine," he whispered, standing up and gently placing his hand on her shoulder.

She looked up at him, and their eyes locked. She felt herself shiver uncontrollably. Nodding, she reached for his hand and squeezed it. Warmth spread through her body, and she looked away. Tom gathered himself and walked to the bar.

Their dinner was over in what seemed like moments. Rebecca realised she had had no adult conversation that didn't include death, ghosts, or murder since arriving in Australia. It felt strange at first, but the conversation flowed as they chatted about this and that, before moving onto other, more serious topics. Their childhoods were similar, in that they both had deadbeat parents and had to learn to depend on themselves. Tom was an only child and never had the pleasure or pain of having a sibling in his life. Divorced once, and with no children, he had lived a secluded life since moving from Sydney almost a decade ago. When Rebecca asked him about his ex-wife, he was quick to explain his desire for a family unit that he had craved while growing up. Unfortunately, he had chosen with great haste, settling for what he described as 'a Loony Tune, nutcase of a woman' who had made his life a living hell for two years before leaving him for another man. At the time he had been distraught, but in hindsight, he was relieved. That had been in his twenties. And since that time, had avoided long-term relationships. Now, at thirty-eight, he was content with his life. Although sometimes lonely. He grinned at her when he said this. And Rebecca smiled back, her heart fluttering, almost ready to take off out of her chest.

"So, what about you?" Tom asked. "Anyone lucky waiting for you back in New York?"

Rebecca laughed. "No, I'm afraid not. There's Antony, my 'friend with benefits' who keeps me company occasionally, but mostly, it's just work, and work-, and work-related social engagements."

Tom chuckled, "You and I are actually very similar, Rebecca... independent, hardworking, alone" ... his voice trailed off, and he stared deeply into her eyes, and once again Rebecca felt her heart would flutter right out of her chest. The urge to kiss him was so strong she had to look away. It would be very inappropriate to kiss the town police detective in the local pub, with locals nearby, pretending to enjoy their pub meal, but who were in fact, "discreetly" watching, and making notes, ready to be told whoever was available to listen as soon as they left the pub. Such exciting times. First a murder, now a new love interest for their favourite cop.

She grabbed her wine and gulped it down.

***

Tom was at a crossroads. He was at a time in his life where was settled and happy. His feelings for Rebecca were causing him some major derailment. He knew logically that he should put any personal feelings in a drawer until he solved the case, but what if he could not solve it? What if Rebecca flew home to New York, and the case turned cold, and he didn't see her again for a long time, or ever? He hated being conflicted, worried that it could jeopardise the investigation. Because Rebecca was leaving soon, he desperately wanted to make some headway.

None of this was her fault though, and he decided to get out of his own head and enjoy her company while he could. Regardless of where it led them.

Rebecca studied him closely. They had a comfortable silence, which is something people could rarely boast about. He drank his wine, lost in thought, and tapped his foot to the beat of the music drifting through the courtyard speakers. She admired a man who drank wine. Her memories of her father were associated with beer. Because of this, she hated the taste, the smell, and the behaviour that was often associated with it. She would always remember the day Helen came home from one of her first dates with Derek, thrilled that he was a whiskey drinker and not a beer drinker. She had ticked that box with delirious enthusiasm, alerting Rebecca to the realisation that their courtship might be serious.

Rebecca usually stayed clear of long-term relationships. Short and sweet was her motto. She never understood why people married young, as her twin had. However, it was not her place to question love. This was more than obvious to her now, as she watched Tom. He smiled at her, and she smiled back. Every time the man paid her any sort of attention, her heart quickened. What the fuck was wrong with her!? Was this just lust? Was she just lonely and sad, wanting comfort in the arms of someone to help her grieve? She thought of Helen and wondered what she would think of Tom. Would she like him?

"So, tell me, what did you know about Helen? I know you said you have only met her a few times, but surely you saw her in and around town occasionally?"

Tom met her eyes. "Are you sure you want to talk about Helen? I don't want to upset you, Rebecca," he whispered.

"You misunderstand me," she smiled at him. "I want to talk about her life, not her death."

"Okay, you got it," he smiled back at her. "Let's go for a walk."

They finished their wine and made their way out of the pub. It was just past nine o'clock, and the dinner crowd was well and truly gone. There were some people left in the public bar, and a dozen on the pokies, but the bistro was ready to close up. They stepped onto the footpath and turned east, walking comfortably along Main Street towards the river end of town.

"Whenever I saw Helen around town, she was usually with Ruth. I had heard how close they were and always marvelled that there was never much gossip about Helen amongst the locals. She kept to herself. If she was in town, she was with Ruth or Derek. She always seemed happy enough, but she was incredibly shy. I remember running into her and Ruth at the local Banana Festival a few years back, and that was the most I ever talked to her."

Rebecca was listening intently. "What did you talk to her about?"

Tom was quiet, trying to remember. "The place was crowded and loud... but I remember talking to Fred first about business, then looking over to Helen, and asking her how she was. I knew she was a teacher, so I asked her if she planned to go back to work." He paused. "This question made her uncomfortable. She had smiled and shrugged, and told me she wasn't in a rush, but I noticed a vibe, call it a cop vibe."

"The first couple of years after she moved up here, I would always ask her how the job hunting was going, and she had always averted the question," Rebecca said.

"I wonder if Derek didn't want her to work," Tom wondered.

"That would be my bet. No wonder she latched onto Ruth. She may have been the only friendship Derek allowed her to have."

Rebecca was silent. Angry once again. At herself. The world. And Derek.

Noticing her feelings, Tom diverted the conversation. "I remember once seeing her at an engagement party too. One of my officers, who no longer works here, Damien Mills, invited me to his engagement party. He had gone to school with Mark, Lou, and Derek, so he and Helen were also there."

"Do you remember what she was wearing?"

Tom started laughing.

"What!" laughed Rebecca, already knowing how silly her question had sounded. "I just want the entire image in my head. The only image I have of her these days is ghostly."

"Well, she looked stunning if my memory serves me correctly. She wore a long, straight pink skirt and a white shirt." He was astounded that he remembered that detail, but she had looked incredibly sexy that night. He said as much to Rebecca, and she laughed again. God, how he loved her laugh.

"I also remember Derek not letting her leave his sight all fucking night," he sighed, "what a dick."

"Do you think he ever hit her?" Rebecca asked quietly, the mood changing.

Tom was silent, thinking it over. "There's always a chance, but I saw no evidence of that, and I heard no rumours of that kind." He shrugged, "Honestly, Ruth probably has a better idea about their relationship."

"Yeah, we've talked about it, but she doesn't think so. I haven't been able to tell if she's just having trouble imagining her son acting like that and therefore denying it, or if she actually doesn't think he would have hit her."

They kept walking, turning the corner onto Commercial Road, past the river, then taking another turn onto Cooinda Road, moving away from the river. They passed the church, and the location Rebecca had seen Helen when Tom had been collecting the car after Chinese for dinner. This part of town was quiet, and Rebecca shivered. Tom instantly put his arm around her, pulling her in close.

"Are you cold?"

"Not really, just remembering seeing Helen here. Feels like a lifetime ago."

"The investigation isn't over, Rebecca; I promise I will do all I can to figure out what happened."

She put her arm around his waist. "I know you will," she whispered.

Together, they kept walking.

{ **18** }

They reached his car long before they were ready to say goodnight. Tom hesitated only for a moment before asking if she would like to come back to his place for coffee. She hesitated only for a moment before saying yes. They decided it would be easier if she followed him there in the rental she still had at Ruth's insistence, with the Cox's footing the bill for her, after she ran out of money. All she had was enough in her bank account to pay for her flight home, and that was it. She was graciously borrowing money from Ruth, with the promise to pay her back as soon as she was back at work. She hated depending on them financially, especially since she was fiercely independent by default, but the last few days had opened her heart to the idea of good people like the Cox's, and she was truly thankful they were offering her help when she so desperately needed it.

Getting in her car, she took a moment to sit and contemplate what she was about to do. "It's just coffee," she told herself. Then laughed aloud. "Whatever," she mumbled and started the engine. She saw Tom pass behind her, and she reversed out of the car space and followed him home.

Tom's home was a delightful little fibro cottage positioned back from the road with a lovely front verandah. She remembered the first time she had seen his home, but to be honest, a lot had happened that day; it was a blur. Tom's home was pale yellow weatherboard with white trim. A white picket fence ran along the property line on all sides. She parked on the roadside while Tom opened his front gate and parked in his carport alongside the house.

He let her into his home without saying much, and he watched her reaction to his humble abode. It had two bedrooms and had been built in the 1920s. It was nothing fancy, nothing luxurious, but it was home to him, and he was proud of it.

"This is lovely, Tom," Rebecca stated sincerely.

The hallway ran down the centre, with the rooms on either side. To the right was the living, dining and kitchen, and to the left were two large bedrooms with a bathroom in between. The backdoor led from the kitchen onto a porch and into his tidy back garden. The house was clean and nicely decorated. He had a brown leather sofa in the lounge room, and there was a lot of timber in the floorboards and door trims. The fireplace flanked the lounge room wall, and personal touches such as art, comfortable throw cushions, and navy-coloured curtains hung against the front windows, and a timber bookshelf stuffed with books sat along the wall that the lounge faced. There was no television, but there was an old record player and another bookshelf that held more records that Rebecca had ever seen. The entire room oozed coziness, and she instantly felt at home.

Tom led her into the dining room, which held an arched doorway into the quaint kitchen at the back of the house. He prepared a pot of coffee and poured a shot of whiskey into each mug before topping up with freshly brewed coffee. He handed her a mug. "I thought an Irish coffee would hit the spot."

They sat in the lounge room together on the comfortable leather lounge. Once again, the conversation flowed. From music to travel to politics and other worldly events, they talked about everything and anything. Before they knew it, it was two in the morning.

Rebecca gasps, "Shit, I should go. Ruth is probably worried about me."

Tom nodded, "Yes, I guess so..."

They stared at each other, and Tom could not help himself. He reached out and stroked her hair. His touch was electrifying, and Rebecca leaned into his hand.

"I... should go," she whispered again. Inexplicably, tears sprang up in her eyes.

"Oh, sweetheart," Tom pulled her into his arms, holding her close and stroking her hair.

And the floodgates opened. She sobbed against his shoulder, holding him tight, trying to anchor herself to him, so afraid of losing hold of him, and she would finally drown in her sea of grief.

He held her for a long time.

She was so drained. So tired. So strung out. She wished more than anything to erase the last two weeks of her life and go back to her old life in New York. But then, she would not have met Tom. Would never have realised how empty her life was, on the other side of the world, surrounded by eight million people, all alone. And she realised then just how bleak her life had been. She had no desire to go back.

They parted ways shortly after. Watching her leave was hard, but Tom knew it was not the time to get romantically involved. He needed to put all his energy into solving Helen's murder.

Rebecca drove away. Full of regret and longing. She drove through the night, the window down, feeling the breeze on her face. The weather was slowly cooling down. It was three o'clock in the morning, and there wasn't another soul on the road. She turned onto the long driveway and slowly made her way up to the homestead. She came to a sudden stop when she saw her sister sitting on the front verandah.

Rebecca sat unmoving, staring at her twin. Helen was dressed in her death clothes, sitting on the front steps with her head down, as though she was inspecting something on the ground. Slowly, she looked up. They stared at each other through the windshield of the car. Rebecca was afraid to move, to do anything. Helen stood up after a moment, and Rebecca slowly stepped out of the car. She kept her eyes focused on her sister.

"Helen?" she asked.

Helen smiled at someone behind Rebecca and spoke, but no words came out. Rebecca could only watch in frustration as her sister talked. It was like watching television on mute, and Rebecca wondered if she was dreaming. She stepped away from the car and closed the door and walked towards Helen, watching her, trying to read her lips as they moved. She was in conversation. But with who?

"Helen, I don't understand," Rebecca whispered these words to her twin, and her voice sounded strange and empty. Even the crickets fell silent in shock. Helen stopped her conversation and turned slightly and looked directly at Rebecca. Helen raised her hand, and Rebecca raised her own to meet it. The connection was close, yet still so far away. Helen smiled at Rebecca, and then she was gone.

Rebecca watched helplessly as her sister disappeared, and within a few seconds, she was alone once again, standing alone in the driveway. She allowed the tears to fall now, and climbed the steps to the verandah, finally letting herself inside. Ruth stood in the hallway, holding a cup of tea, when she saw Rebecca. She plonked her tea down on the hallway stand and moved closer to Rebecca.

"Oh, my goodness, sweetheart, what happened? Are you okay?" She cradled Rebecca in her arms, and Rebecca did not resist, desperate for a human touch.

"I just saw Helen again," she whispered. Hearing the words aloud sounded ridiculous, but she could no longer keep it a secret. Over the last seven days, Ruth had firmly established herself in Rebecca's life, and she felt as though she could trust her as much as Tom. Even more so considering how much she had loved Helen.

"Again?"

Rebecca nodded. "I've been seeing her since I arrived. Today in the river was not the first time."

There was a long pause before Ruth spoke. "Let's sit in the family room, yes? Sounds like a stiff drink and a chat are in order."

An hour later, the sun was slowly emerging, and Rebecca could hear the birds singing and swooping outside as they hunted for breakfast. Tiny splashes in the river as they dove for their breakfast of fish and insects. Ruth was making coffee when Fred wandered, bleary-eyed, into the kitchen. Unaccustomed to his wife being awake before him, he greeted Ruth with a warm hug. He spotted Rebecca seated at the kitchen table that looked out over the back verandah; she looked exhausted, with bloodshot eyes, and visibly pale. He glanced at Ruth, who shook her head slightly, indicating that she would explain later. Fred stood taller and spoke in a soft, clear voice. "Well, isn't it nice to be awake this early with two fine-looking ladies?"

Ruth smiled as she collected a third coffee mug for her husband, and the three of them sat in comfortable silence as they drank their coffee. Rebecca was feeling relieved she had told Ruth about Helen. Not for a moment did Ruth appear sceptical of her story, quickly accepting it as truth. She said the Lord works mysteriously and was not her place to say otherwise. Ruth was concerned Helen was stuck somewhere, unable to move on, and trying to communicate with Rebecca. Ruth now worried about her never being able to find peace.

Tom and Rebecca had discussed the same idea before Helen's had been found, but not since then.

She knew she was not crazy. It made perfect sense to Rebecca that Helen should seek help. Their connection had always been an unspoken energy between them, and Rebecca understood now that Helen needed her twin's help to find peace and move on. Ruth had promised her she wouldn't tell a soul except Fred. They certainly didn't need more gossip.

By nine o'clock that Monday morning, Ruth and Fred were back to their daily schedule, and Rebecca showered and crawled into bed. Every fibre of her body was on edge, and she desperately needed sleep. And indeed, she did, sleeping soundly until three o'clock that afternoon, when she rose feeling refreshed and clearheaded.

She had made a huge decision that morning when talking to Ruth, and after getting the rest she needed, announced to Ruth and Fred that she would stay in Cooinda indefinitely. Leaving was not an option while Helen's case remained unsolved, and she was desperate to make up for deserting Helen in life, by making it up to her in death.

The first thing she did was make a long-distance call to her boss. They spoke for an hour, and she was completely understanding, although sad to be losing one of her best designers. The next call was to Antony. His answering machine picked up, and she left a detailed message along with Ruth and Fred's number for them to contact her. She did not know if he'd call her back, and to be honest, she wouldn't blame him if he didn't. They were only casual friends with benefits who found comfort together amidst the loneliness of the city. While she had been talking to her boss, Ruth had organised a company in the States to gain access to her apartment through the landlord and pack up all her belongings and organise for them to be shipped back to Australia. She had also organised another company to clean her apartment and had paid the rest of her rent and given notice.

It was surreal that she was not going back. However, she realised that this chapter of her life had ended; for the time being. She didn't know what was to come, but she knew now that it was to be in Australia. She was grateful to Ruth and Fred for taking over the arrangements for her to come home, as she knew it would have been too overwhelming for her to even think about, let alone do.

***

On the other side of town, while Rebecca slept, Tom was over at Angela Parker's hostel. Angela had bought the large turn of the century home in the mid-eighties and had turned it into a successful youth hostel. It was a ramshackle building that had endured so many extensions over the decades that it now lacked cohesiveness. The grounds had a natural appeal with lovely native trees and large stretches of vegetable gardens that Angela lovingly tended too. Her land was approximately two acres and sat snug against the river, just southeast of the town. The house sat on a corner, on a river bend. As well as the lovely gardens, there were large willow trees that hung over the river, some with ropes and tires attached that swung idle, waiting for someone to climb on and fly, letting go and landing in the beckoning water. The area had a lot of back-packers, a lot of youngsters who were hitchhiking their way around the country, discovering themselves. Young families also stayed at the hostel, and Angela had built a solid reputation for a safe and fun accommodation.

"I don't know what to tell you, Tom," she said as they stood together out the front of her home. "There has been no suspicious activity across the river. I was shocked as hell when I heard about poor Helen. The evil son of a bitch who dumped her there certainly did it on the down low because I never heard a peep." Angela was a short, wiry woman in her early seventies. She had a long, pointy nose, and a long chin, and she always reminded Tom of a witch. A good witch of course, but a witch all the same. She dyed her hair bright red and was thin and fit. She was as tough as nails. When her husband of thirty years had left her for her best friend of forty years, she had decided there was no point in moping about and just got on with life. Their kids had already left home by then, so she sold the family home and bought the old house on the river, keen to attract younger folk to Cooinda. People gossiped of course, saying she had gone mad, and it would never last, but that was over a decade ago and her little youth hostel was a thriving business. Meanwhile, her ex-husband and best friend were married and hated each other, too proud to admit their mistake, and stuck with each other in misery, or so she'd heard through the gossip grapevine. She hated it; but it validated her feelings about them, and about herself. So un-Christian of her. So, she kept her thoughts to herself and repented for her evil thoughts before bed each night.

"What about around here, Angela?"

"Mmm?" She looked at Tom, startled. "Sorry, got lost in my own thoughts for a second," she chuckled to herself, and Tom wondered if she was feeling okay.

"Around here? Anything unusual been happening, with guests or strange behaviour?"

"Well, things around here are always a little strange., we get some... unusual folk through here, some passing through to Nimbin and not what. Most folks are harmless enough."

Tom began wandering around the property. He needed to check out the spot by the river he had seen Helen standing. He wanted to see the crime scene from a new perspective. Angela walked with him; her chatter was comforting. She was giving him great detail about her fruit trees and what was growing well that season when they came to the spot on the river that Tom believed was where he had seen Helen standing. As soon as he saw it, he got goosebumps. There was nothing particularly different about the spot, except the grass was completely flat where she had stood. Tom noticed it. Stared at it. Angela was oblivious.

"This is a lovely spot by the river. My guests often come out here to this spot to fish. It's nicely shaded by the willow," she motioned to the huge, beautiful tree that stood, with its arms stretched as though it wanted to embrace people, inviting them to be sheltered by its long slender leaf that glistened with silver in the sunlight.

"Okay, so tell me about Josh," Tom asked, staring up at the tree.

"Well, that was just darn strange," Angela replied. "Here one minute, gone the next. And he left all his things here. Lou came out and took my statement, you know." She shrugged, still a little confused about why Tom thought it necessary to follow up on Lou's work.

"Oh, I trust Lou. It's just always professional to have another set of fresh eyes. Since we discovered poor Helen across the river from here, and then Josh taking off..." Tom trailed off and shrugged.

Angela nodded slowly. "Well, he arrived here about a month ago and paid upfront for a month. He was always planning to pass through but needed to stop for a rest and to make some more money. I sent him to Dave at the pub, as they always need people, and Josh told me had bartending experience. He began working, and everything was fine, even made some friends. Told me he was saving money ready for the next adventure."

"Then, a couple of weeks ago, there was a strange phone call for him late one evening. I was the one who answered the phone. It sounded like a woman's voice. When the phone call ended, Josh returned to his room, and I didn't give it much thought. I haven't seen him since. He must have left during the night while everyone was sleeping, but he left his things here. I assumed he'd be back, but so far... nada." She shrugged, and it was obvious she had little else to add.

"Do you remember what date this was? Where are his things? Do you still have them?" He made a note in his notebook to put in a request for Angela's phone records.

"I'd have to look at the calendar to see if anything triggers my memory about the date. As for his things, yep, they are still in his room. It's paid up for another few days."

Tom glanced around wearily. The house was behind them, and as he looked over the old ramshackle place, it really was lovely. The windows on the second story were mostly dormitory style, and all the windows had shutters, which were painted white, contrasting nicely against the pale-yellow paint on the weatherboard.

He was about to look away when something caught his eye. In the far corner of the house was a window. Someone was standing at the window, looking at them from above. Tom squinted in the sun, raised his hand to shelter his eyes to get a better look at whichever guest was having a squiz, but the person had gone.

Tom was shivering, but trying to hold it together, as he turned back to Angela. "Whose room is that one up there?" he asked.

"Why, that was Josh's."

"I'd love to look at his things if that's okay with you?"

"Well, sure... but Lou already did that," she shrugged, "but of course you're welcome to as well.

"I'm sure Lou has done a thorough job and there is nothing to worry about; I just have to be thorough, you know? And now that Josh is a missing person case, well, I have opened up a new investigation."

Angela nodded. "I sure hope nothing has happened to the poor lad."

"Let's not jump to any conclusions, and besides, it's probably as you say. He took off after taking the register cash," he said soothingly. "Let's just start with having a look at his things, eh?"

She smiled and nodded, suddenly looking her age. She turned and motioned for him to follow her, and Tom followed into the house. The kitchen was at the back of the house, and when they walked into it from the back garden, a group of young men and women looked up at them from a large old timber dining table that sat in the middle of the room. There was a great deal of chatter, laughter and the smell of cooking bacon and eggs.

"Ang!" a young guy with long blond hair and a ridiculously tanned and muscular torso exclaimed when he saw his host. "We are having brekkie. Are you hungry? There's enough for your 'friend' here too." The man grinned and winked at Angela, at once making her scold him in a grandmotherly fashion.

"Oh, Andy, you stop that. This is a police officer!" She turned to Tom, shaking her head with an apologetic and slightly embarrassed look on her face.

Tom grinned at the young Andy. "Maybe another time, thanks, mate." He turned to Angela. "It's okay, Ang. I can go up to Josh's room alone. It's the professional thing to do, anyway."

"Yes, of course. The key to the rooms is in my office on the hook by the door. I'll get them now," she scurried off, leaving Tom with the group of young surfer-looking crew who were shovelling food into their mouths like it was the last supper. "Good surf this morning, fellows?" He asked.

The one Angela called Andy nodded. "She's a beauty at the moment, officer. You surf?"

"Not for a long time," he answered with a sigh.

"Ah, mate, get back out there. It like, totally cleanses the soul, man." The other people sitting around the table nodded in agreement, and one of them said, "Right on." Tom thought for a moment they were rehearsing for the movie Point Break with Keanu Reeves and Patrick Swayze.

He left the surfer dudes to eat their breakfast and walked out of the kitchen with a smile on his face. He found Angela walking from her office back to the kitchen. She smiled at him and handed him the key.

"Josh's room is up the stairs, to the right. It's the last door on your left. I'll wait down here; start cleaning up that mess in my kitchen," she said in a cheery voice, and Tom could see why she was so successful at running her business. He could see from the comfortable way the boys were in her kitchen just now that she treated her guests like family and genuinely enjoyed the company of others and also enjoyed looking after people.

Tom quietly made his way up the long, narrow staircase that reached a landing that overlooked the living room. Upstairs, there was a long hallway that led off each side of the landing. There were doors with room numbers clearly printed on them. He turned to the right and began walking down the dark hall.

When he reached the end of the hallway, there was a door to the left, and one to the right. He slowly unlocked the door on the left, as Angela had instructed him. As he slowly opened it, the hinges creaked with age, and he thought he saw movement in the corner of the room as the door widened, revealing a sparse room, with a single bed and a desk and wardrobe.

Hesitantly, Tom moved further in, leaving the door open. It wasn't often that he felt afraid but now was one of those times. He moved closer to the window and peered out, looking down at the sizeable garden and river. On the right-hand side, sitting nestled in amongst the garden was an aluminium shed. There was nothing overly sinister looking about the shed but had the inclination to check it out. He quickly finished checking over Josh's room, which held nothing significant, and left the room, locking it once again behind him.

Angela obviously spent a lot of time tending the flower beds that lined the path from the back porch down to the riverbank. The shed was off to the right-hand side of the path, mostly hidden amongst beautifully maintained fruit trees and other flowering bushes. The garden layout had no rhyme or reason, unlike the Cox's homestead, where they perfectly designed, formed, and maintained all the gardens.

Here, the garden had a life of its own. It had a wild, organic quality about it that Tom loved, and he could see that Angela tended to it with immense pride and respect, allowing it to flourish at its own fruition. The shed blended into the greenery, painted sage green, with a timber door. Ferns surrounded it, and just outside the door was a terracotta birdbath that was currently hosting a magpie mother and infant. They stood on the side of the bath, staring at Tom as he approached. He made kissing noises to them as he reached the shed door. He could tell they were regular visitors as they stayed perched in their spot and then resumed bathing.

With one motion, Tom pushed the shed door open. It creaked grudgingly, and he slowly made his way inside.

The shed was impeccably neat and clean. One side housed gardening tools and supplies, which were all shelved and labelled. The other side was for storage. Neatly stacked boxes labelled with miscellaneous items, a large box labelled 'Christmas tree' with another box stacked on top labelled 'Decorations', all in meticulous handwriting. Tom sighed in frustration and turned to leave, spotting a transparent plastic box tucked behind the tree, which gave him pause.

He pulled latex gloves from his pockets and put them on quickly as he stepped over to the corner of the shed and peered inside the empty container. Inside was a sneaker that was caked in dirt and smeared with blood. Tom frowned, trying to think of all the reasons the sneaker could be here. He reached back into the box, pulled back a quicksilver jumper that revealed a pair of headphones, the other sneaker, and a calico bag. It was empty but written on the outside in neat black marker were the words 'Property of the Imperial Hotel'.

{ **19** }

Tom had taken photos and bagged all the evidence he'd found and was back at the station by early afternoon. Trying not to get excited about the shoes and headphones, he stayed quietly confident he was on the brink of breaking the case. He was back at the station by four that afternoon, filling out his report as Lou bagged, tagged, and logged all the evidence.

"So, what are the next steps?" she asked quietly. Tom stopped what he was doing and looked over at her. He was sitting at Ava's desk while he worked. He saw Lou's expression and realised he hadn't considered she must be struggling with the idea of her friend being a potential killer. "Jesus, I'm sorry, Lou. You don't have to do that if you don't want to. I can finish it all up and get it sent to forensics."

Lou shook her head and shrugged. "It's okay, I can do it. I'm just feeling a tad stupid, is all."

"What do you mean?"

"I should have seen it," she sighed.

"That's crap, Lou. People who have infatuations with others are often particularly skilled at hiding it."

"Well, he certainly was good at that. He never even once mentioned that he even knew Helen."

It was Tom's turn to shrug. "Maybe he didn't know her."

Lou sighed and put down the pen she was holding. "You think so?"

"He could have just seen her around town, or at the pub. Started following her, taking her picture. The fantasy built. Unfortunately, this sort of thing happens more than you realise."

"Okay, so what about the photos left on your car?"

Tom had been thinking about that since he'd been at Angela's. He had gone back up to Josh's room and checked it over again more thoroughly, hoping to find a camera or something else that tied him to Helen's murder. The room had been clean. "I don't have all the answers, Lou. Maybe he didn't mean to kill Helen, feels guilty, so he left the photos for me." He shrugged again.

Lou sighed again. They were both silent for a few moments. "Will you issue an arrest warrant?" she asked.

"Already done," he replied. "Look, why don't you clock off early. Go out with Jenny and have a few drinks?"

Lou smiled at him. "Thanks, Tom, you're awesome."

"I'll see you tomorrow at the funeral. I have both Shane and Ava coming as well and have pulled a couple of juniors in from Lismore to manage the station and any other duties.

Lou nodded. "I'm dreading tomorrow," she said sadly. "I've known Derek since forever. Poor guy. Anyway, thanks for letting me off a bit early. I'll see you tomorrow."

Tom smiled, watching Lou leave. He had noticed she excluded Ruth and Fred. She hardly knew Rebecca, so that was understandable, but he had always assumed Lou knew all the

Cox's well, not just Derek, and he considered the Cox's may not be as nice to the help as they were to friends and family.

***

Fred had summoned Derek that morning to discuss business. He was sitting with Fred in the office at the front of the house when Rebecca had appeared after her long sleep. He had already left, though, when she had decided not to return to New York. Ruth was silently relieved Rebecca was staying, and that her son had not been in the house when she decided. By the time Rebecca had made her phone calls, Ruth had most of the house ready for the caterers in the morning but still needed to go into town to grab a few things, including some basic household supplies, before grieving guests consumed her home. She visited Derek, wanted to extend him an olive branch, and tell him Rebecca was staying. She wanted to get that news out of the way before the grapevine reached him. In Cooinda, the vines ran deep.

Derek was in his kitchen when Ruth arrived at his front door. She banged gently on the security screen before opening the door and letting herself in. Derek poked his head into the hallway from the kitchen. "Mum? What's wrong?"

"I just thought I'd pop in and see if you need anything in town. Rebecca and I are heading in soon." Ruth stood in the hallway. Derek stood at the other end. There was a moment of silence. "So, do you need anything?"

"For her to leave," he said coldly. "Has she booked her flight home yet?"

"Um, no. She has decided to stay a little longer..."

Derek stared coldly at his mother. She could tell he was seething, and she was just confused about why he hated Rebecca so much.

"As long as she stays the hell away from me, Mother."

She nodded. "Believe me, we both want that... son." She almost spat out the word son, turning on her heel and marching back down his front porch steps and disappearing into the cane, furious with herself for believing he would ever change.

Derek watched her go, smirking with amusement. He had to admit it; it was a surprise to see the subtle changes in his mother since Helen had gone missing. He didn't really like it but was also oddly pleased to see her with a bit of courage finally and saying what was on her mind. As long as she didn't do it too often. Women these days. Always thinking they could do and say whatever they wanted. He shook his head and closed the door, heading back to his afternoon drinking and self-wallowing.

Rebecca was quiet as she sat in the passenger seat as Ruth drove them into town. She stared out the window as they emerged from Cane Road onto Main Street and slowly made their way west down the street towards the large parking area next to the old supermarket that had turned into a national brand a few years ago. Ruth still referred to it as 'Blakes', although Mr Blake had long since retired and it was now a 'Coles'.

It was the first time since arriving that she had done anything as mundane as food shopping, but Helen's funeral was the following day, and they were having the wake at the homestead, following the service at the church. Derek wanted to hold it at his home, but his father's reasoning overpowered him, arguing that the homestead had more space for the grieving guests to eat their canapes'.

"How many people are you expecting to come?" he had demanded in a sulky voice.

"As many people that wish to come. I will not turn people away who wish to pay their respects," his father had answered sternly.

"What a fucking joke," Derek muttered. "She barely knew anybody."

"And whos' fault is that?" Rebecca asked, staring at him until he squirmed, gave her a filthy look, and stormed out.

Ruth glanced over at Rebecca as she parked the car. "You okay, love?"

Startled out of her thoughts, she nodded. "Yep, all good," she smiled.

"You don't need to do this with me if you don't want to. Why don't you go for a walk around town? I can manage the shopping."

Rebecca sat for a moment. "Ruth, with everything you have done for me, for Helen, helping you with groceries is the least I can do."

"Oh nonsense. I can't even imagine the turmoil you are in at the moment. Maybe a walk to clear your head will help? This old gal can handle a few groceries on her own," she smiled gently at Rebecca.

"Well, okay, then. A walk might be nice. Considering it's not as hot today." The weather, although still warm and humid, had a lovely breeze, and a walk along the riverfront was a pleasant idea.

"Wonderful," Ruth said. "Meet me back here in about an hour."

Rebecca nodded and stepped out of the car. She wandered out of town before heading toward the river. The breeze was stronger down by the water, and for a while she just sat, staring out into the water rippling up to the shoreline. Graffiti covered the bench on which she sat, but someone had etched two words along the left front bench leg. She stooped low to study it and a chill escaped her when she realised there were two words amongst the other random art. The first one was *'help'*, and the other was *'Rebecca'*. Other graffiti separated the words, and it was a fluke she even saw them. An eeriness descended, as though someone was watching her.

She bolted upright, looking around. The riverfront was quiet. It was past the busy lunch hour when people came out of work to eat or exercise. Now there were just the odd person walking their dog or scurrying by after running errands in town. The words were random, meant nothing. Life, after all, was full of random coincidences that people often tried to pull meaning from. Her heart rate slowed down as she calmly convinced herself not to overreact.

Finally, after a minute or two, she felt she could start walking back to meet Ruth. She turned back towards town, and as she walked, she saw Lou heading towards her. She had her uniform on and looked tired. Rebecca waved shyly, and Lou broke into a big smile when she saw her. "Hi Rebecca," Lou said as they reached each other. Lou reached out and hugged

Rebecca without prompting or awkwardness. "How are you?" she sounded sympathetic, but not pitiful, and Rebecca was grateful for her kindness.

She shrugged. "I'm okay. Exhausted. Still not sleeping the best, unfortunately."

Lou nodded sympathetically. "I can only imagine."

Rebecca changed the subject. "Just finished work?"

"Yep," Lou grinned. "Meeting my friend for an early dinner and a few drinks."

Rebecca smiled. "Sounds nice... well, I better get back to Ruth. She's waiting for me."

"Oh, you're in town with Ruth? How are they doing?"

"As well as expected, hopefully once the funeral is over everything will settle down somewhat."

"Yeah, I'll be praying for you all tomorrow," she squeezed Rebecca's shoulder. "Will you be heading home after the funeral?"

Rebecca hadn't even told Tom her plans to stay in Cooinda yet and felt uncomfortable telling Lou before telling him. So, she shrugged and answered the only way she could on the spot, "Something like that, yeah."

The two women parted ways, each with her own thoughts.

***

Tom had been sitting at Ava's desk staring into space when he decided on a whim to drive out to the homestead to visit Rebecca. He missed her. It was pathetic but resigned himself to his feelings. He finished up his shift and hurried through closing up the station. It was closed on Mondays and Tuesdays, with all calls going through to Lismore. The Cooinda team were on a rotating night shift system where they could stay at home unless they were called out from Lismore. Tonight, Shane was on call, so Tom left the station shortly after six, happy and relaxed. He walked to the gym, did a quick workout, showered and was leaving town just after seven.

The front porch light was on when he arrived, so he parked his car and ascended the porch steps. Rebecca opened the door to greet him before he even reached the front door. Rebecca wore a long floral dress, and her auburn hair hung damp and limp around her delicate face. He leaned in to kiss her lightly on the cheek, and she smelled of fresh soap and moisturiser.

"Did you see me drive up?" He pulled her into an embrace, and she responded in kind, wrapping her long, slender arms around him, running her hand through his thick hair.

"Nope, Ruth has the senses of a wild animal."

Tom laughed heartily, his muscles relaxing.

"You need a drink," she said softly, pulling away from him, taking his hand and leading him into the house. The homestead was quiet, and he suspected that Ruth and Fred had made themselves scarce when he arrived. Rebecca's feet were bare, and she walked softly ahead of him into the kitchen. He noted how at home she was here, and it pleased him.

They sat outside on the verandah. He could tell it had become a favourite spot of hers, as she settled down in a comfortable padded wicker chair, tucking her legs underneath her, nursing her drink. She had poured whiskey neat for him but had chosen a tequila on the rocks for herself. She sipped it steadily, waiting for him to talk. Tom looked around, curious where the Cox's had disappeared too. As though she could read his mind, Rebecca said, "They're over at Silas and Liz's place having dinner." Her head leaned to her left, and he glanced over to where she was pointing. "The business manager and housekeeper's cottage."

"Oh, got it." He pulled her in and kissed her softly on the mouth.

"So, I have some news." She spoke.

Tom raised his eyebrows in expectation. He waited patiently.

"I quit my job. I'm staying here."

Tom stared at her, unblinking. Waiting for her to say: "Just kidding, just wanted to fuck with your heart, big guy!" But she stared back at him, matching his unblinking stance. After a moment she said, "I didn't realise this was a staring competition."

Tom finally blinked rapidly, his brain screaming at him to take it easy. "Wow. This is huge, Rebecca."

"Good, huge or bad huge?"

He broke into a smile and grabbed her in another hug. "Oh, this is good huge. It's awesome huge!" He got to his feet and pulled her along with him. They embraced, and he picked her up, swinging her around. She laughed as her skirt twirled around her legs. Finally, he planted her back on solid floor, tilted her chin towards him, and kissed her passionately. As usual, he took her breath away.

They sat on the swing on the verandah until after Ruth and Fred came back from dinner. The elderly couple spoke to them for only a few moments before excusing themselves to get ready for bed. Rebecca was aware they were being courteous, and she was grateful. She sat with Tom's arm around her shoulders, her head resting against his arm as they listened to Van Morrison on Fred's record player. She was trying not to think about the morning. Every time she thought of Helen, guilt would rise in her throat like bile, and she would think of just how selfish she was being by wanting to be happy. Logic told her it was nonsense. Her heart said otherwise.

Tom left her shortly after, vowing to be there first thing in the morning. He wanted to tell her about what he had found at the hostel that day, but he knew he had to keep the investigation under wraps until the evidence connected Josh to Helen's sneakers and headphones, or they arrested and brought him in for questioning. The funeral would be at eleven in the morning, and Tom suspected Rebecca wouldn't get much sleep. He had asked her if she wanted him there for support, and she had nodded silently, putting her arms around him, clinging to him. He could only imagine what she was going through, and it concerned him she was surviving on too much alcohol and too little sleep. She promised him she would sleep once the funeral was over and she could think more clearly about the next steps she needed to take in her life.

She watched Tom drive away and gently shut the door. She was trying to be quiet as to not disturb Fred and Ruth, and as she tiptoed through the large hallway, she stepped on something sharp, causing her legs to buckle and she fell heavily to the floor, knocking into the elegant hall table that sat along the wall that divided the entrance hall to the Master suite.

"Shit," she whispered. She sat quietly on the floor, folding her legs into a cross-legged yoga position to look at the damage to her foot. Whatever she had stepped on had caused her to bleed on the ball of her left foot. She nursed it with both hands, trying not to get blood on the floorboards, while looking around for something to stop the bleeding. The door to the bedroom opened, and she saw Fred appear, looking down at her with a concerned look on his face. "Oh dear, what happened?"

"I stepped on something sharp," she whispered, "sorry to wake you."

"Nonsense," he said with a smile, "let me get you a washcloth and Band-Aid. Are you okay?"

She nodded and thanked him gratefully as he made his way to the guest bathroom to gather supplies.

Rebecca looked around her, trying to spot anything sharp that was the culprit that caused her injury. Scanning her eyes around the floor, just near the hall table, was a thumbtack, tack side up. She sighed and reached to grab it but accidentally pushed it further under the hall table. She sighed again in frustration and mutters 'bloody hell', sweeping her hand under the hall table in a scoop shape, and pulled the thumbtack, along with a few other objects that hid in the dust that gathered. Rebecca smirked, thinking that if Ruth knew how dusty it was under there, she would be seriously questioning Liz about her competency. She looked at the items in her palm. There was the thumbtack, a button, some lint, and, more importantly, a beautiful diamond ring. She recognised it at once as Helen's and gasped, staring at it disbelieving.

"What do we have here?" asked Fred quietly, returns with the promised cloth and band-aid.

He knelt carefully next to her, and gently took her foot in his hand, and began cleaning it.

Rebecca held out what she had found, and Fred looked closely. It took a moment for his thoughts to register, and he looked at her in surprise. "Is that...?"

"Yes, I believe so. It's pretty unique."

"Yes, yes, it is. Where did you find it?"

"Under the hall table. I was looking for the thumbtack that I stepped on," she explained.

Fred nodded and continued to fix her foot. He carefully cleaned and bandaged her foot, helping her up and into the formal living room. They sat next to each other, and Fred examined the ring silently.

"It's definitely Helens" he announced after a few moments.

Rebecca nodded. "I guess that solves that mystery."

"Mmm," Fred replied distractedly as he studied the ring. "Anyway, my dear. You need to get some rest." He stood and helped her up, walking her to her room. "Sleep well, my dear" he kissed her gently on the cheek, the most affection he had shown her since she had gotten to know him. She felt tears well up in her eyes, and she blinked them back.

"You too" was all she could manage. She moved into her room, tucking her sister's engagement ring into her purse, and finally climbed into bed. She was worried she would not sleep; however, drifted off within minutes, and for the first time since arriving, slept a dreamless, sound sleep.

$$\{\ 20\ \}$$

The church was abuzz by the time Tom arrived. The Cox's knew the turnout would be large. Helen had kept to herself; however, they were a longstanding and respected family in the community, and many people had come just to show their respect. Derek was sombre. Dressed smartly, clean-shaven and clear-eyed, he looked and played the perfect part of the grieving husband. Rebecca almost felt sorry for him. He walked in between his parents as they entered the church, with Rebecca and Tom following. There had been many a rumour about Helen's twin sister, yet few people had seen her. She could feel so many eyes following her as she made her way to the front of the church, and she was glad Tom was by her side, even though she knew it would spark more gossip.

"I don't give a damn" had been his response when she mentioned it to him that morning. She had smiled, secretly relieved that he would be with her all the way.

She sat in the front row with the Cox's; however, Tom sat a few rows behind with Lou, Ava and Mark. Tom, Lou and Ava were all watchful and alert. By the time Duncan came out to the pulpit, the church was full, and there were people spilling out the doors and onto the sidewalk. Rebecca knew Helen had only ever spoken to a handful of them in person, but she was not resentful. Helen had always been a quiet woman, and she knew the people there today were there because they cared about the Cox family, and Helen, even if they hadn't known her personally.

Duncan's sermon was beautiful. Rebecca could see how Helen had taken to him, and she desperately hoped that her sister would eventually find peace with God. She had never really given much thought to God until she had seen Helen's ghost, and even now she was unsure about it all. All she believed was what she saw with her own eyes, and unless she was going batshit crazy, she now believed ghosts existed. And this revelation had opened up many doors for God and the afterlife that she had never contemplated.

Before she knew it, Duncan introduced her to the pulpit to offer the eulogy, and she stood carefully and made her way to the front of the church. Her foot throbbed from the night before, but she welcomed the physical pain, although it could never match the pain she felt in her heart. "Helen was not just my sister; she was my soul mate. We came into this world together. I was the screamer; she was the silent type. Helen was supposed to accomplish so much in her life, and it's hard for us not to focus on what someone stole from her. But I will. Today we will look back at Helen's life and remember her kindness, her intelligence, her genuine love of children and teaching. Her quiet manner meant that she was an introvert, but when you got her in front of thirty 9-year-olds, you could never tell. It has been hard for me to write this eulogy because we have been apart for a few years, but I know in my heart that Helen was loved here," She paused and glanced at Ruth, then continued, "that she found peace and comfort in the Lord, and her new-found family. Whenever we spoke on the phone, which was usually every week, she always sounded happy, content. And what more could a sister really ask for?"

Tom listened to Rebecca as she delivered her eulogy, learning so much about her and Helen, and by the end, there was barely a dry eye in the building. He noticed at one point Jenny looking at her hands, and Lou staring off into space. He realised just how tired they all were and how much they had on their minds. Not everyone was invested in what Rebecca had to say, well, because not everyone was in love with her. He chuckled to himself.

When Rebecca finished, she hobbled back down to her seat in the front and he saw Ruth put her arm around her, and he was pleased that Helen had found a mother that could love her so wholeheartedly, and even more so than her own mother. He suspected this was why Rebecca had no desire to leave. Just like her sister, she had finally discovered what it was like for people whose parents loved them unconditionally.

The rest of the service ran smoothly, and as Derek, Fred, Mark and some other close friends of Derek's carried out Helen's casket, many tears flowed as they played Helen's favourite songs, and a picture reel moved through her life on an overhead projector screen.

Tom almost buckled as Silver Springs by Fleetwood Mac played, and when he saw a photo of Helen and Rebecca on Helen's wedding day, he couldn't stop the tears from escaping. The bride had worn a simple cream satin dress with a lace overlay, which fell to her ankles. A netted hat sat tucked into her thick hair. Her eyes were shining and happy as she held her sister's hand. Rebecca wore an emerald-green satin dress that clung to her figure all the way to the floor. She was saying something to her sister, and they were both laughing.

Rebecca was dry-eyed. The idea of her sister in that box was making her feel sick, and she was concentrating on not throwing up all over Ruth. Her heart was beating a hundred miles an hour, and she had to hold on to Ruth's arm to steady herself as they followed the coffin out of the church. She knew Tom was right behind her, and all she wanted was for this day to be over. She put her head down and tried to concentrate on putting one foot in front of the other until they stepped into the sunlight.

The rest of the day was a blur. She performed her duties as the grieving sister, and she met countless people. It was all small talk, and all she could think about was her sister being lowered into the ground. She had fought with Derek over this issue. He had wished for her to be cremated, but Rebecca was adamant Helen would not have wanted that. When they were seven years old, their mother had fallen asleep with a lit cigarette and almost burned the house and all of them in it, down to the ground. Thank God a neighbour was coming home late from a night shift and had seen the smoke and called triple zero. Just another awful memory that transformed into trauma carried into adulthood. Helen had always been deathly afraid of fire. There was no way she was letting anyone put her through an incinerator.

When she had told the story to Derek, he had stared blankly at her. In that moment she had realised just how little

Helen had talked about their childhood with her husband. But not just him, Ruth and Fred had been horrified at the tale and admitted that all they knew about the girl's childhood was that it wasn't great, and their parents had been "useless" (Helen's words). Rebecca had nodded, telling them not to take it personally. She and Helen had decided a long time ago they would not let their parents ruin their lives, and neither of them spoke to other people about it, as they always had each other to talk to. It had always been like free therapy. And to be honest, the fire story was insignificant compared to other memories locked away in her brain.

By four o'clock that afternoon, the last of the guests had left, and the caterers were completing the cleaning and organising of the china, glassware, and cutlery. Rebecca retreated to her room for a long shower and could not wait to climb into bed and succumb to sleep for a few hours. She was supposed to be meeting Tom for dinner, but to be honest, she was worried she had over-committed herself, as pure exhaustion had taken over her entire body. As she climbed into bed, she told herself she would sleep for a couple of hours and then see how she felt. She fell fast asleep.

At the station, Tom was working on two timelines simultaneously. One for Helen's movements over the last week before she'd gone missing, and the same for Josh. He had tried to find a link between Josh and Helen. Angela had packed up Josh's room and brought a duffel bag and box of his belongings back to the station, where he spent some time going through them as he worked on the timeline. So far, nada. He had found Josh's address book, though which was more like a little black book of women's phone numbers he had previously hooked up with. After each woman's name and telephone number was a number between one and ten, which Tom could only assume were rating hook-ups. He discovered Lou's friend Jenny's name as one of the last entries and saw a solid score of eight. Tom wasn't sure whether he should laugh or gag in repulsion. He made a note to speak to Jenny, though.

He had got a hold of Josh's father thanks to Angela, who needed information of next of kin when checking into the hostel. Josh's father was in Darwin and had not seen Josh in a year or two. Apparently, it had been even longer since Josh had seen his mother. The man was suitably shocked and upset to hear his son was missing as well as the prime suspect in a murder investigation. He promised to call Tom if Josh tried to contact him, and to be honest, Tom got the feeling the guy didn't care that much.

Jerry from forensics rang Tom just after six that evening. Tom answered on the second ring, as he was still the only one still at the station.

"Tom? It's Jerry, mate."

"How are you, mate? Any news?"

"The results of Helen's swabs have all come back. The DNA from the vaginal swab has confirmed that the only match is Derek, which could have been up to two days before she was killed. Of course, this doesn't rule out rape or consensual sex with another partner using a condom."

"Of course," Tom agreed.

"The skin swab analyses from the various parts of her body were all negative. I'll email the report over shortly. But, in short; she'd just been in the river too long, sorry, mate."

Tom closed his eyes. "So, in other words, we've got nothing."

He finished his call with Jerry and sat staring at Helen's timeline. The photos that had been left on his car were time-stamped, allowing him to add them to the timeline in order. Other than the photo taken the night she disappeared, and the ones taken at the church, there were three more, one of her and Ruth at Blakes, and a couple of her and Derek as they came out of a Mexican restaurant in a beautiful coastal town Kinglake, about half an hour away from Cooinda. Tom had recognised the restaurant logo as it was a popular spot for locals to go when they wanted to get out of town and over to the beach.

In the photos, Helen's head was down, and Derek walked next to her, with his arm resting protectively on the small of her back. Someone took the photo from a distance, and the pair stood at a slight angle. The photos were all time-stamped within the last two weeks of Helen's life. The photo in the church started the sequence, and the last photo was time-stamped the evening she was abducted. Staring at the timeline was doing nothing, so Tom called it a night. He packed all the evidence into the evidence locker, turned all the lights off and left the station a little before seven, relieved he was not on call that night.

Tom pulled into his driveway twenty minutes later and saw Ruth's car parked to the right of his driveway. He knew that Rebecca now had the car indefinitely because she had returned the rental. She sat in the driver's seat in the dark, and he couldn't see her face until they both stepped out of their cars, looking over the bonnet of her car.

"I should have called, sorry," she said.

"Bullshit. You never have to call. I'm just sorry you had to wait. How long have you been here?"

"Not long," she shrugged. "I slept for a few hours and then needed to get out of the house. Derek was there, which of course is his right, but I just can't stand the guy." She chuckled.

"Come on in" he locked his car, and she did the same.

They walked into the house, and as he shut the door behind her, she reached for him, kissing him hard on the mouth. There was nothing to do except respond.

He grabbed her, pulling her close to him, devouring her mouth with his own. She smelled of lime and coconut and tasted like tequila. He ran his hands through her hair, and it was all he could do not to tear her clothes off right there in his hallway.

They finally parted, breathing hard, looking at each other with wild eyes. He was sure he had never wanted a woman as much as he wanted her in this moment. His brain, of course, was screaming at him to stop, but he honestly couldn't think of a good reason to.

He slowly leaned in and kissed her again. This time, gently, softly grazing her lips with his own, then moved down her jaw line onto her neck. She sighed beneath him, tilting her head back and wrapping her arms around his neck. She was quivering. Her need for him was insurmountable, and she ran her hands through his hair, down his hard shoulders and arms.

They were both lost in each other. Exploring each other as they stood there until Tom couldn't take it anymore.

"Fuck it," he whispered, turning on his heel and leading her into his bedroom.

Their lovemaking was everything she thought it would be. She realised she had fallen in love with him, something that had not happened to her since she was in high school. She shuddered under his touch, closing her eyes and succumbing to her own feelings. His lips grazed her neck, and his hands slid over her body. He cupped her breasts, lowering his mouth to her nipples, gently sucking, an animalistic growl escaping him. She pulled his shirt off, not even realising how he had removed hers. Gazing at the shape of his arms, she ran her hands over his physique, her fingers grazing his navel, before reaching the elastic of his shorts. Tom looked in her eyes and saw the love and lust that lingered within her as Rebecca reached for him, while he devoured her mouth with his own.

In a moment they were naked and entwined. She could feel him throbbing against her, and she threw her arms above her head, surrendering herself to him. He didn't take his eyes off her as he slowly entered her. Their eyes locked, and they moved in perfect rhythm. He reached over her head and grabbed her hands with his left hand, while his right arm balanced him. She tightened herself and wrapped her legs around him. It was all he could do not to explode inside her right then and there. He slowed down his rhythm, pulled out of her, so his tongue could travel down her glorious body, kissing and nibbling her flesh. Her legs were open to greet him, and he consumed her with his mouth. She tasted sweet as he diligently devoured her until he could feel her tension rise. He brought her to the brink, then pulled away, and plunged back deep inside her. She screamed with pure ecstasy as they came together. They held each other tightly, their sweat mingling, and their hearts raced in unison.

They lay quietly together, still naked for a few moments, before she smiled lazily at him and excused herself, going to the bathroom. She splashed water on her face, cleaned herself up, and stared at her own reflection. She thought she would feel guilty for enjoying such intense lovemaking, but she didn't. This had been nothing like Antony, who had been a worthy fuck, and a mate, but not much more. Once again, she marvelled at just how empty her life had been until she met Tom, and she suspected he felt the same.

As she turned towards the bathroom door, she saw movement in the mirror's reflection. She froze, waiting, but nothing else appeared. If Helen was there, she was keeping herself hidden. She smiled to herself and whispered, "It's okay, sis, I'll tell you all about it later."

She opened the door, turned off the light and walked back to the bedroom, unaware of her sister watching her from the bathroom door.

{ 21 }

As they sat together in bed, Tom wearing his boxes and Rebecca in his shirt, eating vegemite sandwiches, and drinking peppermint tea, Rebecca filled him in on the Wake, but more importantly, she told him about her discovery of Helen's engagement ring the night before. Helen had lost it, and Rebecca suspected she might have been too afraid to tell Derek. Fred planned to tell Derek about it that evening. She was hoping he would respond better to his parents while she was not there. Obviously, their feelings for each other were mutual, and her being in his presence brought out the worst in him.

Tom filled her in on as much as he could legally, which wasn't much. He knew he couldn't share information with her, especially now, and she didn't ask. There was no way she would jeopardise his career or Helen's case, so they talked about other things. She was funny, intelligent, emotionally vulnerable as well as stoic and confident. He found it sexy as hell.

The witching hour had begun by the time Rebecca drove to the homestead. It was the last thing she wanted to do, preferring to stay in Tom's safe arms. However, she knew it would not be the best idea just yet.

Once back home, she showered, allowing the warm water to cleanse her soul, and climbed into bed, throwing the sheet off, and ensuring the ceiling fan was gently buzzing above her. Unable to sleep, she contemplated her life. She was unsure whether she wanted to stay in Cooinda forever, worried the country life would not suit her long-term. However, for the first time in her life since Helen had moved away, she felt surrounded by family, and she understood why Helen had stayed. It had not only been for Derek. It had been for Ruth and Fred. They were the parents they had always dreamed of, and she was so happy that Helen had found that in the last few years of her life. It was all she had ever wanted; it was why she had married Derek so young. She had craved a family and craved being surrounded by people who loved her. And even though Derek was a narcissistic arsehole, Helen obviously felt satisfied with the love Ruth and Fred had offered in his place.

She did not know what her future with Tom looked like, but she knew, without a doubt, that Ruth and Fred would always be in her life. This thought made her smile as she closed her eyes and drifted off to sleep.

***

Tom woke up wondering if he had dreamt the night before. He closed his eyes, remembering the softness of Rebecca's skin, her full lips, her irresistible taste. He knew he should regret making love to her, but instead it was fuelling him to continue. The case needed to be his number one priority. He needed to solve it, not just because it was his job, but because he couldn't stand the thought of moving forward in any kind of relationship with her, knowing she would always be heartbroken.

He showered and shaved and swung by to pick up Lou by eight. Considering he had slept for about two hours after Rebecca had left, he was surprisingly chipper. He supposed getting laid for the first time in two years would do that to a man. Lou was ready and waiting outside the station. They decided to both see Janice about the photos because Lou was a member of the congregation, and it would help the investigation having a second pair of eyes there, as well as a friendly face.

Lou climbed into the passenger seat with a tired grin. "Morning, boss," she said, handing him a cappuccino.

"You are truly a saint," he said as he took a huge gulp, closing his eyes and savouring the caffeine as it warmed his throat and kick-started his heart.

Lou was quiet on the way to Duncan and Janice's home. Tom glanced over at her several times, concerned that something was on her mind. It was a brief trip though, and before he knew it, they had found parking on Prince Avenue, a few blocks back from the church where the Manse was. It was a stately home that the church had purchased in the nineteen-sixties. Duncan and Janice had been in residence since the late eighties. They had three children who had flourished in the country life, and Tom suspected the family had no desire to leave Cooinda. The back of the manse held a home office attached to the garage, and both Duncan and Janice were sitting in an area to the left of Duncan's desk. On the far-right side of the office was a large bookcase, stuffed with more books than shelves. Tom didn't know Duncan or Janice very well, and formally said hello to them both. Lou, on the other hand, leaned in and hugged Janice fiercely and kissed Duncan warmly on the cheek.

After the four sat down, Janice was eager to show pictures of her newest family member. Tom didn't interfere, knowing how mundane chatter was important for the investigation, He needed Janice to be comfortable and trusting of him. Often witnesses had a lot more to say and remember when they were relaxed or off guard. He let the conversation flow naturally, and after about half an hour, Lou naturally steered the conversation from grandbaby photographs to the photos that had been left on Tom's car.

"Yes, Duncan only mentioned this to me after I arrived home." Janice said. She was a tall, willowy-looking woman, with soft, flawless skin and thick dark hair that was greying slightly around the roots. She possessed a graceful and soothing nature that Tom liked instantly. "All these terrible things happening while I've been gone, it's almost like I've come home to a completely different town," she said sadly.

"Do you mind looking at the photos? We are baffled about who took the photos, why they took them, and why they left them on my car."

Janice was listening and nodding intently as Tom said this. Lou handed her the photos, and they watched quietly as Janice looked through the photos carefully. After a few moments, she stood up and walked over to the overstuffed bookshelf, where she removed a rectangular box and brought it back to the table. Inside were about three lots of developed photos, still in their envelopes that the chemists used to put them in once developed.

"These are the photos I've taken at the church over the last couple of months. Of church services and related events like the church picnic and different youth group activities." She pulled them out and spread them on the coffee table in the middle of the four of them. They all leaned slightly in, studying the images laid out before them. It didn't take long for Janice to pick out a handful of photos to look at more closely. There were a few that she had taken over on a few different Sundays when special occasions had happened, such as a specific choir event or a christening. The photos of the christening seemed to interest her in particular. There were about six of them, and Tom watched her closely as she looked at them, and when she asked him for the photo of the Cox's and Helen in church, Tom had it ready to hand it to her.

"Yes, I thought so." She was staring at two photos, side by side. "This is the same day. See, Sheryl Winslow in the last row is wearing a red and black floral blouse with her hair in a high bun in both pictures. The one I took is from the front, and the other one, your photo, is from the back. You can also see in my photo Ruth, Fred, and Helen, all standing in the fourth row, and even though you can't see much of them, you can tell that they are all wearing the same clothing in each, as well." She handed the two photos back to Tom.

He could clearly see what Janice meant. It wasn't just Sheryl, but you could tell by the entire congregation, where they stood, and what they wore, that two different people had taken these photos on the same day, just from two different angles. And just like the photo left on his car, it looked like just another church service.

Until Lou piped up, "Oh, I remember this service. It's the one I brought Josh to. See?"

From over Tom's shoulder she pointed to her own head, which was on the same side that Helen was sitting but right in the back row. Janice had been at the front of the church when she had taken the photo, making Lou's face slightly blurry because of the distance. Tom could also see a tiny, blurry headshot of Josh standing next to Lou.

"You didn't tell me you took him to church."

"I had actually forgotten, sorry. I took him only that one time, and to be honest, he was bored out of his mind. He never came along again." Lou sounded a little upset as she spoke, and Tom suspected she was upset with herself for forgetting an important detail like that one.

"Do you remember him acting strangely at all? Did you see him talk to Helen, or did he have a camera with him?"

"No camera, and I'm almost positive he didn't talk to anyone except me and Jenny. He wanted to leave straight after the service. We had lunch at the pub, if my memory serves me correctly."

Tom sighed. Once again, he had connected Josh to Helen, but it was only circumstantial with no evidence or proof that he was the one who had been stalking her.

Tom and Lou thanked Janice and Duncan for their time and headed back to the station.

Back at the station, Tom began writing the report from the visit and logged the photo of Josh into evidence.

Lou collected their lunch, and they sat at Tom's desk, eating deli sandwiches. She had been thinking about Josh coming to church with her and Jenny and was animated as they ate.

"I just feel like this is it, Tom," taking a bite out of her chicken sandwich, and chewing rapidly. "Why else would Josh come along to church? He obviously wasn't interested in our faith."

"I agree. But if you didn't see him, take any photos, there isn't really a connection to Josh being Helen's stalker. It's purely a theory."

Lou nodded, "I know. But at least it means we may be on the right track. I just keep praying this is the beginning of the end of this case, and that poor family can finally be at peace. I can only imagine what Derek and his folks are going through."

"Agreed," said Tom, and silently added Rebecca to that list.

***

Derek was having a bitch of a time trying to sort out Helen's clothes. Everything he touched reminded him of her, and his emotions were jumping from sadness to fury depending on the moment. How dare she leave him? She was supposed to be there for him, always. He thought of smile, her delicate features and quiet, obliging demeanour. She had always been willing to please him, always subservient.

Every single item of clothing he pulled from the cupboard smelled of her, and his grief was infuriating him. He was unsure if he was even ready to sort out her clothes, but he was worried her bitch sister would try to claim them for herself. If he could get rid of them now, she wouldn't be able to do anything about it. Just as this thought crossed his mind, there was a knock at his door. Muttering to himself, Derek called out, "Just a sec," scooping Helen's clothes from the bed and throwing them back in the cupboard. He left the bedroom, pulling the door behind him. From the hallway he could see straight to the front of the house, and there stood Rebecca. She was by herself.

Puzzled, he ambled to the door, opening the screen outwards, forcing her to take a step back. Her hair tumbled around her shoulders, and he could see a trickle of sweat beading through her skin, lazily making its way down her hairline. She smiled at him nervously.

"Hi Derek."

"Hi?" He was baffled because she stood on his porch.

"Can I come in?" she asked softly.

Derek didn't say anything, instead, he took a step back so she could come inside. She stepped into the house hesitantly, as though she were entering a place with a sign that said, "ENTER AT OWN RISK."

They stood awkwardly in the hallway before Rebecca finally spoke, "How are you doing?"

The question caught him by surprise. He shrugged. "About as well as expected," he paused, running his hand through his hair. "You?"

"About the same, I guess." It struck her just how little she knew Derek. When he and Helen had been dating, he had been very subdued, reserved, almost rude. She had never seen what Helen had seen in him, yet over the last two torturous weeks, she had seen glimpses of the man her sister had fallen in love with. She knew he must be hurting.

"Would you like a coffee, tea?" Derek waved her through the hallway into the kitchen. It was the first time Rebecca had been into her sister's home, and she was feeling her presence as she walked into the kitchen. There was a solid timber island in the centre of the room, with a potholder hanging above it. Pots and pans and decorative trinkets hung from it. They swayed as they entered, although the day was still and breezeless. The far wall of the kitchen had two timber double-hung timber windows that were adorned by timber shelving. Rebecca saw the neatly organised shelves; with plates, glasses, and other china, was out of place. The sink was on the wall that looked over the back deck, with another larger double-hung timber window. To the left of the window was a little wooden sign hanging on the wall that said, *"Bless this house."* On the fridge were three photos held up by magnets.

Rebecca walked over and examined them as Derek filled up the kettle, placing it on the gas stovetop to boil. There was a photo of Helen and Derek. They were sitting together in what Rebecca assumed was a local restaurant. Derek had his arm around Helen and was pulling her in close. She looked happy and relaxed, with her head leaning in towards her husband. They certainly made a striking couple, and Rebecca could almost feel her heart constrict with pain. The other two photos were of Helen with Ruth and Fred. In each photo, her eyes were bright and alive, and it pained Rebecca to know she would never see that light in her eyes again. Whenever she closed her eyes, she saw only her sister lying dead on that cold steel table. A tear escaped, and she quickly wiped it away.

Derek was eyeing her as he poured water into the French press, and he a sudden pang of guilt engulfed him.

He cleared his throat and said softly, "Go into our study, and have a look at her collage wall" he nodded towards the hallway where a bedroom door stood opposite the kitchen.

Puzzled, she nodded and wandered across the hall. Derek used one side of the study for his work. There was a desk and filing cabinet and a large schedule board hanging on the wall behind the desk that organised the cane farming and mill schedules.

To her left as she entered the room, there was a craft space that Helen had used. The wall to her left was a beautiful collage wall with homemade crafts and photos that Helen had carefully pinned to the wall. Rebecca stared in wonder at her sister's masterpiece, which she had taken great pains to create. There were several photos of her and Helen throughout their lives. Their parents had rarely photographed them as children; their grandmother usually stepped up to the task. One photo was of their first birthday. The girls sat side by side on their mother's lap. Helen's chubby face stared at the camera with a serious expression, while Rebecca held her arms out. Neither of the girls looked comfortable sitting with their mother, who also looked uncomfortable. The level of discomfort in her mother's eyes made Rebecca chuckle.

The other photo was of their sixteenth birthday. They had spent this birthday at their grandmother's house, and it was one of the best memories the girls had of their teenage years. For two weeks, Nana had loved and cherished them, and the photo reflected their happy, carefree days they spent with her.

They had decided that holiday that they were going to move in with her, and their grandmother had agreed. Two weeks later, Nana had died in a head-on collision as she drove to her weekly Bible reading group. She remembered how Helen had cried a river of tears. She was always so much more in touch with her emotions, and her grief had been a stranglehold on her heart and mind for months afterwards. Rebecca had been the one to support and care for Helen; her own grief was tucked behind a solid wall where she always tucked away her feelings, being careful not to display an emotion that her parents could use against her later. Of course, their mother used her own mother's death to get maximum attention and was constantly irritated by Helen's grief. It was just one more thing Rebecca always tried to protect Helen from. Their mother's narcissism bordered on sociopathy.

Suddenly Derek appeared behind her, holding out a cup of coffee. He handed her a cup, gesturing towards the photo of when they were in their early twenties, living in Melbourne, not long before he had met them. "That was her favourite photo," he said solemnly, as though revealing a deep secret. She stared at the photo and then turned to face him.

Behind him stood Helen. She had a sad look on her face as she looked at her sister. Rebecca froze, staring at her.

Derek, puzzled, looked behind him, only to see the other side of the study, his desk, his things.

He turned back to Rebecca. "You, okay?" he asked.

She nodded, afraid to speak, afraid her sister would vanish again.

He nodded and shrugged. "Well, maybe we should sit down?"

She knew he didn't want her in the study alone anymore, and it made her curious about what else was there.

"Okay," she agreed, sipping her coffee, her eyes firmly planted on her sister. When she reached the door, Helen had faded, staring at Derek sadly while she slowly but surely ceased to be seen. Rebecca stared at the hollowness, contemplating why Helen had appeared there. Outside the window, views of the cane fields and, in the distance, stood the sugar mill. Blinking furiously, Rebecca tried to shake off the intruding uncanny feelings that crept to the surface.

Derek led her to the back verandah, and once again they sat awkwardly in silence, while sipping their coffee.

Finally, he spoke. "So, I hear you're staying longer than planned?" His voice was smooth as silk; however, there was a slight edge in the undertone.

"Um, yes. I want to stay for a while. I can't bear to go back yet, and unfortunately my job couldn't keep my position for me, so I have resigned." She studied him closely as she spoke, curious to see his reaction. He must be furious, although she was unsure why. Until a few moments ago, she had been pretty convinced he had nothing to do with Helen's murder. Maybe he couldn't stand looking at her. That she could understand. It must have been difficult to look at her and know how different she was from Helen. It caused a myriad of emotions.

"Stay? Indefinitely?" his voice was incredulous. "Why?"

She laughed, "Derek, I know you hate this town, but I think it's charming."

He grinned. "Try growing up here."

Rebecca laughed again. "I'm pretty sure it's not that bad."

Derek shrugged, and she could tell he was getting bored and wondering why she was there.

"So, Fred was going to bring this back, but I came instead," she smiled nervously as she handed Derek Helen's engagement ring. It glinted in the daylight. A puzzled expression appeared on Derek's face. "Is that what I think it is?"

"Yep, the night before the funeral I stepped on a thumbtack, and I fell beside the hall table. I found this lying underneath it."

Derek stared at it. He seemed confused. Rebecca waited patiently.

"I'm surprised she didn't tell me she had lost it. She loves this ring." Derek reached out and finally took the ring from Rebecca. He glanced at her sadly and corrected himself, "loved."

"I don't want to sound like a bitch, but you would have been angry if she had told you she'd lost it?"

For once, Derek didn't react. Instead, she saw his eyebrows furrow as he thought about her question. "Maybe?" he answered. "I do have a habit of losing my temper sometimes."

"Sometimes?"

Derek actually grinned before shrugging. "It's been a hard couple of weeks."

"I get it Derek, I've lost my temper countless times since arriving here," she continued, "look, I know you don't like the idea of me staying, but I just can't go back to New York and pretend to go back to my old life. Every night I dream of her; every day, I see her ghost. I'm barely functioning." She knew Derek would assume she spoke metaphorically about the ghost, and he nodded, as though he understood.

"I know why you'd want to stay; it's just hard for me, seeing you, especially at my folks' place. It's like she's not dead. And then I remember, and it all comes flooding back." It was the most honest he had been with anyone about his feelings, and she nodded; she understood.

"I just have to stay there until I figure out what I'm going to do. And they make me feel welcome. I understand why Helen loved them so much. You are lucky to have such amazing parents."

"Ha!" It came out snidely. "I know they aren't anything like your folks, but believe me, they aren't saints."

"Well, I guess none of us are...."

He nodded, and they were both silent for a moment.

Rebecca motioned to the ring before speaking again. "Do you remember the last time you saw her wearing it?"

He shook his head, looking at it, as though it would unmask some big dark secret. "I don't remember. It's not exactly the sort of thing a guy pays' attention too I'm afraid."

Rebecca sighed. "Well, okay. I had a feeling it meant nothing significant."

"Yeah," Derek agreed, although his voice wavered in uncertainty. "Do me a favour though?" He asked, handing the ring back to her.

"Okay?" her voice was weary.

"Ask Tom to run fingerprints?"

She took the ring with surprise. "Good idea. It'll take a while. But I guess, time is what we have."

{ 22 }

By the time Rebecca walked back to Ruth and Fred's, it was early afternoon, and the sun was low in the sky, beating down aggressively, targeting anyone and everyone who ventured outdoors. It was the beginning of March now, and Rebecca wondered what the weather was like in New York. Freezing, she suspected. She had always hated that time of year in the city. Cold, dark, and miserable, impossible to get a cab. The heat in Cooinda, however, warmed her skin as she walked through the trail in the cane that led from Derek and Helen's cottage to the homestead. Since arriving in Cooinda, her skin had turned a golden-brown colour, and her auburn hair had become sun-streaked and a few shades lighter. She had lost a few kilos as well, certainly not with any effort on her part, but she had been smoking a pack of cigarettes a day, drinking too much, and not eating enough. A change was needed now that she was staying. Her life had been out of her control since arriving, and the idea of getting organise made her anxious, probably because organisation in her mind equalled 'moving on.' How could she move on without Helen?

As she emerged from the cane, the first thing she noticed was Tom's unmarked, police-issued sedan parked in the driveway. Her heart fluttered as she ascended the front steps, and a stupid grin broke out on her face when she heard his voice inside the lounge room. She remembered their evening together, and the flutters in her heart became a pounding. All three of them looked up and smiled as she entered the formal living area where they sat.

Tom was sitting opposite Ruth and Fred, and on the coffee-table were some photographs. She knew he had been to see the minister and his wife today, and she stared at them, hope spreading openly across her pretty face.

"Sweetheart, how did it go?" Ruth asked softly, knowing full well that her son would not be easily swayed. She admired Rebecca so much for wanting to try.

Rebecca smiled. "Better than expected, actually." Without thinking, she sat next to Tom, comfortably placing her hand on his knee as she reached over to peer at the photo.

"I was just asking Fred and Ruth if they recognised anything about this photo," Tom paused. "How did what go?"

"I visited Derek, hoping to make peace," she smiled wearily at him, pulling at his heartstrings.

"And?"

"Well, he actually asked me to pass it on to Tom." She laughed at Ruth and Fred's amazed expressions.

"Pass what on to Tom?" Tom asked pleasantly.

"You know I told you I found Helen's engagement ring under the hall table." She took it out of her pocket and showed him.

Tom took the ring from her gingerly. "Yes, I remember."

"He asked if it was possible, you could run prints?"

Tom stared at the ring, deep in thought. "I'm not sure that this has to do with anything. She may have lost her ring and forgotten to tell him. Or was too afraid too."

Rebecca nodded. "That may be true, but something is weird about this to me. Like, ghost weird."

Tom glanced at the Cox's who were nodding in agreement. "I take it you two know?"

Ruth nodded solemnly. "It's like having our very own ghost hunter in the family," she said with a serious face.

Tom was unsure how to respond until he saw the slight crack of a smile on Ruth's face.

They all broke into relieved chuckles. "Well, I'm glad we can all have a laugh at my expense," Rebecca said light-heartedly.

Later that evening, Tom and Rebecca sat together comfortably in the family room. Dinner had been served and eaten, and Ruth insisted she and Fred could clean up, telling them to stay put as she topped up their wine glasses. Rebecca was studying the photo from the church again. "I can't believe Lou forgot she'd taken Josh to church," she said finally.

"Yeah," said Tom. "I think she's pretty upset with herself for forgetting. Considering the circumstances."

Silence filled the air as Rebecca thought about what Tom had said. Her voice wavered ever so slightly as she spoke, "Ruth mentioned to me that sometimes she and Helen felt like they were being watched when they were in town. What I don't understand is why Josh would leave the photos on your car before taking off."

He put his arm around her, pulling her close, and absent-mindedly kissed her on the forehead. "We'll figure it all out, I promise you," he whispered.

Ruth and Fred quietly observed Rebecca and Tom while putting away the clean dishes. "Rebecca is not going back to New York," Ruth said to her husband quietly.

Fred thought for a few moments as he put the casserole dish in its place in the cupboard above the oven. "Well, that's wonderful news. Did you offer her to stay here until she gets on her feet?"

Ruth nodded. "She wants to stay here...is that okay?

He stopped, putting down the damp tea towel, and reached for his wife, gently pulling her into an embrace. "Of course. I know how much it means to you having her here, but please remember, she's not Helen, my love," he whispered. Ruth pulled back from him, gazing at him.

"I know, Fred. She is a completely different woman, but she and I have formed a bond, and we are both grieving. She has been a godsend to me. Derek is so self-involved he hasn't even considered how much we are grieving Helen. At least Rebecca sees. She understands."

Fred nodded, pulling her into him again. "I'm sorry, my darling. My intention isn't anything sinister. I just don't want you to get hurt again." She nodded against his chest, tightening her arms around him.

23

Tom dusted Helen's ring for prints first thing the following morning, and with Lou alongside him, they followed the procedure to prepare the fingerprint evidence ready for transport. There were several prints found on the ring and had to assume not much would come out of the exercise considering multiple people would have managed it since it was found. He was unsure of why Derek wanted to check it but was happy to run the prints either way. He was paranoid because he had made no actual progress on the case, and he knew the family would be devastated if the case turned cold.

Soon, other work overwhelmed him. He was due in court that afternoon for a domestic disturbance case, and there were still a few other incidents about cow tipping that he needed to look into. When he first came to Cooinda, he thought cow tipping had been a joke. He found out the hard way that teens around the area were really mean to cows when they were drunk and bored, and it often caused problems for farmers in the area. Tom just felt really sorry for the damn cows. He sometimes wanted to tip over a sleeping teenager to see how they would like it, but he suspected people would disapprove.

Meanwhile, Rebecca had started her day excited and positive, ready to look at a couple of places to potentially rent.

It was a nightmare. The first place was an apartment by the river in an old turn of the century weatherboard place that had once been one enormous home, before being divided into flats, probably in the sixties or seventies. It was a cute little place, but it was on the ground floor, and when she walked through it, she could clearly hear toddlers (or elephants) running around above her.

The second place was a duplex, and although it was a newer build, it was lacking air conditioning, and she left the place dripping with sweat. There was no way she could live in an oven. By lunch time she realised she wouldn't be able to find a decent place with air conditioning and sans elephants until she had a job, so she visited the only recruitment agency in town. They were less than positive about the idea of her finding a job with her skill set in town and suggested she try the Gold Coast or even Brisbane. She had no desire to leave Cooinda and left feeling dejected. When she arrived back at Ruth and Fred's, the three of them sat and 'regrouped', as Fred put it.

"What does design involve, Rebecca?" he asked her in a serious tone, the savvy business owner shining through. She ran through the elements of her job, explaining what she did and what her skills were. They were both suitably impressed.

"What about photography, or art?" Ruth asked.

Rebecca thought about it. "You're right," she answered. "It's the perfect long-term solution. Starting my own business would be a dream come true. I just don't have the luxury or the time to do so, not without a part-time job, anyway. Do you think I should try the local cafes or pubs?"

Ruth and Fred exchanged glances, and Fred nodded. "We may have a solution for you if you are interested," Ruth said.

Rebecca raised her eyebrows, shaking her head emphatically. "I don't want any charity."

"This is not charity. It would be a business proposal. Fred and I have been discussing what we should do. As part of our business, we have quite a few rental properties, both residential and commercial. We have been considering for a while now the necessity of removing the listings from Derek and managing them ourselves. He's been slipping in his work responsibilities, and Fred has had to take over a few things. We were thinking you could manage the properties for us while you try to get your business off the ground. You are obviously an extremely competent businesswoman."

Rebecca thought about it. "What would be involved?" She asked, curiosity getting the better of her.

Fred explained everything to her, and she understood it wasn't too complicated. Overseeing the rental agreements, organising cleaning and maintenance on the properties, and conducting inspections when needed. It certainly wouldn't be exciting work, but it would be something to do while she could concentrate on her business idea.

By the end of the day, she had agreed to work for them as their property manager and had settled on a modest salary. She could work from home and agreed to remain with them until she was settled. There was a study in the back of the house she could use. It would only be about twenty hours a week. This also gave her plenty of time to pursue her photography and art. She had not picked up a piece of charcoal or paint brush since she had arrived, and she was looking forward to the soothing rhythm she always found in painting or drawing. By the time she drove into town to meet Tom for dinner, she was feeling happy and excited, and for the first time in a long time, back to her normal self.

Tom was late to dinner, and when he arrived, he appeared flustered and distracted. Rebecca knew he was working hard to break the case, and she felt bad that she'd had a good day when he was busting his arse to find her sister's killer. They walked into the local Chinese restaurant and were shown to a private corner table. They ordered drinks, which arrived with a saucer with two fortune cookies accompanying them.

Rebecca opened hers first: '*Once you make a decision, the universe conspires to make it happen.*'

Tom's read. "*Be careful who you trust. Salt and sugar look the same.*"

"Wow, that one is a little dark," Tom jokes.

Rebecca looked serious for a moment. Then, she broke into a smile. "Just take it with a grain of salt," she winked at him, and he laughed, relaxing along with her.

They talked about everything; from her new job to his day ... to more serious issues, such as her visit with Derek and Helen's ring. Tom explained the procedure of getting the prints analysed, telling her it would take a few weeks. Finally, she started talking about seeing Helen in Derek's study again.

"What do you think she was trying to tell you?" he asked.

Once again, he validated her love for him. Over the last few weeks, he had never doubted her when she spoke of seeing Helen. It made her loved, but more importantly, sane.

"It was like she wanted to get my attention while I was in the study. She was looking at Derek. I don't know; it was just a sense I got." She took a sip of her wine and looked at the contents of her glass. "She's always wearing the same thing. It's like she's stuck here, waiting for me to figure it out."

"I've been thinking..." he paused, unsure of how to proceed. "I know there's absolutely no evidence of it, but do you think Josh and Helen were maybe involved?"

"It's certainly not an unreasonable question. I've thought about it myself countless times. I just don't think there was any time for it. Between Derek and Ruth, you have accounted for all of her time. And I don't think she was the type to cheat. No matter how unhappy she may have been."

Tom nodded. "Yeah, that's what I thought. I just thought I should ask. They may have had a lover's quarrel, and he lost his temper...." he sighed and shrugged. "It's so frustrating."

"I'm pretty sure I can help you unwind," Rebecca grinned.

He looked at her, a twinkle in his eye, "oh really?"

She giggled and threw her napkin at him. "Let's get out of here," she said with sudden lustful urgency. She didn't have to ask twice.

Later that night, as they lay entwined and exhausted in each other's embrace, she thought about her new life. It felt strange, moving on, living, loving, all the while knowing she was potentially living in the same town as the person who killed her twin. Most nights she begged Helen for just one more sign to point her in the right direction. She could always sense her presence, even when she didn't appear. It had been the same in the States. There were certain times when their connection crossed oceans, and they knew the other was needed. She now believed that their connection crossed more than just the vast planet but also crossed over between the physical and spiritual planes as well.

24

She had told herself that she wouldn't stay the night at Tom's house, and she had no intention of doing so. However, she had drifted off, content in his arms, thinking, "just for a little while," and the next minute (or so it seemed) she was stirring to the smell of coffee percolating. She threw on his shirt and wandered into the kitchen, looking around her as she did so.

Cabin was the word that came to mind when she examined his style and décor. Everything was neat and, in its place, with no clutter or unnecessary items. The kitchen was spotless and sparse, with a peninsular bench with a timber bench top separating it from the dining area. Timber blinds hung on the window above the sink, and Tom had painted the walls a fresh lemon colour. The kitchen cabinets were off-white, and the floor was a warm grey slate. Rebecca sat on one of the timber stools at the peninsular bench and watched him.

Shirtless, Tom moved around his kitchen with ease, collecting mugs and milk from the fridge, removing the coffeepot from the base, and pouring two cups, adding a dash of milk (already knowing and remembering how she liked it) and gently sliding it towards her.

"How come you are still single?" She asked.

"Am I?" he studied her, another one of his grins making her blush.

"You know what I mean," she replied sheepishly as she sipped her coffee. It was delicious.

He shrugged, "My ex-wife traumatised me."

"Sorry, we don't have to talk about it."

Shaking his head, he sighed. "It's okay. The divorce was the main reason I moved here. It was an incredibly destructive relationship with a bitter and unforgiving end. I needed to get away from her and my family."

"Why your family?" she paused. "You haven't mentioned them before."

Tom sipped his coffee for a moment, thinking. "There is no easy way to say it, but my wife had an affair with my father. They are now married. She is now my stepmother."

Rebecca almost spat her coffee out. "What!"

Her reaction made Tom laugh. "Yep, that's most people's reactions."

"I'm so sorry; that was so insensitive of me, but holy shit."

"Yeah, so to sum up, I don't talk to most of my family much anymore."

"What about your mum?"

"She passed away when I was sixteen. It was my dad and me for a long time. Then I met Laura, my wife, when I was twenty-two. We were married at twenty-four, and she was married to my dad by the time we were thirty. It was around the time I received the wedding invitation that I knew it was time for a sea change."

"They invited you to the wedding!" Once again, Rebecca almost spat her coffee out.

Tom laughed again. "They were so puzzled why I hadn't 'gotten over it' by then. Anyway, I think it scared me for a long time. Until you came along."

She smiled and reached for his hand. "Well, don't worry, I only have eyes for you."

When Rebecca arrived back at the homestead that morning, it was only a little after eight in the morning. The air was humid and damp after the rain overnight. Although the temperature was in the mid-twenties, the humidity was in the eighties. The morning was grey and still.

She stepped out of Ruth's car. There was an unfamiliar car in the driveway, and she ascended the front steps wondering who would visit so early in the morning. Ruth and Fred were exceedingly early risers and were usually already out on the farm or doing other business by then. She quietly let herself in and was heading towards her room when she heard a familiar voice. Rebecca stopped, tilted her head and listened for a moment. As recognition crept into her brain, she broke out in a grin, turned and saw Mark standing in the kitchen with Fred and Ruth.

Rebecca made her presence known by clearing her throat. The three turned towards her, and Ruth smiled.

"Good morning, my dear. Late night?" Rebecca saw the twinkle in Ruth's eye and knew she was teasing her.

She grinned in return. "You could say that." She winked, and Fred chuckled

"Honestly, you two," was all he said.

Mark laughed and reached out to give Rebecca a brief, firm hug. "Seems like you're settling in just fine."

Rebecca rolled her eyes. "Yeah, I'm okay."

Mark turned serious for a moment. "He's an exceptional man, Rebecca. One of the best. I'm so happy he's found you."

"Me too," she replied softly. "Anyway, what on earth are you doing here at this time of the morning?"

"Fred's farm manager, Silas, called me a couple of hours ago. Something bit their dog. A brown snake, most likely."

Rebecca did not know Silas or his wife Liz very well, although she had certainly gotten to know Liz more since moving into the homestead as she was the Cox's housekeeper and there most days. Silas ran the management of the sugar cane harvesting, and the couple lived in the other cottage on the property, on the other side of Derek and Helen's place.

"Oh no! Is Roger okay?"

Mark shook his head, a sad look on his face. "Unfortunately, he didn't make it. Silas and Liz are devastated. I feel awful."

"I'll take her some flowers, I think," said Ruth, and Fred nodded in agreement.

"Let me know when you go over, and I'll come too" Rebecca felt saddened. Silas and Liz had the most beautiful cattle dog. He had been intelligent and affectionate. Every time he'd come to the homestead with Liz, he'd always come up to Rebecca for cuddles, and even as a cat person, it hadn't taken her long to become smitten with him.

"Lou's over there now. She was pretty upset when Liz called her."

Rebecca glanced at Ruth, a puzzled expression on her face. "Lou?"

It took Ruth a minute to realise the confusion. "Of course. No one has told you. Louise's mother, June, worked here for years. June and Liz were close friends and of similar ages. After June passed away, Liz became full-time, and Silas from seasonal worker to full-time manager, and moved into the staff cottage. Anyway, Lou has known Silas and Liz like family, and she adored that dog. It's just so sad."

Rebecca returned to her room shortly afterwards to shower and have a nap before getting some work done. Before she excused herself, she had an idea. "Mark, are you and Ava free tonight? Why don't we take Lou out? I bet she could use some cheering up."

Mark grinned widely. "What a great idea. I'll call Ava when I get into the office, and we can get it organised. Can you find out if Tom's free?"

Rebecca nodded, smiled, and wandered towards her bedroom enjoying the contentment. Her heart still ached for Helen, but she realised that would always be the case. She walked down the hallway, glancing at a photo of Helen that was framed and hung alongside a dozen other pictures Ruth had hung with care. As she smiled at her sister's photo, a candid shot of Helen smiling and holding a wooden spoon in Ruth's kitchen, the house started to rumble. It first came from the floor, as though a subway train was passing underneath the house. Mark, Ruth, and Fred appeared in the hallway, and they all looked nervously at each other, unsure of what to say or do.

Fred was about to announce that it must be an earthquake when, one by one, the photos began flying off the wall. Each one stopped mid-air, then crashed to the floor. The protective glass of each frame smashed into pieces, breaking and flying in the air. Rebecca yelped, jumping away from the wall, and grabbed hold of Ruth's outstretched arm. Mark instinctively put his arm in front of Ruth and Rebecca, and they all moved out of harm's way. They all stood staring at the mess on the floor. The rumbling noise dissipated, and the house was quiet.

The blood had drained completely from Mark's face, and Rebecca was concerned that if he turned any greyer, he would be dead.

Twice in his life, Mark had questioned the spiritual aspect of life beyond his religious upbringing. The first was when he had met Ava. Surely such beauty was not of this world. And the second time was when he watched the picture frame hover a moment, suspended in the air, before crashing to the floor.

Finally, his pulse slowed down again, and he looked at Ruth, Fred, and Rebecca. They didn't speak, for there wasn't anything to say. Ruth looked stunned, while Fred trembled beside her. Rebecca was staring at the smashed glass as it lay glistening in the filtered light of the hallway.

Slowly, Mark knelt to look at the pictures on the floor. They all had one common denominator. They were all photos of Derek.

{ 25 }

Mark was rattled. All the way back to his office, his legs jittered, and he smoked three cigarettes in less than three kilometres of driving. He had left shortly afterwards, mumbling about patients, as Fred had knelt to clean up the glass, saying in an unconvincing tone that the picture hooks must have been rusty.

Back at his office, he sat drinking a cup of instant coffee, waiting for his assistant to open the clinic for their first furry patient. It was a little after eight in the morning when Ava turned up for her morning chit-chat before starting her day. He was often called out to local farms to care for stock and other farm animals, and this morning he'd left her sleeping soundly before the sun was up.

It was Ava's day off work, and she liked to jog around town, buy a coffee and pop in to say hi before going home to shower. Now she sat perched on the edge of his desk, her revealing sports bra and singlet top straining against her breasts as she unintentionally drove him to distraction while he described to her what had happened at the Cox's place only half an hour before.

Ava stared at him; her adorable wide eyes focused on his. He reached up and caressed her breast without thinking. She reached out and swatted his hand away without thinking. "Are you trying to tell me that a bunch of pictures flew off the wall and crashed to the floor right in front of your eyes?" she asked in an incredulous tone.

"That's exactly what I'm saying," Mark sighed and stood up from his desk. "We need to talk about this later, though. I have a sick kitten waiting to be seen, and your breasts are very distracting." He gently kissed her on the lips as he pulled her up from her perch. "Also, Rebecca thought we should go out with Lou tonight to cheer her up. Can you organise that?"

"Why? What's wrong with Lou?"

"Roger died this morning."

"Oh shit. Poor Lou. Yep, I'll call Rebecca as soon as I'm home and organise something. I'll let you know." She kissed him once more before sailing out of his office, always enjoying the way he looked at her arse as she left a room.

***

Rebecca was barely out of the shower when Ruth announced Ava was on the phone. She picked up the receiver next to her bed, yelled "Got it!" and waited until she heard Ruth hang up the living room phone.

"Well, hello. First Mark, and now the lovely Miss Ava. Aren't I a popular lady this morning?" Rebecca grinned into the phone, happy to hear from her new friend.

"Do you really think I wouldn't call after a poltergeist literally threw photos off your wall?"

Rebecca laughed. "It's not my wall."

Ava giggled. "Mark only told me the cliff notes before he had to start work. Can you fill me in? Meet me for lunch?"

Rebecca looked at her clock. It was a little after nine. If she got in a quick nap and a couple of hours of work, she could still meet Ava. "Yep, is one o'clock okay with you?"

"Whenever suits you is good for me. Mark also mentioned you wanted to organise something tonight?"

"I did say that, yeah. He told you about Roger dying?"

"Yeah. So sad. He was a cute old thing."

"Well, he told me how close Lou was to the family, and to the dog. I feel sorry for her. Thought she could use a night out? Ask Jenny along too?"

"That sounds lovely. I spend so much time with her at work that we have little time to socialise. She's always with Jenny. It's a great idea to get to know them both better. And now that I have you, I'm no longer the third wheel!"

Rebecca laughed, shaking her head. They organised where to meet for lunch, and Ava said she'd call Lou at the station to see if she was keen for dinner. Each hung up the phone feeling a little more connected to their lives in Cooinda.

***

Tom was exhausted and supposed no sleep and too much sex would do that to an old man like himself. He needed to have a stern talk with himself about the dangers of behaving like a teenager when he was on the downhill slope to forty. Figuring out a way to have more daytime sex would also help.

He sat at his desk, staring at the crime scene photos laid out before him. They were compiled into groups: photos from his windscreen, the one photo Janice had let him keep, the autopsy photos, and the crime scene photos. In his hand was Helen's autopsy report. He read it over for the millionth time that morning. Nothing new jumped out at him, and he sighed in frustration.

The day was quiet. Lou was in the bullpen writing up a report from a theft call out in a town on the outskirts of Cooinda. Shane was on patrol and would be gone until the afternoon. Tom was due in court later in the day on a DUI case from a few months before, but until then, he was using his time wisely by staring at photos. Waiting for something to jump out at him. Nothing was jumping out at him.

Lou appeared in his doorway. "I just got off the phone with Ava. She wants to know whether you are keen on a night out. It was actually Rebecca's idea." She smiled at him.

"Oh, okay, sure. What brought that on?"

"Do you know Liz? She works for the Cox's."

"The housekeeper, sure."

"Well, I've known them since I was a kid. Remember, I told you my mum worked for the Cox's too when she was alive?"

"Yeah, of course. Is Liz okay?"

"Oh, yeah. But her dog Roger died. I was over there this morning. It was awful. He was sixteen years old, and I've loved that dog since he was a pup. I would always go over and walk him after school before mum, and I headed home for the day."

Tom noticed tears welling up in Lou's eyes again and felt a pang of sympathy. "That's awful, Lou. I'm so sorry."

She smiled. "Well, Rebecca thought a night out might cheer me up. Isn't that so thoughtful?"

"It comes to her naturally," Tom smiled in return. "Anyway, I'd love to come. Just tell me when and where."

***

Rebecca arrived before Ava on their lunch date. After getting off the phone to Ava, she discovered she couldn't sleep and stared at the ceiling for a while trying to figure out how to accomplish daytime sex so she could get more sleep at night. Her whole body was out of whack, and she found it too hot to sleep. She finally climbed out of bed and got some work done. It was a beautiful day, and just after midday, she walked into town instead of driving.

She dressed in comfortable clothes after freshening up and waved goodbye to Ruth, who was in the garden doing... garden-y things. Ruth had warned her about snakes in the cane, and when she set off through the farm, she was watchful. She could've walked on the roadside, but decided this route would be more peaceful, and even exciting. The quiet country life was a stark contrast to New York, and sometimes she yearned for midnight dumplings or listening to her Indian neighbours fight loudly as they cooked their spices. The potent smell would waft through the entire building, and she was sure her hair and clothes constantly smelled of garlic. But now she missed the cultural side the city offered. The most outrageous food she'd eaten since coming home was Chinese food, and even then, the most exciting thing on the menu had been chicken and cashew stir-fry.

Her walk through the cane was uneventful, and she emerged from the Cox's farm near the river, next to the park she and Tom had sat in her first day in town after seeing Helen at the pub. Within minutes, she found the cafe Ava had suggested, ordered two coffees for herself and her friend and found a place to sit.

Ava arrived shortly thereafter, and the next two hours were a whirlwind of chatter. Ava had a clever knack of drawing Rebecca out of her shell, and she laughed more than she had in years. It didn't take Ava long to fish for details about Rebecca and Tom, and by the end of lunch Rebecca felt like they were old friends. She couldn't remember the last time she'd had a girlfriend to confide in. It had always been Helen.

A little before four in the afternoon, Ava dropped Rebecca at home, and the women parted ways, already looking forward to their evening out. As Rebecca climbed out of the car, she saw Derek come out of the homestead. Surprised to see Ava, and unsure of how he felt seeing her and Rebecca together, completely infiltrating his life, he smiled politely. Mark and Derek had been buddies since they were boys, but he had never spent a lot of time with Ava because the two men mostly saw each other at their weekly poker game with a couple of other mates from school. He knew Mark and Tom were friends, which irritated him irrationally. There was also the rumour Rebecca was seeing the cop, which completely infuriated him. He had never trusted authority figures, and now his mate was marrying a cop, and the woman identical to his dead wife was dating a cop. How was that even allowed?

Rebecca waved courteously to Derek as she got out of the car, and Derek gave her a superficial smile in return. And then Ava got out of the car.

"Hi Derek." She knew the complications of Rebecca and Derek's relationship, but Derek was Mark's oldest friend and had just lost his wife. A hug at the funeral was the last time she had seen him, and she sometimes felt guilty for not reaching out more. She followed her philosophy of 'no time like the present' when she hugged Derek, while the three of them stood awkwardly on the driveway.

Ava even said, 'Nice weather,' to which Rebecca had to stifle a laugh. The next thing that came out of Ava's mouth was not so funny.

"We're going out tonight, Derek. You should come along."

Rebecca stared at Ava as though she'd just grown a second head. Then blinked and smiled sweetly at Derek, nodding. "Yeah, you might feel better once you get out."

Derek looked from one to the other, then shrugged. "Yeah, I might. I'll see how I feel." He waved goodbye and was in his car and down the driveway within minutes.

Rebecca stared at Ava. Ava stared at the ground. "Sorry," she mumbled.

Rebecca laughed. "It's okay, Ava. I understand that he's Mark's friend."

Ava sagged in relief, looked at her friend with a wicked grin and said, "Alrighty, let's find you a smashing outfit to wear tonight."

***

Ava had chosen a pub just over the border in a beachside town that was a common spot for the locals of Cooinda to populate. Live music played as Tom and Rebecca arrived. The outdoor seating was quieter, so they sat down while waiting for everyone else to arrive. A cool breeze came in from the ocean, and Rebecca relaxed.

When Ava and Mark arrived, Lou, Jenny and Shane were with them, and Rebecca secretly sighed in relief that Derek was not with them. The group moved inside to a lounge area. Within an hour, the women were having a riot getting to know each other. Lou and Jenny were fun to hang out with, and Jenny was a natural comedian, constantly making everyone laugh.

There was a stark difference between Rebecca's friendships with her colleagues in New York, who were often polished and poised, always ensuring their carefully crafted persona was on display, to the three women she now sat talking to as the musician played acoustic ballads of The Eagles, Crowded House and Jimmy Barnes a few metres away from them.

Jenny, more animated than usual, often splashed her wine as her hands flung about while she told a ridiculous story about losing her underwear at a party while hooking up with some 'rando.' Lou sat next to her best friend, shaking her head with a smile, watching as the others chuckled over Jenny's story. Sometimes Lou wished she had confidence like her friend.

When the musician sang a 'Hunters & Collectors' song that Rebecca loved, she stood and grabbed Tom's hand, pulling him onto the makeshift dance floor by the stage. She clung to him as they swayed to the music, and Tom felt more alive and content than he had ever felt before. Ava saw her friend drag Tom onto the dance floor, and before the song was over, she and Mark also swayed to the music as Jenny, Lou and Shane made their way over to one of the pool tables. As Lou racked the balls, she heard a familiar voice from behind her say, "Count me in." She turned to see Derek and smiled.

Jenny clapped her hands when she saw him and yelled over the music, "Good to see you, mate!"

Derek grinned and shrugged. He looked around and asked, "Is Mark here?"

Lou nodded her head and looked towards the dance floor where the two couples clung to each other as a '1927' ballad played. Derek stopped when he saw Rebecca and Tom, but quickly shrugged off his reaction, trying not to stare at Rebecca as she danced with the cop. He sighed and turned back to the pool table, grabbed a cue stick and grinned at Jenny and Lou. "Alright, let's play." Shane stared at Derek and wondered if he'd become invisible.

Ava, Mark, Tom, and Rebecca made their way back to the pool table when the musician stopped for a quick break. They collected fresh drinks from the bar, and Rebecca spotted Derek as she weaved her way through the crowded pub. She inwardly sighed, not wanting Ava to see how much Derek triggered her, as she knew Ava already felt bad enough for asking him along. At the pool table, Rebecca grasped Tom's hand, and he squeezed it reassuringly.

"Derek!" Mark greeted his friend with a clap on the back. He was the usual man - clueless to the discomfort of inter group nuances - and was happy to see his friend. Rebecca discovered it was probably a blessing that Mark was unaware of the awkwardness. The normalcy helped her relax, and within a few minutes, the chatting resumed to normal, and they all continued enjoying the banter and jokes as the group resumed their game of pool.

It was around ten o'clock when the pub's lights flickered. The musician was back on stage performing his last set for the night when the room turned dark. He faltered in his rendition of 'Take it Easy' by The Eagles, unsure to keep playing or not. The power was not out completely, but the lights continued to flicker, causing a disorienting effect for the patrons as people looked around the pub nervously.

Rebecca was standing next to Tom as she watched him play his round at pool when the lights went out. She was about to grab Tom's arm when the bright lights hit her eyes again. The room seemed brighter than it had been a minute ago, and she squinted, wondering whose idea it was to resort to over-head fluorescents that harshly exposed a woman's every fault and flaw behind meticulously applied makeup. She was about to joke as much to Ava when she saw her friend standing on the other side of the pool table, bleeding. Ava stared blankly at Mark, who continued to cue up the ball on the table, oblivi-ous to his fiancée as she bled from a long gash on her forehead.

Rebecca felt panic rise and her chest tighten when she re-alised no one else in the pub was aware of the trouble. Tom especially. He laughed at something Lou had just said, and Mark and Shane grinned, shaking their heads at the shared joke. The lights buzzed around her and flicked out again, plunging the pool room into darkness once more. This time, it stayed dark.

Rebecca grabbed onto the edge of the pool table, and her hand landed on something soft and wet. She tried to snatch her hand back, but her body felt like tar. In the darkness, she felt something crawl up the back of her hand that lay submerged in a thick liquid she couldn't see. Closing her eyes, she calmed her breathing and knew that whatever was happening around her; it was surely a hallucination. Desperately wanting to keep her head as clear as possible, she counted to ten in her head, slowly inhaling and exhaling as she counted. Whatever was on her hand moved onto her arm, and she felt a tear well up in the corner of her closed eyes.

"Rebecca, babe. You okay?" Tom had noticed Rebecca standing by his side, her hand clenching the pool table, eyes closed. She was whimpering, and he glanced around nervously at the lively room. Everyone else seemed to be oblivious of Rebecca. He moved closer and put his arm around her shoulder, hoping that anchoring her to him would bring her out of her panic attack.

Rebecca could hear Tom's voice, yet it sounded far away, like a long-distance phone call. She opened her eyes. The pub was gone, and she stood alone on a dark road in the middle of the bush. There were no streetlamps, and the moon was full, casting its light on the trees that surrounded the narrow dirt road, creating shadows that moved in the breeze. She slowly turned around on the spot where she stood, looking at the nothingness before her as the road stretched on to nowhere, trees and shrubs lining the side of the road like a cavalry of soldiers. Her eyes adjusted in the moonlight, and she saw a figure standing a short distance from her. Taking a hesitant step, she moved forward, trying to see who was staring at her, and tripped on something large and soft. Afraid to look down, afraid to take her eyes off the person ahead of her, she glanced down and saw Ava lying crumpled at her feet, a bullet wound revealing blood and brain matter.

Rebecca let out a scream, but a groan emerged instead. She looked back up at the blurry figure ahead of her. Now, she thought she could see who it was and was about to recognise them, when she heard Tom's voice calling her name. Blinking, she turned towards his voice, and was back in the pub.

Disoriented, nauseous and dissociated, Rebecca swayed, blinking rapidly, finding her bearings. She felt Tom's firm hands settled on her shoulders and steadied her. He pulled her into his warm familiar chest and held her and stroked her hair until he felt her breathing steady.

After a few moments, she leaned back and looked up at his handsome face. His look of concern melted her heart.

"I'm okay," she whispered, glancing around self-consciously. To her surprise, nothing was different. Her friends continued to laugh, play pool and drink. Derek was heckling Mark as he lined up his shot, and Ava and Lou laughed at Shane and Jenny, who were back on the dance floor.

Puzzled, Rebecca looked back at Tom. "No one noticed?"

"Your panic attack?" Tom whispered. "Of course not, it only lasted a minute," he smiled, "and I was here to protect you." He winked and pulled her into him again, holding her tight. And she realised it had all been in her head — the lights flashing, Ava bleeding, the pool table turning to mud.

Now that she had returned to the living, she tried to conjure in her mind the person she saw in her hallucination. She knew them; it was on the tip of her tongue, but the harder she tried to envision it, the blurrier it became. She sighed and silently prayed she wasn't going insane.

{ 26 }

Over the next week, Rebecca was mostly at Tom's house. She found she could do her part-time job just as well at Tom's, and Ruth and Fred had no desire to interfere with new love. Tom had completed the required paperwork regarding his relationship with Rebecca. His boss, Angelo, had called and confirmed there would be an inquiry to determine if Tom should recuse himself from the case, but for the moment it was business as usual. Angelo ended the call saying he was happy for him - considering his history with women. Tom swore he could hear the man laughing through the phone.

The wind howled as they got out of the car at Tom's place after picking up groceries the following Friday evening after their night out. It was cool since a cold snap had hit Sydney in the last week. The area copped the tail-end of the cold weather, making the early mornings, around dawn, and the evenings cool.

The breeze whistled through the trees as Tom walked up to his front door, with Rebecca behind him, digging her cigarettes out of one of the grocery bags. He knew she would shower, then sit outside on his porch, smoke, and drink a cup of coffee, winding down after her day. He had discovered over the last few days that sometimes she liked his company, some-times she needed to be alone, to cry, to contemplate, to create.

That evening he observed her as she came out of the shower. She wore long yellow and white floral culottes that flowed around her ankles, along with a white, almost translucent sin-glet top that clung to her breasts. Her outfit revealed the deep golden colour she'd developed. Her skin glistened now as he looked at her while she made her coffee and headed out to the porch. She glanced casually back at him and said with a smile, "You coming?"

He nodded and followed her out onto the porch. Rebecca carefully placed her coffee on the railing and leaned against the balustrade. She really loved his home. It was quiet and iso-lated. Tom moved up behind her, and put his arms around her, and his lips to her ear. "How was your day?" he asked casually.

Rebecca tried to restrain herself from moaning, but he was just so damn appealing. She could feel his hardness pressing into her arse, and her pulse quickened. She tilted her head back against his firm shoulder, exposing her slender neck. Tom brushed his lips across the soft slope from her ear to her shoul-der, in the mood to tease her. He loved to feel her quiver be-neath his touch, and his fingers crept down her arm, and onto her waist. He held her tightly as he ravaged her neck.

He made love to her right there on his front porch. Their mating was furious, and when they finished, Tom leaned into her, panting, waiting for his heart rate to stabilise. "I swear you're going to kill me one day."

Rebecca chuckled, reaching down to pull her panties back into position. "Hey, I was just standing here drinking my coffee... which is gone." She looked around the porch and spotted it on the grass in front of the verandah. "Oops," she laughed.

Tom buckled up his pants again, and moved away from her, quickly descending the front porch steps to collect the now empty mug. "Come on inside. I'll make you another one. I need to start dinner too."

"Considering it's dinner time; I may as well skip straight to vodka."

"Good idea" Tom winked, grabbed her hand, and led her into his home.

A short while later, they sat comfortably on the lounge watching television: Rebecca with vodka and Tom with beer.

"Do you think the case will ever be solved?" Her voice was soft, husky. Tom glanced over at her and noticed the cloud that settled over her as it often did in her moments of grief. He pulled her into him and held her. "I hope so, babe. It's not unusual for these cases to take time."

"Do you still think Josh killed her?"

Silence followed for a moment. "I really don't know at the moment. Lou seems to think so."

"Tell me again why she thinks so?" Rebecca gently pulled away, stood and walked to the sideboard where Tom kept his liquor.

She glanced at his beer. "You need a top-up?"

He shook his head. "No, thanks."

Rebecca poured herself another vodka, set the bottle down, added ice, and moved back to the lounge.

Tom continued, "Lou remembers Josh asking her a lot of questions about Helen one night. Not long after he came to town. Said he'd seen Helen come into the pub one night and couldn't stop commenting to people how beautiful she was."

"Have you had any luck in recovering his trail?"

"No, all I can confirm is that he has contacted no one, including either of his folks."

Rebeca raised her glass, studying the clear liquid as it gently rattled the ice against the glass. As she stared at it, an image emerged in the glass reflection. Her heart jumped, yet she remained silent, steady, her eyes glued to the vodka glass in her hand. She could not see through the clear liquid to the living room beyond. Instead, she saw a shape take form like clouds when they take form in the sky. She could see tall trees around a timber cabin. She squinted, trying to see the tiny reflection more clearly, but the more she tried to study the image, the blurrier it became. In a moment, the image had faded altogether, and the vodka was once again clear. Rebecca sighed, threw back the glass, and gulped the spirit in one quick move, the liquid warming her throat.

Tom studied Rebecca closely. He was silent, waiting for her to reveal to him what she was experiencing. He knew her well enough to know when she was experiencing a vision, or premonition, or whatever it was. Since the episode at the pub, he was far more watchful of her, worried about missing the signs as he had that night. Finally, she planted the glass down firmly on the coffee table and looked at him. She shrugged. "I saw trees and a cabin in my glass' reflection. I recognised nothing, although it reminded me of what I saw when I was at the pub. It was similar scenery. I mean, my hallucination at the pub was about Ava. I don't even know if it had anything to do with Helen."

As she said her sister's name, Tom's car alarm sounded outside. Obnoxious in the silent neighbourhood, it made them both jump. Wincing, they stood and moved towards the front door. Tom cautiously opened it and stepped out onto the porch. Rebecca followed behind him. Tom did not remember locking it, and as they moved slowly off the verandah and towards the car, they were both on high alert. Tom reached the door first. The alarm stopped abruptly as his hand touched the door handle. The silence was deafening. He opened the driver's door and looked inside, not sure what he was expecting to see. Rebecca stood behind him, looking over his shoulder. He shook his head, and said, "There's nothing here." Tom straightened up, and closed the driver's door, this time locking it. As he walked back towards the house, Rebecca came face to face with her sister in the car's reflection window. Helen was standing behind her, a ghostly body double. Her hair was caked with dirt; her face distorted in the reflection. Helen and Rebecca stared at each other. Rebecca could not tell if her sister saw her or saw right through her.

"I'm here, Helen." Her voice was but a whisper in the cool night air.

Tom turned back to Rebecca, who stood motionless, staring at the driver's side window, her lovely face white and glowing in the darkness. Rebecca resisted the urge to turn around, knowing the reflection would be her only window into Helen's world.

Tom glanced around. The night was black. The moon was only a sliver, and the wind caused the trees to whisper and reach out to each other. He desperately wished he could see what Rebecca saw. Helen had only shown herself to him the day they found her on the riverbank. And even then, he was unsure if his brain had just been playing tricks on him. He waited for Rebecca to say something.

Afraid of cutting the connection, Rebecca finally smiled at Helen. Helen stared back with sad eyes.

"I miss you" There were so many other things Rebecca could have said. Yet, in that moment, that was the most important.

Helen hung her head. And slowly, she disappeared.

Rebecca crumpled to the ground and shook. Tom knelt beside her and enveloped her in his arms. Together, they rocked back and forth. Her grief was so raw he could feel it grating her insides away. After a few moments, the trembling subsided, and she became calm once again. He stroked her hair. He wanted to tell her everything would be alright yet knew it was not really the truth. Just hope. Rebecca finally pulled away and looked at him. Her face was raw, her bottom lip quivering, and her hair fell over her eyes. He felt a stirring within and recognised it might be love.

They stood and together walked hand in hand back into the house. Rebecca stood in the doorway, peering into the night. Finally, she sighed and closed the door to the world outside. A few feet away, Helen watched through the front window as her sister moved into the living room and embraced Tom. She put her hand up to the window, pressing it against the glass. If Rebecca had looked at the window at that moment, she would have seen the handprint on the glass slowly fade.

{ 27 }

Six kilometres up the river, Derek sat on his verandah, whiskey in hand, staring at the rippling water. It had been four weeks since Helen had left him, and his life continued to fall apart. He knew he should pick himself up but honestly didn't care. The once spotless home was now a messy house. Dirty dishes piled in the sink, and rubbish overflowed from the bin. The cupboards were bare of food, and he survived on whiskey and the occasional meal his mother dropped off for him. His father spoke to him that day about getting back to work. Until now, they had given him space. They understood he was grieving, but it was time to 'get back on the horse'.

The horse could go fuck itself. He was already making plans to get out of town. He'd had enough. They had shown their true colours since his wife had died, and he realised their betrayal would continue now that Rebecca was staying in town. He thought of a Helen duplicate on the other side of the cane, living with his parents, fucking that cop, and working one of *his* jobs was about all he could manage, and he knew he couldn't stay in the house alone much longer. He planned to ask his parents for the money that was rightfully his and buy a business in Sydney or Melbourne. Something that was his that he could build on his own. Enough of this sugar cane bullshit.

He threw back his drink in frustration and stood, ready to call it a night. As he walked inside, the doorbell rang. He glanced at his watch. It was after midnight.

When he reached the front door, he looked through the peephole and sighed. Muttering to himself, he opened it and stared at the person standing on his porch.

"I thought I told you never to come here," he hissed.

The woman stared back at him. "I know, and I'm sorry," she whispered. "I just had to see you."

Derek opened the door further. "What makes you think anything's changed?"

She shrugged. "You're alone now. And I know you're lonely. I just wanted to help make you feel better" she hung her head, annoyed with the tears spring up in the corner of her eyes. She wiped them away furiously. "But if you don't want me, that's fine." She turned to leave, but Derek caught her hand. It was soft and smooth, and her unblemished skin glowed under the porch light. She was wearing a short floral dress that brushed dangerously against her bare thighs as turned away from him, and he glimpsed her smooth bare arse. He felt his resolve crumble and pulled her towards him.

"This will be the first and only time you are welcome here for this. Do you understand?" he grabbed the back of her hair, pulling it and forcing her to look up at him. Her eyes were a mixture of lust and fear, and Derek felt himself harden.

"I understand," she whispered hoarsely.

He dragged her inside and slammed the front door with his foot. He pushed her to his arm's length and stared at her. She stood quietly, submissive, as he peeled her dress from her body. She was nothing like his Helen. But she would have to do. Her eyes were glued to him, begging him to love her. It made him furious. He grabbed her roughly, turning her so she was trapped against his front door. Before she had any time to protest, he ripped her flimsy underwear off her, entering her before she spoke. He fucked her hard and fast. The woman whimpered, and Derek knew he was hurting her, but he didn't care. She had turned up at his home. Was she expecting him to invite her into his bed, where he still wept for his dead wife?

He climaxed within moments, and withdrew from her, leaving her sagging against the door, breathing fast. She kept her head down, and her eyes avoided his as she got dressed. Derek walked into the kitchen and took out a beer. He waltzed back into the hallway, where she stood in the same spot. He took a long swig of his beer before he said, "It's time for you to leave. And never come back here again. I will see you at our regular spot on our regular day. Understand?"

The woman nodded timidly. "I understand." She turned and fled.

* * *

Ruth was still up, sitting in her favourite armchair and knitting a jumper for her friend Margaret. Since Helen's death, she had become a bit of a night owl. Most nights she would climb into bed, close her eyes, and instead of sleeping, a picture show would play in her head. Helen would beg for help, for life, and then a faceless man would appear, put his hands around her throat and squeeze. The images that played out in Ruth's head always varied but always ended the same. Deep down, she knew she blamed herself for Helen's death. The dear girl had asked her countless times to accompany her on her jogs, but Ruth was past the age of serious exercise and felt it was important Helen had time to herself. And now she was gone forever. Gone were the days she and Helen spent together, cooking, going to town to buy groceries, singing together in the church choir. Wherever Ruth needed to go, Helen would always go with her. The two of them against the gossip. She had formed a close bond with Rebecca, for which she was thankful, but it would never be the same. Rebecca was an extremely independent woman and didn't need to rely on Ruth the way her sister did.

A sob caught in her throat, and she blinked the tears away furiously. She unfolded from her armchair and moved into the kitchen, flicked on the kettle. While she waited for the water to boil, she meandered around the house. Fred was a heavy sleeper. He rose at four every morning and had done so for the last forty years, and it meant he had learned to sleep through anything if it guaranteed him the precious few hours of sleep each night.

Ruth opened the front door and peered into the night. The air was cool, and a breeze blew across the cane, whistling a sorrowful tune. She stepped out onto the front porch, letting the screen door gently slap the wooden door frame. With her arms crossed, she gazed at the heavens. It was pure chance that she saw the headlights turn off the road a kilometre away. The car veered to the left, heading to Derek's place, and within a moment, was out of sight. Ruth stood, staring at nothing, thinking of her son, knowing that he was in a downward spiral, and not understanding what to do about it. Fred believed in stoicism. Yet, it was a different day and age now, and society encouraged dealing with grief openly.

Except Derek did nothing openly. He thought he was so discreet. Little did he know, she saw and knew everything that happened in his life. She knew he abused Helen, drank excessively, cheated with whores, and lived his life the complete opposite of the way Ruth and Fred raised him. He was her only child. She had wanted a house full of children and had only carried Derek to full term after four miscarriages. He had been so perfect. Such a delightful child, willing to help, always wanting to please. He had followed Fred everywhere, closely observing his father in adoration. Fred had loved every minute. Until puberty had hit. She wasn't sure what had happened to their family after that. Derek had just drifted away. He suddenly hated the farm. Hated working outdoors alongside his father. Hated spending time with his mother. As soon as he could, he moved away. Choosing to attend the university of Melbourne and stayed there until he had come home with Helen five years before. Oh, Helen. There were few moments that where Ruth was not thinking about her daughter-in-law. She had been a ray of light in the darkness of Derek's shadow.

Derek was suffering, yet there was no longer a connection between them, and she had no idea how to bridge the gap that grew larger every day. She had spoken to Fred about it, and although his stoic behaviour shone, had expressed his remorse and regret when it involved their estranged son.

As she made her way back inside, she wondered who was now sleeping with her son, in Helen's bed. She locked the front door and made her way to bed, her heart sick.

{ **28** }

Rebecca was at Ruth's early the next morning. She had barely slept after her fresh encounter with her sister. She was desperate to tell Ruth. It had been a few days since she had been back at the Cox's. She and Tom had been in a bit of a love bubble but realised just how much she missed Ruth.

They sat on the back porch, sipping coffee as she told Ruth about Helen's appearance to her the night before. Ruth listened intently. She accepted what Rebecca said as a kind of truth and believed in the afterlife, believed in some higher power. She and Helen had formed a bond over it and had always enjoyed conversations about religion and ethics. To not believe in ghosts seemed silly, considering she believed in God and his teachings. This, along with the 'twin factor', had been all the information she needed to be convinced Rebecca was communicating with her sister. It must have been so frustrating not to be in control of it. She listened and occasionally nodded in encouragement.

Rebecca had written the encounter down in her journal, something Tom had suggested she begin the week before, after the pub incident. She had also drawn the encounter and showed it to her now. Her ability to draw never ceased to amaze Ruth. She looked at the sketch of Helen. Her hair fell in whispers around her face, and Rebecca had even captured her sister's large, sad eyes.

"Do you think she is actually sad?" Ruth whispered.

Rebecca thought for a moment. "If she is stuck somewhere, unable to move on, watching us miss her every day, which must be awful. Just awful. I think she has been trying to get messages to me every single time I've seen her. I just need to figure it all out. Her communication skills leave little to be desired," she grinned at Ruth.

Ruth laughed. "These pesky ghosts who don't have the decency to talk."

They were both silent for a moment, sipping their coffee and thinking their own thoughts. After a moment Ruth asked, "how's things with Tom?"

For the first time that morning, Ruth saw Rebecca's face lighten. Her sister's murder was always primarily on her mind, but she needed to let her feelings for Tom shine through, otherwise she'd go insane. It made Ruth ache for her. Dealing with so many conflicting emotions all at once must have been exhausting.

"Things are great with Tom," Rebecca answered. "It feels right with him. I never thought I would depend on a man for comfort and love. Our dad made sure of that. But it's different from Tom. He understands me without words. He senses me. The way... the way Helen did."

"Wow," Ruth whispered, "that's rare, Rebecca. Don't let that one go." She smiled and reached out, gripping her hand, and squeezing tight. They sat in silence, each in their own thoughts; until Liz appeared for the day, ready for her daily schedule, and prompting Rebecca and Ruth to do the same.

***

The open file of Helen's autopsy was in front of Tom that morning as he sat at his desk. Helen stared, unblinking, at him. With one hand, he fanned out all the autopsy photos before him. He sighed in frustration as Ava came into his office to say she was going on patrol. He waved goodbye to her distractedly, and then realised that staring at Helen's face would get him nowhere, he decided it was time to follow up again with Dave, the owner of the pub. Josh had only worked there for a short time before he disappeared, and he had already talked to him, but he felt as though he needed to check some boxes again to be sure.

Dave had been born and raised in outback New South Wales and moved into Cooinda in his thirties after he purchased the local pub, which he had been running so long that he knew everyone and everything. He loved a good laugh and enjoyed a chat with his patrons, even on the nights he wasn't officially working.

Tom approached him as he was opening the doors to the service entry. "Hi Dave."

"G'day there, Tom. I haven't seen you for a few days. I can imagine life's been hectic?" Dave said sympathetically.

"Yeah, you could say that mate."

"You here to follow up on Josh?"

"Well, there haven't been many leads to follow regarding Josh, and I guess I hoped someone could give me a clue. Is Jenny here today?"

Dave grinned and nodded. "Jenny is always here," he said as he moved about the bar, getting out limes and lemons from the fridge, pulling clean glassware out of the dishwasher, placing them on their shelves.

"Jenny!" Dave hollered towards the back of the bar. Within a minute, the door labelled 'staff only' opened and Jenny appeared.

She saw Tom and beamed. "Hey Tom. Recovered from our night out?" she asked while Dave looked on with a slightly puzzled look.

Tom laughed, "Yeah, I can handle my own. It was a fun night." He glanced at Dave before he asked; "Um, Jenny, could we please have a moment to chat in private?"

Jenny was baffled. "Yeah, of course. Out the back?"

Tom nodded and followed Jenny as she opened the door she'd just come from and led Tom down a short hallway and through another door. Suddenly blinded by the daylight, Tom shielded his eyes and noticed they were in the loading dock at the side alley of the pub.

Jenny sat down on a nearby milk crate and lit a cigarette. She pointed to another crate, and he pulled it up next to her, sitting on the uncomfortable plastic storage container.

"So, what's up?" she asked cheerfully. Tom wondered if she was ever not cheerful. Her constant happy façade was a default setting that made Tom feel exhausted just being in her presence.

"I need to talk to you about Josh."

Jenny frowned. "Okay? What about him?"

"I know you slept with him, and I'm curious if you could enlighten me as to why he's left or where he might have gone?"

"Oh, my God," Jenny groaned. "How do you know we slept together? I haven't told anyone. Not even Lou."

"I found a 'little black book'" Tom used quotation marks when he said this, and Jenny got the implication.

"Fuck, well, isn't that embarrassing," she blushed slightly before she sighed. "Okay, so you want to know if I know anything personal about him because we fucked?"

Tom cleared his throat. "Well, yeah, I guess I do."

Jenny was quiet for a few moments, contemplating her time with Josh before he disappeared. Finally, she said, "He seemed nice, Tom. Easy going, casual. Enjoyed the ladies' company. He was a good-looking guy and knew it. I must admit it surprised me when he stole the cash from the safe."

"Is there anything else that you can think of in hindsight that was maybe unusual, but you didn't notice at the time?" Tom probed.

Jenny was silent again. She smoked her cigarette, staring at the ground as she did so, creating love hearts as she exhaled the smoke.

"Okay, so the only thing I can comment on is I thought it strange that he and Lou became friends," she shrugged, feeling bad for her best friend.

Tom frowned. "What do you mean?"

"Well, they were so different. Lou is so serious and hard-working. She doesn't sleep around or go out partying or drinking like Josh likes to. I just thought it was odd they had anything in common to talk about, but the few times we hung out together they were thick as thieves."

Tom's skin crawled as he listened to Jenny speak, but he wasn't sure why. He kept his cool.

"Well, okay, I appreciate you taking the time to chat. Let's keep this just between us, maybe?"

"Absolutely," she smiled.

They both stood, and Jenny flicked her cigarette to the ground, twisting her foot over it. "One more thing, Tom," she said, "this little black book. What else does it say about me?"

Tom grinned and flushed slightly. "It says you're a solid ten," he winked as he fibbed, before he made his way back into the pub, leaving Jenny with a stupid grin on her face, feeling oddly proud of herself.

A few moments later he found Dave, and waved goodbye, but his friend stopped him, waving his hand to call his friend over to where he stood near the bistro kitchen. Tom made his way over to Dave, who guided him over to a more private spot, away from prying staff ears.

"I've been thinking about Josh since you got here, mate."

"And?"

"Well, it may be nothing, but the day he disappeared he had mentioned to me he was seeing a woman and asked me not to say anything to anyone. I had never seen him with anyone, and to be honest I assumed he was making his way through every waitress in the joint, so I was a bit surprised. He told me he had to finish work early that night because he was meeting up with her. It must have been quiet because I just checked the timecards, and he clocked off at nine PM that night instead of midnight."

Tom stopped for a moment. "Wait, he clocked off early on his last shift he ever showed up to?"

Dave frowned. "Was that his last night?" He looked down at the timecards he was holding and started flicking through them.

"Dave, that was the fourth of February, yeah?"

Dave nodded. "Yeah, you're right about both. It was the fourth, and it was the last shift he showed up to before he took off."

"Okay, thanks Dave, I have to go."

"Tom, wait" Dave held out something, and Tom took it from his friend. It was a black canister that held undeveloped film.

"You may find it didn't even belong to Josh, but..." he shrugged, "I found it lying near his locker, wedged under a chair."

As soon as Tom closed his hand around it, uneasiness crept into his belly.

"Thanks." He gripped the canister tightly in his hand, trying to keep his excitement at bay, and glanced at another staff member who rushed in and threw her bag behind the bar. She barely looked at him as she then raced out to the bistro, grabbing a box of condiments, and throwing salt and pepper shakers onto the dining tables, readying for patrons. Tom said goodbye to Dave and Jenny, who had reappeared, and left them to their jobs. It was eleven in the morning, and he knew the pub was about to open for the day.

It was all he could do not to bolt back to the police station. Within a short walk, he was back behind his desk, with the door to his stuffy office closed. He rolled the canister in his hands, staring at it, trying not to get his hopes up, but already knowing that was too late. There was a rubber lid confining the contents within, and he slowly popped it off. It landed on his desk. He peered inside and looked at the roll of undeveloped film. Was this it? Was this the break he needed in Josh's or maybe even Helen's case? He tipped the canister, and the film fell into his hand, and he stared at it, pondering. He thought it best he kept this added information to himself until there was something to share.

There was a one-hour photo developing place up the coast half an hour that he had used before. He decided it was best to go there as there would be fewer locals there, and he could wait the hour. He got there shortly before one in the afternoon. The weather was perfect. He wished he had more time to appreciate the finer things in life, such as weather. He sighed at the prospect of sitting by the river, a line thrown in, enjoying nature.

He considered a life not lived as he strolled into the shopping centre that housed a supermarket, along with several fashion shops, a bank, a discount store, and a food court. The idea of shopping on a weekday, having lunch with friends, and being stress free was a foreign concept to him. Tom sighed to himself, then forced his brain back to the task at hand.

The pharmacy sat next to the food court and had a section for film processing. He dropped off the film to the young and pretty assistant, who smiled absently at him while she handed him a receipt stub and told him he could collect the photos in an hour.

Tom wandered around the shops for twenty minutes before settling into the food court with a coffee and a salad. The least he could do was eat something while he waited. Exactly sixty minutes later, he sauntered back into the pharmacy to collect the film. He had wanted to sprint but restrained himself. The young girl smiled brightly at him as she rang up the purchase and tucked the envelope of photos into a bag, wishing him a lovely day. Once again, it took his restraint not to tear open the bag before he got to the car, but he managed, congratulating himself on his self-control. He drove out of the shopping centre's carpark to look for a secluded spot, praying the photos held something more interesting than a day at the beach, or a night out with friends. He prayed this was a lead that actually led to something solid.

By the river was a lovely park that Tom pulled up next to. He turned the engine off and wound down his window. Nearby, a mother's group sat on picnic blankets. The women chatted and laughed as they hugged and fussed over their babies. On the playground, young children screamed in delight, some in frustration, when something didn't go their way. The background noise of normalcy soothed Tom's nerves as he pulled on a pair of latex gloves, reached into the envelope and pulled out the glossy four-by-six photos.

He stared down at Helen's smiling face. She was sitting on her verandah with Ruth. Her face was lit up, and she was talking about something that made her happy. It was a photo of Derek and Helen's house from a distance, and Tom could tell a zoom lens was used; not that he knew about that sort of thing. Taken from the side of the verandah, he could see cane poking into frame, and he guessed the photographer stood amongst the cane fields to stay hidden.

The next three photos were much the same, but the fourth was of Helen and Derek. Josh had been closer to the house this time, and it was dark outside. Tom could see the living room through the back window, and a shiver crept up his spine as he studied the photo. Helen was in her underwear and standing in front of Derek as he examined her. Tom shifted uncomfortably in his seat. The image was in profile, and he could see the casual manner in which Derek observed his wife. It was lustful, and objective. Tom moved on to the next photo. It was Derek standing behind Helen. They were both naked now, and Helen was bent forward, with Derek directly behind her. He held her by the hair, and she looked... resigned. Tom moved quickly on to the next photo.

This one caught his eye. Derek was looking up, out the window, towards the camera. Had he seen Josh standing outside his living room? Tom couldn't tell. It was plain to see that it was nighttime, perfectly disguised in the dark. Had Derek spotted Josh that evening? See him take photos of him and Helen in their most intimate moments?

Tom sat quietly for a few moments, contemplating the possibility. Was it even Josh who had taken the photos? Dave had given him the roll of film. It may not have belonged to Josh at all. Tom considered who else worked at the pub and realised he couldn't rule out anyone until he collected prints. Tom sighed, knowing the connection was flimsy, and prayed Josh's prints

were on the canister. He needed to bounce his ideas off someone. He started up the engine and made his way back to town,
deep in thought.

{ 29 }

Lou sat at her desk, deep in paperwork for a case that was about to go to trial the next week. Distracted, she glanced up as Tom made his way over. "Hi" she said with a glance, then back to her work.

"Hey, do you have a moment?"

"Sure," she finished what she was writing and put her pen down. "What's up?"

"Um, in private?" he asked, pointing towards his office.

"Oh, sorry, of course." She smiled and jumped up, following him in and closing the door behind her.

"So, I was at the pub this morning and Dave gave me a roll of film he found near Josh's work locker. He wasn't sure where it's from or if it's even Josh's."

Lou's eyes widened. "Oh, okay. Did you get it developed?"

"Yeah. Sorry I didn't tell you. I wanted to see what was on it first. It could have been nothing."

"Was it?"

"Well, it proves someone from the pub was taking creepy photos. There are pictures of Helen and of Derek. In their home."

"Bloody hell," was all she said.

"So, I have a theory. If Josh took these, maybe he was obsessed with Helen for a reason?"

Lou looked thoughtful for a moment. "Like?"

Tom shrugged. "Maybe they were having an affair, and there's just no proof of it."

Lou looked credulous. "Most people can't hide that sort of thing. They try, but eventually it comes out. And she was an incredibly meek person. She barely left her in-laws' side," she shrugged. Tom knew she was right. It was a long shot that Helen would have an affair with Josh. From what he knew about her; it just didn't fit her personality.

"Well, Dave from the pub suspected Josh was seeing someone. Just didn't know who. Any ideas?" he asked Lou cautiously. He didn't know what he was hoping to see in Lou's expression or reaction, but what Dave had told him earlier had him thinking that maybe Lou had feelings for Josh or had even been seeing him. Did she know where he had taken off to and was keeping it from him?

She looked at the pictures that Tom had handed her, flipping through them slowly, studying them, thinking. "I don't know about any girlfriend, but maybe Josh had just seen Helen around and become infatuated. People who stalk usually have a fantasy in their heads about what is happening. And often the fantasy is so far from reality that it's laughable." She paused for a moment, studying the picture of Helen and Derek having sex. In a disgusted tone, she continued, "I bet you anything Josh was just your regular sicko who became obsessed with Helen. I mean, she was beautiful, sweet, and, most infuriating to a stalker, unavailable."

Tom had to admit Lou's argument made sense. Even if she had a crush on Josh, it meant nothing, apart from the fact she'd fallen for a player instead of a nice guy like she deserved. It all fit; Josh had kidnapped Helen because of an obsession. Had killed her. It could even have been an accident. Dumped her body and took off, with the cash from the safe to help him stay hidden. Something was still making him feel uneasy, but he couldn't put his finger on it yet. "Why would Josh leave photos he had taken on my car?" He said the question aloud, yet it was more to himself. If life as a cop had taught him anything, it was that gut instincts happened for a reason, and if he followed them, they were usually correct.

Lou thought, her eyebrows furrowed. "Maybe guilt? Maybe someone else found them and, when they heard about Helen missing, left them on your car so as not to get involved..." she trailed off, and Tom nodded.

"Well, let's follow this lead to start. See where it leads us. If Josh was obsessed with Helen, maybe there are some other clues. We should go back to the youth hostel and go over it with fresh eyes. Also, let's go through all his belongings again. Maybe we missed something. I'm also going to go to the pub and talk to the staff. See who's willing to submit fingerprints to us."

Lou nodded. "Tell me what you want me to do."

Tom looked at his watch. "How about I go to the pub, and you head to the hostel? Ava will be on call tonight, and Shane is working over at Lismore for a few shifts while someone's on leave."

Lou nodded. "Of course. I'll keep in touch."

***

By the end of the day, Tom was exhausted. He was meeting Rebecca for dinner and was looking forward to the day's end. Dave had called a staff meeting, and through it, Tom had discussed the collection of prints, and why it was important. All the staff had volunteered their fingerprints, and now only the missing staff who could not attend needed to be contacted. Dave agreed to call and leave messages.

Forensics had collected the print cards, film and the canister in their afternoon collection run, and by five was in his office, where he had brought back all of Josh's belongings. There was not a huge amount to go through, and the feeling in the pit of his stomach returned. The feeling he got when a case was about to go to shit. His frustration was raw, and he was hoping to find something to connect Josh to Helen's murder. He knew he should not get emotionally attached, but he understood this case was different. These were his people. It wasn't just because of Rebecca. He also cared about Ruth and Fred. He cared about the people who trusted him to keep them safe.

Just before six, he walked into the reception. Lily was getting ready to divert calls to the Lismore station and close up for the night. "Hey Tom," she said, and smiled as usual.

"Hi Lil, have you heard from Lou?" he asked, slightly concerned she hadn't checked in.

Lily shook her head, about to reply, as Lou burst through the front door. Her face was bright with excitement, and Tom felt a flutter in his stomach.

"What?" he asked her.

"Your office," she replied, "now."

Lou had hit the jackpot at the hostel, combing through Josh's room. "Angela gave me free rein. She wants this over probably more than us. She's sick of all the gossip associated with her business."

Tom nodded, trying to wait patiently, but ready to burst. "So? What did you find?" He didn't think he'd ever seen Lou look smug, and it almost made him chuckle. He really needed to nominate her for a promotion. He just hated the idea of her getting transferred to another station.

"There was a floorboard that was broken, with stuff hidden under it. Just like in the movies," she exclaimed.

"Oh my God, are you for real?"

"Yep, cross my heart," she said with a wave of her hand signalling the cross over her chest.

"How did you find it?"

She paused for breath. Her face was bright, and her breath ragged. He was worried she was about to have a stroke. "Maybe you should sit for a second?"

Once again, she waved at him dismissively. "I'm fine."

He waited. After a few moments, she spoke. "I just knew there had to be something. Whatever was going on, surely there had to be something to show it. Whether he was taking photos because of an obsession, or because of an affair. It's just too much of a coincidence that he disappeared when Helen did."

"Okay," he nodded slowly, "so, the question still stands. How did you find it?"

Lou grinned sheepishly and then slowly shrugged her shoulders as she answered. "I just jumped up and down a lot. You know. To test the floorboards."

There was silence for a moment before Tom burst out laughing. "Wow, Lou. That's fucking genius."

She broke into a relieved grin, then looked down at her hands. "Thanks, Tom."

"It's officially killing me. What did you find?"

"I left it there for you. I didn't want to touch anything or disturb the scene. Once I found the broken floorboard, I looked under it, then replaced it and came straight back here."

He waited.

"It is a box. Like a petty cash lockbox."

He deflated, and Lou saw his expression. "I swear it's something though, Tom. Why else would Josh hide it under the floorboards!"

She was right. He stood up and grabbing his keys, he said, "Grab the camera and all the evidence gear. I'm going to make a phone call. I'll meet you at my car."

$$\{ \ 30 \ \}$$

Tom and Lou arrived at the house just after six in the evening. The old hostel loomed in front of them as the sun hung low in the sky, and a cauldron of bats escaped a massive old gum tree, flying so low they both ducked. The bats screeched past them in search of food.

"Ang said she would be here." Tom said softly as they approached the front door. Angela opened it before they could even reach for the handle. She smiled at them, ushering them in. She offered them tea or coffee, and they both declined politely, and headed straight up to Josh's room once more.

Lou was right. The floorboard was easily noticeable when he entered the room. Tom was annoyed with himself for not noticing it initially, and he worried Rebecca distracted him more than he liked to admit. He knelt down; the floor creaking under his weight and studied the floorboard closely. He reached his arm out distractedly to Lou; "Can you please pass the camera, Lou?" She had placed it in his hand before he finished his question.

Before removing the floorboard, he snapped a few photos of it still in place. The nails were missing from one end of the plank, and when he pushed his hand against the opposite end of the timber, the other end flipped up grudgingly. He stood up and replaced the rug that had previously covered the floor. He took more photos. The digital camera lit up the dim room, casting shadows. An eerie sensation settled over him. Tom cleared his throat. "Alright then, let's have a look, shall we?" He passed the camera back to Lou, pushed the rug back with his foot and kneeled down again. Within a minute, the floorboard came up, and underneath, snugly nestled in the floor joists, was a lockbox. It was one commonly used by businesses for their petty cash. He had slipped gloves on as he had approached the room, so now, as Lou took more photos, he reached in and pulled it out of its home.

He stood up and dusted his pants off. A dresser stood near the bed, underneath the lone window that allowed guests to watch the river scenery beyond. A large dogwood tree stood outside the window, and the wind caused it to brush up against the windowpane. The noise crept inside and made Tom shiver involuntarily. Ignoring the spookiness, he placed the lockbox on the dresser and studied it carefully. There was a padlock guarding the contents, and before he could even ask, Lou handed him a pair of bolt cutters. In a moment they were both staring expectantly down at the contents.

Inside, there was a passport, some cash, a few letters, a bunch of negatives from rolls of film, and a stack of photos. The photos were of nothing in particular. Josh had obviously taken photos of the area after moving to Cooinda. Tom held up the negatives to the ceiling light and could see the outlines of the pictures. There was some of the surf, and also of some sort of gathering he had attended. He actually recognised a few negatives from the event called the Fruit Festival, which the town held every year. It had taken place only a couple of weeks before Helen died. If he'd had the photos instead of the negatives, he probably could have found himself in the background of a few of them. As he scanned through the negatives, he wondered where the printed photos had ended up. He figured Josh had taken them when he left town, but he was confused about why he would leave his passport. Maybe he'd been in a rush, afraid to come back to the hostel, and already had the photos on his person when he fled.

Tom continued rummaging through the lockbox and saw the most important item since the beginning of the investigation. A zip-lock bag with a lock of hair in it. Tom carefully studied the auburn colour strands that were covered in dirt, and more importantly, dried clumps of blood. He suddenly felt a lump rise in the back of his throat. He had found Helen's hair.

Tom needed to remain professional. He tucked the hair back into the lockbox, sealing it shut once again. "Okay, I'm going to head straight to forensics. I want this analysed straight away."

"Want me to do that?" Lou asked, always at the ready to prove her dedication.

"No, it's okay, I can do it. Chain of custody looks better coming from me."

Lou nodded and returned to the task at hand of packing up the camera gear.

When they had finished, they made their way outside. It was dark, and a cool breeze moved through the flowerbeds and trees that surrounded the house. An odd sensation settled over

Tom, and the hairs on his arm prickled in anticipation. He stopped and looked around, peering into the dark, waiting for the uneasiness to leave him. Instead, a hollowness buried deep into his chest, making it difficult to breathe. "What was wrong with him?" He needed to get it together. He shook it off and continued to the car.

Tom desperately wanted to go to dinner with Rebecca but decided to call her and tell her he had too much in the way of paperwork. He wasn't ready to tell her about the hair and wanted to head to Lismore to talk to Jerry personally.

Back at the station, Lou clocked out, and Tom greeted Ava as she began her shift. He sat at his desk, with Ava watching, he put gloves on and read the letters before bagging them. The letters almost sealed his decision. Josh had stalked and then killed Helen. The letters were full of sick declarations of love. There were five of them, and by the time he got to the last one, which was dated only days before Helen was abducted, the fantasy had become sick and twisted. Tom had to stop reading it before its end. He called Jerry and asked him to stay back late so they could talk when he arrived, and the forensic pathologist agreed, not bothering to tell Tom he rarely left the office before ten or eleven most nights, anyway.

It was just after seven when Tom hit the road. It was over an hour's drive, but he was happy for the late-night distraction as he knew it would be difficult to keep it all from Rebecca until he was certain he had something absolute to tell her.

Tom pulled into the forensic labs and offices at eight-thirty. The streetlights flickered as he climbed out of his car and made his way into the building, which was manned twenty-four hours a day with security. He signed in at reception and collected his visitor pass while he waited for Jerry to come out of his cave to collect him. He only had to wait a few minutes before he saw the pathologist scurry into the waiting room, beckoning Tom, waving to the security and shaking Tom's hand, all in a flurry of motion that reaffirmed just how busy the man was. Although his actions indicated an air of importance, his smile was warm and genuine, instantly putting Tom at ease about bothering him so late at night. He said as much, and Jerry's response was: "Tom, I respect a man who works off the clock. It shows dedication and diligence. Two important factors in our line of work." He grinned and beckoned Tom into his cramped, sterile office.

When Jerry had ended his phone call with Tom earlier, he had fished out all the evidence from Helen's case that had trickled into him over the last few weeks. As the forensic pathologist for the entire region, it often took him months to get results back, and Helen's was no different. He was still waiting for the DNA results; however, he had spent the last couple of hours looking over some of the other evidence he had already run tests on. He had Helen's clothes, one shoe, and a lot of biological and trace evidence. The latent fingerprints were also in his possession, and he now collected the prints Tom had collected from the pub staff, the roll of film found at the pub, and all the contents of the lockbox. As the two men chatted about the case, and then onto more personal chatter, Jerry ran the prints through NAFIS. The prints Tom had collected from staff were clean prints that took minutes to upload into the system and attach identifications to. The other prints were not as neat, and the matches could return multiple results. Within an hour, Jerry had run them all and printed all the results out for Tom to take with him. He now had clear prints of a long list of people that he could use to clear and reduce his suspect list.

Tom said goodbye to Jerry, who promised him to put another rush on the trace evidence of what Tom had found in the lockbox and DNA results, and he climbed into his car. He was calmer now he had all the print results in his hand. He drove home with the window down and The Counting Crows playing on the stereo, positive about the case for the first time since they found poor Helen floating in the river.

{ **31** }

Rebecca was disappointed when Tom called to cancel their dinner. She meandered around the homestead and finally sat out by the river and do some drawing. It was late afternoon; the weather was calm and hot, but the breeze off the river made it a nice place to sit. Liz saw what Rebecca was doing and before long had brought outside a picnic blanket, comfortable camp chair, cushions, cheese and biscuits on a platter, along with a pitcher of iced tea. Rebecca tsked at her, thanking her for being so thoughtful. Liz had smiled shyly and hurried back to her duties.

Rebecca hesitantly started to sketch the scene before her, trying to capture the dense humidity, the ripple in the water and the last of the summer. Soon, she became completely absorbed in her own world, ignoring everything except the river before her.

***

Derek was in a bad mood by late afternoon. His father had been coming down hard on him in the last few days. He was exhausted and desperate to leave town. Everywhere he ventured, he was reminded of Helen. And to top it off, he saw Rebecca every day. Didn't anyone understand how hard it was for him to see her? It was like having Helen there, but not there. He knew it was irrational to hate Rebecca so much. Deep down, he knew exactly what was going on. He didn't hate her. She was sexy as hell. Just like his Helen. It pissed him off that she wasn't Helen. He ached for Helen every day. The idea of Rebecca going about her day, doing what she wanted. Well, it was his worst nightmare. Often, he thought back to the night he had gone to the pub. At the time he thought it was a good idea, he got out with his mates again, and he missed Mark's company. He knew Rebecca would be there, and he had considered it a stepping stone to peace, but it took him by surprise how difficult it had been to see her with Tom.

He sighed in frustration as he made his way home after he and Fred had been out in the fields most of the day. The cane was struggling with no rain, and Derek hoped the afternoon storms would pick up now that summer was nearing its end. He wanted out of Cooinda, and he needed to make some decisions about his life. Would he buckle down and work his arse off for the next few years to appease his folks? He was worried they would not let him slide into oblivion with his inheritance without a fight.

After he showered and sat on his deck, smoking a cigarette and drinking a whiskey, he wandered over to his parents' house. It was almost seven in the evening, and the sun was low in the sky. He was nervous as he made his way through the cane to the homestead. The strolling was a façade. He was sure his father was watching him. Lately, he was sure someone was always watching him. A few evenings ago, he had even yelled into the cane fields, sure someone was out there, quietly observing him. Of course, no one had answered. He had immediately felt like an idiot.

As he climbed the front steps of the verandah, he could hear Rebecca laugh. It was a hearty laugh that made him pause. He wondered what they were talking about. He stood quietly to one side of the screen door and listened to his mum as she spun a story about Helen.

It was years ago, and they had all been having lunch together on a Sunday. It was shortly after he and Helen had moved into town after getting married in Melbourne. Helen had wanted to make lunch for them all, and had spent hours cooking a Shepards pie, knowing it was his dad's favourite meal. She had carefully filled the pie dish with the meat, and then carefully layered on the mashed potato. It was a true masterpiece. The rich aromas had filled their cottage, and Helen had glowed with pride. Derek, Ruth, and Fred had sat around the dining table, eager to dig in. As Helen had been pulling out the pie, the dish had wobbled in her hands, and the lot had 'plopped' out, landing in the bottom of the oven.

Derek smiled at the memory, and at Rebecca's laughter.

Then he heard what his mother said next. "I tell you though, if Fred and I hadn't been there, I'd say Derek would have been furious with Helen. The poor girl looked terrified and was white as a sheet when she dropped that dinner. I was so naïve about what their relationship was like at the time, and I was perplexed." She paused. "Fred must have sensed something though, because after only a moment, he started laughing. His beautiful belly laugh that's contagious. Before long, we were all laughing, and Helen relaxed. I helped her clean up the mess, and we all had Chinese for lunch instead."

Derek stood silently; his hands clenched in fists. He remembered Helen dropping the dinner, and he remembered laughing along with everyone else, yet he didn't remember reacting angrily. He didn't remember Helen looking afraid of him and was furious with his mother for telling such lies to Rebecca. No wonder the woman hated him. He realised this bullshit had to stop. He took a moment to calm down, and then knocked lightly, and entered the house.

Rebecca and Ruth looked at him with surprise when he entered the kitchen. Neither of them had heard him come through the front door. The room smelt like roast pork, and Derek's stomach rumbled.

"Hello Derek," Ruth said warmly, standing up to greet her son, and silently hoped he had not heard what she'd said a few minutes before.

Rebecca was refreshed after her evening sketching by the river. Her work now sat on the sideboard in the family room, and Derek spotted it as he hugged his mother.

"Where did this come from?" he asked, walking over to get a closer look.

"Rebecca sketched that today. Isn't it beautiful?"

Derek stared at the black and white charcoal drawing. Rebecca had captured the river perfectly, along with the gentle slope of the grassy bank, the pelican floating peacefully along the shoreline, and the most precious part; Helen. Rebecca had drawn her sitting on the grass, her hand stretched out towards a pelican as it meandered towards her. She had captured her twin's uniqueness in a way that ensured one would look at the picture and know it was Helen, not Rebecca. Derek's chest tightened, and he cleared his throat. "This is beautiful, Rebecca. You're so talented. Just like her." He glanced at her, embarrassed.

"Thanks, Derek. It's been a while since I've used my creative brain. I didn't realise how wonderful it would be." She paused for a moment, then added, "Want to stay for dinner?"

He paused, then nodded. "Thanks, that would be nice. I actually came to discuss some work issues with Dad. Is he around?" he looked at Ruth.

She nodded, "just in the shower. He'll be out shortly." Derek nodded and sat down in the nearest chair. He couldn't take his eyes off the drawing.

Ruth hesitated. "Or is there something I can help with?"

Derek looked at her doubtfully, then glanced at Rebecca, who pretended to not pay attention as she cut thick slices of the bread she had made that morning and lay them out on a baking tray, ready to add the garlic butter before putting them in the oven. She, of course, was listening.

"It's doubtful, but I guess I can chat with you anyway." He paused, took a deep breath, and tried to ignore Rebecca. "I want to leave town, Mum." He rushed on before she said anything. "I hate it here since Helen. Everywhere I look, I see her. I just... feel like a change in location would be beneficial for me."

Ruth was silent for a moment. It was a delicate situation, and she was unsure how to proceed. It took all of her strength not to glance over at Rebecca and to remain focused on her son. "Where were you thinking of going? What are you thinking of doing?"

Derek sighed and shrugged. "Something that's not farming."

Ruth nodded. "It was never your cup of tea."

Derek suppressed a stir of hope that was forming in the pit of his stomach. Maybe talking to his mother first was the right idea after all. "Yeah, it certainly never lit my world on fire."

"Why are you telling me this, Derek? I assume it's money you need. It certainly isn't our permission or our approval."

Derek's anger flashed. "It's not like anyone would miss me, Mum. It's pretty obvious you don't care about me at all. You only ever cared about Helen."

Ruth shook her head, and Fred's loud snort of incredulous laughter that came from behind him. It was all he could do not to charge over to his son and shake some sense into him.

Derek swung around in his chair and confronted his father, who now stood behind him, freshly showered and shaved and looking ready to work another ten-hour day. The old man was a machine. It took the wind out of Derek's sails. "Sorry, dad" he said meekly. On the inside, Derek was furious he could not stand up to his father.

Fred looked at his son, trying to find the little boy behind the man that sat before him. "How about we sit down and have a nice dinner together" he said, an edge in his voice only Derek could hear.

The dinner was relaxed and comfortable thanks to Ruth and Rebecca. The women chatted about nothing in particular, and it wasn't until Ruth was serving up apple pie for dessert she'd made earlier in the day, as Rebecca cleared away the main dinner plates, that the discussion about Derek moving was mentioned. Rebecca excused herself, uncomfortable being involved in the discussion reserved for family. She also sensed Derek didn't want her there.

"I'm going for a walk. It's a nice evening," she smiled, wiping her hands on the dishtowel before hanging it back on the oven handrail. "I'll be back soon."

Her sandshoes lay at the back door, and she slipped them on before she smothered some insect repellent on her exposed skin and headed out the back door, letting the screen slap gently behind her. She headed down the back porch stairs and walked towards the cane.

She meandered through the fields, listening to the rustling of the cane, before finding a spot by the river. The rocks protruded from the water's edge, and she perched precariously on a rock and watched the water. Fish occasionally jumped out of the water, and just off to the left, an old man sat in a tin boat, his line thrown in. Now and then, he would wind in the line, hook the bait, and throw it back in. Rebecca watched, almost mesmerised by the movement. Her thoughts drifted back to when Helen and she were teenagers.

She had decided one day that they should learn to fish. They chose a spot on the Yarra River near where they had lived in Prahran, a suburb in Melbourne. For hours, Helen had diligently hooked her bait and thrown her line in. Repeatedly, it would get snagged, and she would pull it back in and try again. They had caught no fish, and Rebecca had gotten bored after about twenty minutes and fallen asleep on the picnic blanket, they had brought with them. Helen always laughed at the memory as they got older. Rebecca was the spontaneous one with the great ideas, such as fishing, and Helen was the one who always followed through. After that day, Rebecca had never fished again, and Helen had gone out regularly on her own, enjoying the solitude and the methodical process of the sport.

Now, all these years later, the ripple of the water, and the splash of the fish made Rebecca's heart ache for her twin. She finally stood up, dusting the dirt from her pants, turning back towards the cane. Movement caught her eye. She froze. From her left, the cane stirred, its whispers reaching out to her, sending a chill down her spine. She closed her eyes, waiting for the chill to pass, but when she opened them, Helen was standing in front of her.

Rebecca stumbled back in fright and fell on her arse, too shocked to even scream. But it was her twin who was terrified. Her hair was wet and plastered to her face; her running gear was sodden, and blood streamed down the side of her face. Rebecca sobbed, but Helen became frantic. She looked around, beckoned to her sister and finally opened her mouth and screamed. It was silent in the afternoon calm, yet the message was clear. Her sister was screaming for her to '*run!*'

Rebecca scrambled to her feet, panic rising in her throat as she turned around to run back to the homestead. She had only moved a few feet before someone moved silently up behind her. She sensed the rush of movement, and a sharp pain on her scalp, and then blackness as she crumpled to the ground.

{ **32** }

Derek left the homestead and began walking home. The moon was full, and so bright it lit his way. After Rebecca left, he and his parents had talked. The conversation had been amicable, and he was happier than he had since Helen had left. A few things had come out of the conversation; the first was that he could leave; the second; he could access some money to open a business; the third, his parents had to be investors. He had pondered the idea of still being accountable to them and countered with the proposition of them being investors for the first two years, and if the business proved successful, he could finally become financially free. They counter, counter-offered with the requirement of his paying them back the original loan amount to begin with.

It was the first time in a long time that Derek had considered a relationship with his parents — an equal, fair, unconditional one - may be feasible. He considered the possibility as he walked back home and was so deep in thought he actually tripped over Rebecca's shoe. He stared down at it, confused. Then, he looked around him to see if there was anybody nearby. He bent down and picked it up and saw the blood. A chill crept up his spine, and he glanced around again.

"Rebecca?" he called her name, but it came out as a croak. He cleared his throat and tried again. "Rebecca?" This time it was louder, and the frogs that had been croaking in the cane nearby halted their conversation. Derek's initial concern was snakes. Both brown and red belly blacks were out in force this season, and the death of Roger was still fresh on his mind and everyone else's who worked at the farm. He looked at the shoe again; the sight of blood sealed his decision to look for her, and to do it quickly.

The dark, wet patch of blood by the rocks was not even dry when Derek came across it a few minutes later. The moon shone brightly, illuminating the blood, and it glistened. He stared at it and glanced around for any other clues. The river lay in front of him, and he saw a boat not far away. A man sat at the back of the tinny, steering the motor, heading away from Derek. And he was going fast. Too fast. Was Rebecca in that boat? Had someone taken her? What the fuck was going on? He held onto her sandshoe tightly, turned and raced back to his folk's place.

Ruth was surprised to see Derek barge back into the living room as she and Fred sat in their favourite armchairs. Fred was already engrossed in a book he'd just picked up in town that he'd ordered the month before called 'The Professor and the Madman: A Tale of Murder, Insanity and the Making of the Oxford English Dictionary', and Ruth sat quietly in her own armchair knitting a quilt she had planned to donate to the church fair that was coming up. Arvo Pärt's 'Spiegel im Spiegel' played softly on the record player, and the pair were comfortable in their evening routine.

When she saw her son, Ruth sat up straight, staring at Derek as he thrust a shoe towards her. "This is Rebecca's. I can't find her anywhere, Mum. She's gone." His voice wavered, and he was on the verge of losing control. Ruth worried about his mental state as she tried to stay calm. She glanced at Fred, and they both discarded what they were doing and stood up. Fred reached out and gently took the shoe from his son, studying it. A deep frown had settled on his weathered face.

He handed it to Ruth. "Is this Rebecca's?"

Ruth was nodding before he even finished the question. She looked at her son. "And you looked everywhere?"

Derek nodded. "I also saw a boat speeding away."

"What do you mean?" Fred's voice rose slightly, and Ruth stood up, heading for the phone.

"The shoe was near the river, Dad, as well as blood on the ground and on the rocks. And the boat was going way too fast. It might mean nothing, but it's a weird coincidence."

Fred nodded, agreeing with his son. "Okay, we need to get Silas and Liz to help. We need to spread out and look for her. Ruth can stay here and wait for Tom."

Derek nodded, heading for the kitchen. "I'm going to put the shoe in a bag so no one else touches it. It's evidence."

***

Ava was the one who got the call out. She was already in the police cruiser coming back from patrol and answered the radio. She was at Ruth and Fred's within ten minutes, confusion and dread settling over her as she climbed out of the car. Ruth and Liz were standing on the driveway waiting for her.

Ruth was holding a bag with something inside she couldn't quite see.

"Hey folks, how are we?" she asked gently. All she had been told is that someone had not come home after a walk.

"Oh, Ava. You need to call Tom. Rebecca was out for a walk after dinner, and then Derek found her shoe when he was walking home." Ruth spoke quickly, thrusting the bag at Ava, who took the bag from her with a credulous look. Until she spotted the blood, which was caked along the top of the white sandshoe and plain to see through the plastic. It wasn't a 'smidge' of blood. The blood was dark brown now that it had hardened over the shoe as though someone had sloshed paint all over it and left it to dry.

She looked up at Ruth, now alarmed. "What do you mean she was out for a walk? I thought she was with Tom tonight?"

"He cancelled their plans. I'm not sure why. Anyway, she and Derek were both here for dinner. Then Rebecca left for a walk. Derek, Fred and Silas are out looking for her now. Derek said he saw a boat speeding away from near where he found the shoe. He also found blood splattered on a rock by the river." This finally broke Ruth, and she began sobbing; her whole body shook uncontrollably.

Liz guided her to the steps of the porch and sat her down gently while Ava rushed back to the car and radioed the station. She put a call out to all officers who were on call, asking for them to meet at the Cox's. She then ran into the house, passing Ruth and Liz, explaining she needed to use their phone. Liz nodded while Ruth continued to sob into her handkerchief.

In the kitchen, Ava called Tom's house. It was nearly eight in the evening, and she was frustrated when he didn't answer. She left a message telling him to come to the Cox's as soon as he could. She then rang Lou and Shane, who were both off duty. Lou didn't pick up, so Ava left a message on her machine, but Shane answered on the first ring. He said he'd be there as soon as he could. She then rang Mark, who also answered, and promised to be there as soon as possible. Ava hung up, turned and ran back outside. The ladies still sat on the steps.

"I need to go out to where Derek found the shoe. Can you point me in the right direction, Ruth?"

As she asked this, she heard a voice from behind her.

"I can take you, Ava."

She turned and saw Derek standing on the edge of the driveway, having appeared from the cane beyond.

Ava nodded. "Great, let's go." She turned back to Ruth and Liz.

"You both need to stay here. There will be more people arriving soon, including Shane and Mark."

The women nodded wearily as Ava and Derek headed back into the cane.

****

Tom was home shortly after one in the morning. He was bone-tired but also so wired he knew he wouldn't be able to sleep. He made a cup of tea and sat down with the list of names for each fingerprint alongside it. As he looked over it again, he became tired. Nothing was jumping out at him, even though he knew he had to look for it and not wait for it to jump out at him.

He leaned back in the chair and took a sip of his tea. Thinking. Something wasn't right. Something was right in front of him that he couldn't see. He sighed, stood up and walked over to the kettle. As he flicked it on for a second of tea, his brain finally switched on.

"That's it!" he yelled at the quiet, empty room. He strode back to the dining table and looked over the evidence lists again. Every item that had been swept for fingerprints was listed alphabetically. Tom moved his finger down the list until he came across Helen's engagement ring that Rebecca had found. He moved his finger along the line to where it stated if prints had been found; and if those prints were in NAFIS. Clear as day, it said, 'Gold/diamond ring...no prints found.'

Tom tried to ignore the excitement build in his gut as he thought back to when Rebecca had found the ring under the hall table. In theory, the ring should have had at least four people's prints on it: Helen's, Rebecca's, Derek's and his own. But it was clean. Someone had wiped it clean. He remembered bagging the evidence and locking it away until it was sent to Jerry. So, it meant that someone at the station had wiped it clean after he'd bagged and tagged it.

Tom reached for the phone to call Rebecca. He picked up the receiver and heard the familiar dial tone that showed he had messages. Maybe she'd called him? He dialled one-o-one and heard the familiar automated voice. Instead of hearing the computer animated voice announce he had one message; it told him he had eight missed calls. Nerves began to intrude as he dialled five at the instructions and listened.

"Tom? It's Ava. You need to get to the Cox's as soon as you get this. Thanks, mate." The hair on Tom's arms prickled as he dialled for the next message. "Tom, it's Ava again. You need to call me or come to the Cox's. Noone knows where Rebecca is."

Tom didn't listen to the rest of the messages. He slammed the phone back into the cradle and was out the door, grabbing the pages with the fingerprinting information as he ran.

He pulled into the majestic driveway within fifteen minutes, utilising his siren and cursing his decision to move out of town eight years ago. Fifteen minutes wasted in the fucking car. There were half a dozen cars already parked in the dimly lit driveway, including Ava's cruiser and Mark's truck. Before he could even climb out of the car, Ava was there to greet him.

"Have you found her? What happened? Where's Derek?" He knew he sounded frantic, probably even out of control. He knew he needed to stay professional and was failing miserably.

"We haven't found her, Tom. I don't think she's here. I think someone has taken her." What Ava said was followed by confused silence.

"Wait, what do you mean? How do you know? Tell me everything, please." His words came out as a plea, and Ava could see his fear.

"She was out walking after dinner. Derek found her shoe a short time later, and it had blood on it." Tom was about to interrupt her, but she held up her index finger. "Let me finish."

Tom took a deep breath and nodded.

Ava lowered her hand. "Derek's time is fully accounted for. He was at the homestead with Fred, Ruth and Rebecca for at least an hour or two having dinner, and was still there talking to Ruth and Fred, which is when Rebecca left. She wanted to give them privacy while they chatted. Derek left about half an hour after Rebecca and tripped on her shoe on his way home. He picked it up, saw the blood, and looked for her immediately. He then found fresh blood on the ground and on the rocks by the river. At the same time, he also saw a boat speeding away from the area. He raced back to the house, and the police were called." Ava stopped and finally took a breath, letting Tom digest everything she'd just told him.

"The boat? Has anyone followed this up yet?" Tom glanced at his watch. It had been hours since it had all happened, and he couldn't believe he'd been meandering about, talking to Jerry, listening and singing along to the Crows on his way home. It made him feel nauseous.

Ava nodded. "Yeah, Shane got onto that straight away, and the answer actually found him. The guy in the boat was old Dick Shaw. He was speeding because he saw someone hit Rebecca from behind. He was speeding home to call us." She let the news sink in. "Tom; we have a witness."

Tom looked at Ava sharply, his brain going a hundred miles an hour. "It was Lou, wasn't it?" He said this quietly, and it surprised him even as he said it.

Ava tilted her head and narrowed her eyes. "No. By Dick's description, I believe it may have been Jenny. Why did you think it was Lou?"

Tom shook his head, upset that he had been on the money. "I still think Lou's involved. She could be covering for Jenny somehow. Tonight, I was over at the forensics lab with Jerry. I got the information back from all the fingerprints on the items from the crime scene, plus all of Helen's personal items, including the ring Rebecca found. Do you remember that?"

Ava thought for a moment and said, "Yeah, Derek asked if you could run prints. You bagged it and put it in the safe until forensics collected it the following morning."

"How many sets of prints did we think would be on it?"

Ava shrugged, "At least three or four, considering how many people had handled it."

Tom nodded. "It came back clean. No prints detected. Someone had wiped it clean."

Ava's eyes widened. "And you think it was Lou?"

"No one else has the code to the safe. Except me and my senior constable, Louise Hunt."

"Fuck."

"Yep."

Tom and Ava walked inside the homestead to let the others know what was going on. Mark looked at them both incredulously, finding it hard to believe that Lou and Jenny could have anything to do with Rebecca being taken.

Liz sat quietly on the lounge, deep in thought, before she said, "It does sort of make sense. Neither Jenny nor Lou ever seemed to have a pleasant word to say about Helen. They always referred to her as a snob or a lazy wife. I never thought much of it, assuming one of them had a crush on Derek."

Tom looked over at Derek when Liz said this, and he saw the man had turned deathly pale.

"Derek, what is it?" Tom urges.

"Oh, Derek. You didn't?" This came from Ruth, who sat with Fred, holding his hand trying to calm her nerves. Derek glanced at his mother, then looked down, shame replacing fear on his pale face. He nodded.

Tom was still confused. Until Mark piped up. "Derek, have you been sleeping with one of them?"

Derek sighed, finally looking up. He saw that the entire room was staring at him and judging him. It made him furious. "What?" he said sulkily. "I'm no saint, and I did my best. It still makes little sense why either of them would want to hurt Rebecca."

Tom shook his head angrily. "Are you really that stupid, Derek? If they are actually behind this; if they have kidnapped Rebecca; there is a damn good chance they also killed Helen."

Derek's eyes shot open as the penny dropped. "No. No, there is no way Lou or Jenny would hurt Helen. I thought you were on the brink of announcing it was that Josh guy?"

Ava was confused. She put her hand up to interrupt the conversation. "Okay, wait. Derek, you need to clarify who you slept with? Lou or Jenny?"

Everyone in the room looked at Derek expectantly. He knew the blush under his skin was rising from under his collar, up his neck and into his face. He lowered his head and mumbled, "Well, both of them."

Ruth gasped dramatically, and Ava sighed. Derek looked up again. "Oh my God, it's not as if I slept with them at the same time!"

"Oh, bravo, Derek. Well done for cheating on your wife with only one woman at a time." This came from Shane, who stood behind Tom. His usual quiet, easy-going manner had been replaced with enough furry to strike Derek with one look.

Tom casually moved a foot or two over, to place himself in front of Shane. The last thing he needed on his hands was a fight. He held his hands up to disarm the masses. "Look, I still think Josh is involved. I just haven't figured everything out yet. I know for a fact that Jenny and Josh had slept together, though."

Ava piped up. "Remember in your report you wrote Jenny thought it was strange that Lou and Josh had become friends?" she shrugged. "Even if it makes little sense yet, the connection is there. Now we just have to figure it all out. That includes motive."

Tom nodded. "You're right, Ava."

He turned to Derek. "You need to stay here with your mum and dad," he turned to Ruth and Fred, "don't you let him leave your sight." He turned to Mark. "You need to go to my place and sit by the phone in case Rebecca gets away and calls me." He scanned the rest of the room. "Shane, head back to the station and organise for Dick and the composite artist, Shannon, to come in as soon as possible to do the composite while it was fresh in Dick's mind."

Tom looked over at Ava. "Okay, you and I are going to head to Lou's right now." He threw her his keys. "But I need you to drive. To say I'm not at my best is an understatement."

***

Lou lived just outside of town in the home she had grown up in. Her parents had passed away within twelve months of each other when she was in her late teens, and, as an only child, was left the entirety of her parent's estate. It was a fibro two-bedroom cottage with a quaint verandah and a picket fence that surrounded the entire block of land. Lou was proud of the one thing her parents had left her, and the lawn was always immaculate. The outside porch was decorated with potted plants, hanging flowerpots and a pretty little wind chime that announced the breeze when it came for a visit.

It sang softly now as Tom climbed the three front steps from the footpath onto the verandah, and he glanced around cautiously, wanting to stay quiet. He motioned to Ava to head around the back of the house, and she nodded, her weapon drawn at her side. The street was still and empty, as it was the witching hour, before the roosters had even stirred. Tom knocked on the front door as softly as he could, when in fact he was holding himself back from physically breaking the door down.

Instead, he waited a moment with his ear to the door, listening. He couldn't hear any noise inside, so he slowly turned the handle to find it locked. He moved to the window next to the front door and peered in. It had a sheer curtain hung over the space, so he had a slightly distorted view of Lou's living area. The home was like other homes in the area built during the forties and fifties, with living spaces and rooms divided by hallways and walls. Tom moved around to the side of the house where the kitchen was and peered in through the kitchen window. He saw movement at the back of the room, to his right-hand side, and froze, until he saw that it was Ava; her head poked carefully through the back door. He waited a moment for his heartbeat to subside to a normal rate, then hurried around to the back of the house, and followed Ava through the back door, and into Lou's house. The two stood in the kitchen, silent and waiting. Everything remained quiet in the morning's dawn. He closed the door and locked it so no one could come in after them before they moved further into the house.

The kitchen was quaint and meticulously kept. He always knew Lou was a clean freak, but the extent of her cleanliness made him grimace as he looked around the room, careful not to touch anything. It reminded him of a display home, with a vase of native flowers displayed on the kitchen counter, lace curtains on the window, parted neatly in the middle and held in place with pink ribbon. There were canisters neatly lining the counter that had printed labels for coffee, tea, sugar, flour and rice. Tom moved through the home, feeling intrusive, and more than a little sick. He had never suspected Lou of being unstable. He paid attention to anything that might have been out of place, or to something that could tell him where Lou, Jenny and Rebecca were.

Within minutes, they had finished looking in the living areas, and nothing seemed out of place. The only places left to check were the bedrooms and bathroom. He nudged the first door in the hallway open with his foot, still careful not to touch anything, and stood in the doorway staring into Lou's bedroom. It was as he expected. Pristine and perfectly in place, with floral curtains hanging at the window and a lovely wrought iron bed against the opposite wall. A green and pink floral quilt covered the bed, and about a dozen pillows were placed strategically to look as though someone had thrown them casually on the bed.

Tom had always appreciated Lou's complete and utter fastidiousness, as it made working with her calming and incredibly efficient. But now it was like a neon sign flashing in his face. The exceptionally clean home that was decorated like a magazine was more than slightly off-putting, and he glanced at Ava as she followed him into the room. She stared around her and finally broke the silence.

"Geez. Does anyone actually live here?"

He frowned and shook his head. "It's bloody strange. That's for sure. A neat bedroom doesn't make you a murderer though," he reminded Ava as she moved further into the bedroom, opening the wardrobe.

"Yeah, but a dead body does," she replied quietly. She turned around and faced Tom and said as quickly as she could, "It's not Rebecca."

Tom's eyes widened, and he rushed over to the wardrobe. Before he could even ask who it was, he saw with his own eyes. Jenny. She was crumpled like a pretzel at the bottom of the wardrobe. Her knees were up near her chin and her arms folded across her breasts. Her eyes were open and stared into her own abyss.

"Jesus Christ" was all Tom could manage as Ava finally turned away, tears escaping her eyes. She thought of their recent night out and how Jenny had danced without a care in the world. How she had always waved her hands widely as she spoke, so animated, so full of life. Ava sat down on the floor, not caring that she was a cop. This was too personal. And she was now deathly afraid for Rebecca. If Lou could kill her own best friend, there was no telling what she could do to her. She began to hyperventilate and put her head down towards her crossed legs.

Tom turned to see Ava begin to panic. He knelt beside her, rubbing her back.

"It's okay, Ava. You'll be okay. Just breathe through it." He continued to rub her back and speak to her softly, talking her through it. As Ava gained control of herself, a photo on the bedside table caught Tom's attention. He moved in closer to peer at it. It was a photo of Lou, Mark, Derek, Jenny and Cain Lewis in high school. He didn't know the location of the photo, but they all stood together, with their arms linked, laughing at something someone said. Tom noticed the photo was slightly crooked, and he couldn't help himself; he picked it up to study it closer. Everything else was so perfect, yet this one photo was not. When the frame moved, the photo slipped out-of-place even further, and he could see another photo tucked behind it. He reached to the back of the frame and pulled on it slightly, causing the frame to slip away from the glass. The photo that was tucked behind the one at the front fell to the carpet and landed face down. Tom placed the frame on the bedside table and bent over to pick it up.

The photo was much newer than the high school photo it hid behind. Lou appeared to look closer to her current age. She was holding the camera in an outstretched hand; the lens turned to capture her own face. It was a close-up portrait of Lou passionately kissing Derek as they took a candid selfie. He realised then that this casual affair for Derek; meant a whole lot more to Lou. She was not only in love with him but ob-sessed. She wanted him all to herself, sick of taking photos of the man she loved, and then hiding it from the world.

Rebecca slowly came to. Her head pounded, and when she tried to open her eyes, her vision blurred. She closed them again and groaned, but that hurt too, so she stopped.

"Rebecca? Hon?" Lou's voice was soft, concerned. Rebecca slowly opened her eyes again. The room slowly spun while her eyes slowly adjusted to her environment. She winced in pain, feeling a sharp pain in the back of her head. She tenderly reached out and touched her scalp. There was a lump, and she could feel the wound already scabbing over.

"What happened? Where are we?" Her vision slowly cleared, and her eyes adjusted. Although there was not much to adjust to. They were in a darkened room, and she was lying on an old bed. Lou was sitting beside it in a vintage armchair. She no longer wore her uniform, and she sat on the edge of the chair, her hand gently resting on her arm.

"We are safe."

"What... what do you mean safe?"

"You don't remember anything?"

Rebecca tried to think. Her head pounded at the base of her skull, and she winced every time she spoke. There was a heavy metal band playing in her head. She hated heavy metal.

"Apparently not. What is going on?" Her eyes finally focused, and she saw Lou sitting next to her, a look of concern on her face. There was a warm blanket tucked firmly around her, and her head rested on a comfortable pillow. She glanced around the room. All she saw were timber walls, old timber furniture and old electric lanterns placed around the room. There was a boarded-up window on the other side of the bed from her, which kept the room dark. The glow from the lanterns cast eerie shadows across the room.

Lou was grasping her hand, gently stroking it with her thumb. Her friend had a concerned look on her face, and Rebecca calmed down at the sight of her soft, caring face.

"I'm so confused. What happened and where are we?"

Lou withdrew her hand and wiped her fringe back from her eyes, tucking it behind her ears. "Derek tried to kill you; that's what happened. I have no idea why, but I had to get you out of the homestead and somewhere safe. We are at my aunt's old cabin. No one has been here since she died fifteen years ago. I thought it would be the best place to bring you until I sorted out what the fuck was going on."

"Wait, what do you mean Derek tried to kill me?" Rebecca was confused, and she wished her head would quit pounding so she could think. She tried to remember back to earlier in the evening, but the last thing she remembered was dinner at the homestead and then sitting by the river. She closed her eyes and tried to remember more. It was then she remembered Helen appearing to her, telling her to run. Right before she blacked out.

Lou was looking at Rebecca closely. "I was nearby, visiting Liz and Silas. Thank God I heard something going on and decided to go into the cane to find out."

"Oh, my God" was all Rebecca could muster. "Have you called Tom? He's going to be worried sick." She saw Lou hesitate, and a look of guilt crossed her face again.

"No, not yet. I haven't. There isn't a phone here. I was waiting until you woke up and I knew you were okay before I left to find a phone booth."

"Why would Derek want to hurt me?"

"I don't know, honey, but he won't get away with this, though. Let's hope he's already in custody. I'll head out soon and call Tom. Hopefully, we can sort this out." She squeezed Rebecca's hand and stood up.

"Okay, you keep resting. There is water next to your bed, and if you feel like getting up, you'll find tea and coffee in the kitchen. Not much else though, I'm afraid. I've only ever been out here a handful of times over the years. Will you be okay by yourself?" She looked hesitant about leaving, and Rebecca smiled weakly, and not reassuringly, at Lou.

"I think I'll be okay. I'll just stay in bed. My head is pounding; do you have any painkillers?"

Lou nodded, reached into the drawer in the nightstand and pulled out a packet of dusty Panadol.

"You're in luck," she said, handing them to Rebecca. "Okay, so I better go before Tom organises a full-on search party for us." She grinned. "Take it easy, okay?"

Rebecca nodded and closed her eyes while she tried not to panic. Everything was so surreal. She heard Lou quietly leave, and a tear rolled down her cheek. She turned onto her side and pulled the soft duvet up to her neck, desperate to go back into a dreamless sleep.

Instead, her thoughts raced. Why would Derek suddenly want to kill her? What had she done? The only thing she could think of was that she had come close to some information that he was hiding, but she didn't know what. Her mind wandered back over the last month since arriving in Cooinda, but her head was pounding and muddled, and her heart filled with fear. What if Derek had followed them here? Maybe he was waiting for the moment Lou left so he could come in and finish the job.

Heart pounding, Rebecca gingerly sat up on the side of the bed. She reached for the Panadol and water and swallowed four at once, not caring what the directions recommended about dosage. She stood up, still in the clothes she'd been wearing at dinner, and walked towards the only door in the room. Lou mentioned no one had really been there since her aunt had died, but the room was lovely, with old family photos on the wall, a pretty floral rug on the floor, covering most of the old timber flooring. There was an old fabric armchair next to the bed that Lou had been sitting in, and an antique wardrobe and dresser, next to the mostly boarded-up window. Moonlight filtered through, but Rebecca could hear the early morning songs of the wildlife. She guessed it was almost dawn.

Rebecca stood staring at a vase of flowers on the nightstand. They were beautiful and fresh, and the way they were arranged implied that Lou had picked them herself. Why on earth would Lou have flowers next to the bed if no one had been there in years?

Feeling unstable and weak, she made her way around the wrought-iron bed to the bedroom door and carefully turned the knob. The door creaked loudly as she pulled it open and slowly peeked through the doorway. On the other side was a sitting room. She opened the door fully and walked out of the bedroom. The living room was like the bedroom, with antique furniture, beige curtains that hung at the windows, and old Persian rugs covered the timber floors. There was an empty fireplace with ash and wood in the hearth. Once again, Rebecca stared at the fireplace, overcome with uneasiness. Someone must have been out there recently to leave flowers and use the fireplace. Come to think of it, why would Lou tell her there was tea and coffee to drink if it was fifteen years old?

The kitchen was at the back of the house, with a counter that ran along the wall from the back door. The bench was old timber, and there were cupboards underneath, and a sink under a timber-framed window. Shelves were on either side of the window, with small bric-a-brac decorating them. Separating the kitchen and living room was a square timber table with tartan padded cushions on the chairs.

The cabin living area was no larger than twelve by fifteen feet. There was only one other interior door that led off the living room other than the room she had just come from, and Rebecca hoped it was a bathroom. She walked over to it and opened the door to find a tiny bathroom with a pedestal sink, a shower stall and a toilet. She quickly used the toilet and washed her face with warm water and looked at herself in the oval mirror that hung from the wall above the vanity.

Her hair hung limp around her shoulders, and her eyes were fleshy and swollen with large dark circles under them, making her appear older than her twenty-nine years. Her skin had a pasty quality, and she looked grey. She was pretty sure she was grey on the inside too. She sighed heavily, she turned off the faucet and dried her face and wondered how on earth she had ended up there? She touched the lump forming on her scalp and winced in pain. What was she going to do? For the first time since arriving from New York, she wished she had never come home. Despising her poor decisions, she moved slowly back into the living room and stopped, staring at the table in the centre of the room.

One of the antique chairs had moved away from the table, as though someone had pulled it out to sit down. Nervous, she glanced around the room. "Lou?" Her voice sounded meek and hollow. Silence answered her. She shook her head and assumed the concussion had made her a tad cooky. She walked over to the kitchen, pushing the chair back into place as she did. She filled the old kettle with water and placed on the gas stove that was along the back counter. She found matches in a small dish and lit the stove. There was movement in the corner of her eye. She froze.

Once again, the chair had moved away from the table. Rebecca stared at it for a moment, and a visceral sound escaped her. She slowly glanced from her left to her right. Suddenly the air felt icy, and the hair on her arms bristled with goosebumps. She absently rubbed her arms, hugging herself, and walked through the open living area toward the fireplace. The room remained cold and silent. Rebecca could not help shaking as stood by the window and pulled the curtain back to stare outside. It was beautiful. The sky was bright with a full moon, and a hint of breeze caused movement in the darkness. She was aware of the contrast to her inner turmoil as she stared, deep in thought; about Helen, about Cooinda, about what was happening to her.

Finally, she sighed and turned back towards the kitchen when the kettle whistled. In the corner of her eye, she saw movement.

Helen was there.

She was sitting in the dining chair that had slid away from the table. As Rebecca watched, Helen stood and walked towards the stove and its whistling kettle. She bent slightly, pushing her auburn hair away from her face, and blew out the burner. Without looking at Rebecca, she walked towards the bathroom and disappeared.

Rebecca stood frozen as she watched her sister walk away. Slowly she glanced back at the stove, where the kettle now stood silent, the flame extinguished by an apparition. She shivered uncontrollably and quickly sank into the armchair near the window. Her heart was pounding, and she needed to think. Although not the first time she had seen Helen, this was the first time she had behaved differently. Her movements had been more fluid, and Rebecca wondered if her sister had become tangible. She wished she could hug her.

Finally, she stood and walked into the kitchen and looked around for paper and a pen. She was lucky enough to find what she needed in the second drawer she rummaged through. She made herself a cup of black coffee, heaped with three sugars she also found in the cupboards, and sat down to make a list of all the times Helen had appeared since arriving in Cooinda.

Within minutes she had compiled her list, and she sat back to look at the piece of paper in front of her. Every time except today, Helen had been wearing her running gear. At no other time had the temperature of the room changed. She had almost seen the frigidity in the air. At no other time had Rebecca felt scared or threatened. Today, however, had been completely different. Helen was wearing her running gear, but it was not torn or dirty. She had not been bloody, and her hair flowed around her shoulders rather than being pulled back with a hair band. And today, Rebecca had been scared when she had seen Helen. Not afraid of her, per se; but afraid none the less. Something sinister lurked in the air, and she knew Helen was desperate for her sister to see it.

With her coffee, she gingerly made her way over to the old couch and curled up to sip her drink and make sense of her thoughts. There were hundreds of pieces of information floating around in her head that she needed to fit together. She kept glancing up at the stove, hoping Helen would reappear, but the room remained empty. Why had she appeared to her here at all? Tom was convinced Josh had killed Helen, that he had stalked her. Maybe it was something else. She stood up in frustration, picked up her coffee cup and took it to the sink where she rinsed and set it on the bench. When she turned around, the chair had moved again. Rebecca stared at it.

Then an urge to sit it in the chair rose in her so strongly that she gingerly walked the two feet to the chair and sat down. Her heart was racing, and her hairline had developed a bead of sweat that threatened to escape down the side of her cheek. She waited, not sure what to expect next. The room was silent. Finally, in exasperation, she threw her hands in the air and said to Helen, "Now what?"

An invisible force seized her arms and forced them together behind the chair just as she was about to stand up again. In a panic, she looked around and saw no one.

"What the fuck?" she said, trying to move her arms. She became frantic, desperately trying to gain control of her hands that were bound by force. An unseen entity then pushed her feet apart with a grip so strong that she yelped in pain. She watched in awe as an invisible rope tied her ankles to the chair legs. Bile rose in her throat, and she let out a strangled whimper. She was deathly afraid and worried she was about to pass out from fear.

"It's okay, Rebecca." The whisper came from directly behind her, close to her left ear. She could feel Helen's breath on her cheek, and an involuntary sob escaped.

"I need you to see." Helen's voice was soft and calm.

Slowly, Rebecca's heartbeat slowed. She took a deep breath and relaxed against the invisible restraints that held her to the chair, and she closed her eyes.

"Okay, Helen," she whispered, "show me."

{ **35** }

Rebecca slowly opened her eyes. She was on a dark road, and she the warm breeze brushed against her face. It was a strange sensation; she knew she was sitting in the dining room chair in Lou's cabin, yet she also stood on a dark road, her arms and legs free. Rebecca looked down at her feet and saw she was wearing runners noticed a Walkman attached to her side. She looked around the dark empty night, and the realisation came. She was Helen, and she was on Cane Road.

"I need to run," she thought. "I need to run. Hard."

She jogged, the solid road under her feet made her alive and free. "If only I could keep running," she thought to herself. "If only he would let me go." She sighed and tucked her head down and ran.

The night was sultry and sweat trickled down Rebecca's face as she ran. The strangest sense had come over her, an out-of-body experience that had captured her soul.

"Just relax," a voice whispered in her head. It was Helen.

So, Rebecca relaxed and allowed herself to be happy to be running. She loved the solid rhythm of running and heard her sister's thoughts while she did. She prayed the experience would not end too quickly. She stopped short when she saw the car that was stopped at a weird angle on the side of the road. The passenger door was open, and she'd almost run into it.

She could see a man and assumed he had broken down. She smiled, shy and only slightly startled. She said something to the stranger but couldn't understand the words.

The out-of-body experience allowed for a multitude of feelings. As though there were layers within her. She could perceive her own thoughts, yet her actions and thoughts were those of her sister. She heard herself speaking yet didn't know what was being said.

The next few moments were muddled. Rebecca could only concentrate on the fear and shock, as she was shuffled into Josh's car without reason. She wanted to say things to him, yet she knew he wasn't actually there. She was nauseous.

When they drove away from town, Rebecca was scared. She thought of Derek and sadness gripped her soul. "This must be it," she thought.

She glanced at Josh, a stranger in her eyes, but not in her heart.

He was relaxed, humming a tune on the radio. The cranberries? He looked over at her and grinned.

"I'm looking forward to tonight."

Rebecca's eyes widened. The man was insane.

When Rebecca lifted her head again, she was back in Lou's cabin and was shaking all over; a combination of exhilaration, and fear over what she'd experienced. The cabin remained quiet, and she was desperate to see Helen. But she was alone. Her hands and feet were free again, so she stood and walked over to get a glass of water from the sink.

She turned back, to see Helen now sitting in the chair. Rope bound her arms and legs, and she was wearing her running gear. Rebecca noticed the Walkman now sat on the table next to her. There was blood on her face from a cut on her hairline. She was staring at Rebecca now, with a look of amusement.

Rebecca was afraid to look away. Helen talked, yet she could hear no words. Rebecca knew that whoever Helen was talking to; was in her past. Rebecca didn't need to hear her sister to see that whatever she was saying was antagonistic. Her eye had a sparkle that reminded Rebecca of when they were young, and Helen was trying to piss her off. The twins loved each other fiercely, but boy, they could get on each other's nerves as teenagers.

Suddenly she saw Helen's head jolt backwards, as someone slapped her hard across the face. Rebecca winced and stepped forward. Her illogical side told her to warn Helen not to antagonise Josh, but instead, her sister vanished.

Rebecca turned and slammed her glass on the counter and walked into the bedroom to find something to put on her feet. This was ridiculous; she needed to get out of there. She flung open the antique wardrobe, hoping to find some of Lou's shoes. But the wardrobe was empty. Except for one thing — a Walkman, sitting by itself on the one shelf in the wardrobe.

Rebecca stared at it and finally comprehended as all the pieces fell into place. Helen had actually been there. She had sat in the kitchen chair in Lou's kitchen. Josh had abducted her, but Lou, for some reason, was involved. She backed away from the wardrobe and turned to leave, only to see Lou standing in the doorway, blocking her only exit. She stared at Rebecca, who smiled brightly, while her insides screamed in fear.

"Oh, you're back. I was looking for some shoes so I could come and find you. I was getting worried," Rebecca smiled weakly, reached out behind her and closed the cupboard door.

Lou stared at her for a moment longer, unblinking, unsmiling. Then her face broke into her usual smile, and she moved further into the room.

"I'm so sorry I took so long. However, Tom will be here shortly. I found a phone, called him and Ava. Then I called Ruth."

"What did Tom say?"

Lou stared blankly at her for a moment, then spoke. "I told him Derek attacked you and I brought you here for safety. He said he would find Derek, then come here."

Rebecca marvelled at how calm and convincing Lou was as she spoke and would have believed her if she had not just seen her sister's Walkman in the cupboard behind her. She was desperately trying to stay calm, as her tried to reconcile the idea that Lou was involved in Helen's death. She was so confused; but knew it to be true. Helen had given her enough signs to know that this was what she had needed her to see. Now she just had to figure out the why. And get out of the place alive. One thing at a time.

"What time will Tom be here?"

"Soon. He was going to pick up Ruth and come and collect you. He's so worried." As she spoke, she hurried over to Rebecca, gently took hold of her arm and guided her back to the bed.

"In the meantime, you need to lie down again. I'm worried you still have a concussion. You seemed confused and scared when I walked back into the room. What were you doing while I was gone?" She asked casually, but Rebecca could almost hear the menace dripping from her words as Lou settled her back into the bed, tucking the blanket around her feet and then rearranging the pillow for her.

It was all Rebecca could do not to bolt out of the bed and out the front door, but she needed to keep Lou talking. If she had killed Helen, she had to find out why. Lou sat on the edge of the bed and looked worriedly at Rebecca.

"Is there anything I can do? Want another cuppa?"

Rebecca shook her head. "No thanks. I'm tired. I just think I'll close my eyes. Why don't you tell me about growing up in Cooinda?"

Lou chuckled. "Really? It'll be the most boring life story you've ever heard."

Rebecca shrugged. "What else is there to do?"

Lou laughed, "Okay, you asked for it. I was born in Cooinda. My parents were far from wealthy. I was an only child, and we lived in a modest house. Mum actually worked for the Cox's."

There was silence after this. Rebecca opened her eyes and saw Lou staring at her.

Rebecca said, "Such a small town. Everyone knows everyone. What did she do for them?"

Lou stared at her for a moment longer, then smiled again. The woman's ability to change her expressions so completely within seconds impressed Rebecca. A true psychopath, she suspected.

"She was a cleaner. Worked in their house for years. Dad was a local farmer. He would contract out to different farms each season. Sort of a 'jack of all trades' guy," she paused, and Rebecca could see that Lou was lost in the past.

"They both died too young."

"I'm so sorry to hear that."

Lou snapped out of her trancelike state. "Yeah, well, shit happens." She shrugged.

"So, you really only have your friends? Your job?"

"Yep, guess you could say that."

"Anyone special?"

Lou stood up abruptly. "I think I'll make a cup of tea. Are you sure you don't want one?"

Rebecca didn't answer, just stared at her. There was a moment of silence between the two women. Rebecca broke it for good.

"Why did you bring me here, Lou?"

In an instant, Lou's demeanour changed. Her face became rigid, furious.

"You damn well know why I brought you here."

Once again, Rebecca was shocked by the instantaneous change in her friend. But kept her cool manner, determined to find out the truth without getting herself killed.

"No, sorry Lou, but I don't. We both know you are the one who knocked me out. We both know you haven't called Tom. But only one of us knows why you want to hurt me."

Lou screeched. She lashed out with such speed and intensity that it completely threw Rebecca off guard. Before she knew what was happening, Lou had punched her hard across the face, causing her head to hit the wrought iron bed frame and bring tears to her eyes.

"Don't fucking lie to me, you stupid slut!"

Rebecca stayed silent. She kept her head down, thinking furiously about what could make Lou think she'd hurt her somehow.

"You're the same as your fucking slut sister. Just waltz into town, take whatever the fuck you want. Even if it doesn't belong to you."

Rebecca's brain was racing with so many thoughts she had to still herself for a second. She closed her eyes. "Tom?"

Lou's shrill laugh told her immediately this was not about Tom.

"Derek?" she asked hesitantly.

"Ding, ding, ding, give the woman a prize!"

"I'm sorry, don't give me anything. I honestly don't understand what you are upset about. Everyone knows I can't stand Derek. The guy is a complete narcissistic arsehole."

The second punch was so hard that Rebecca knew her nose was broken. Blood sprayed out in front of her, and she raised both hands to her face as tears welled in her eyes.

"Don't attempt to fool me, Rebecca. Just when I thought I had gotten rid of the wife. The fucking sister-in-law shows up and makes herself comfortable."

"You killed my sister? Over Derek?" Rebecca stared at Lou with pure hatred. Her face was throbbing, and she was on the verge of panic. And anger. She wanted to kill this bitch.

"Ha! I put her out of her misery. I knew Derek was too good for her. He just didn't see it. He was so in love with her, even though she treated him so badly," she shrugged casually, "he would never have left her for me. But now, I will treat him the way he deserves. I've always loved him. Everything would have been perfect if you had just stayed out of the fucking way."

Before Rebecca could say anything, Lou reached down to the bottom drawer of the bedside table and retrieved a set of handcuffs. She grabbed Rebecca's hands and yanked them painfully above her head and locked her to the frame before she had the chance to struggle or defend herself. Fear was now cemented in her gut, and she knew there was no escaping unless someone figured out where they were. Rebecca closed her eyes and had a stern word with herself not to cry. Surely, Tom would figure out what had happened to her?

Her head was pounding, and she could already feel her entire face swelling from the hits she'd taken. She thought of Helen, also trapped in this house. And realised — this is where she died. A sob involuntarily escaped, and Lou smirked.

"You're pathetic, just like Helen." She turned and stalked out of the room, slamming the door shut behind her, leaving Rebecca alone to ponder how the hell she was going to get out of there.

{ **36** }

It was three in the morning by the time Tom and Ava drove back to the homestead. Tom had called Viraj and Shane to come over to Lou's place and wait until the forensic team arrived to secure the crime scene. He wasn't sure where Jenny had been killed, but Lou's house was now a no-go zone for the foreseeable future. Shane had arrived, looking shocked and sad. He and Jenny had always gotten along, and Tom suspected he may have even had feelings for her at one point. The poor guy appeared stoic, but Tom knew he was breaking up on the inside as they watched

Viraj and his assistant load Jenny into the van.

Viraj made his way over to Tom, shaking his hand with a sad look on his face.

"You okay, mate? I heard you knew her."

Tom nodded. "Yeah, I'm okay. But I have to go. Rebecca's missing."

Viraj nodded. "Of course. I just can't believe this was Lou. You think you know a person…"

***

Tom discovered how quickly town-talk travelled, with word already gotten back to the Cox's by the time Tom and Ava arrived. They found Ruth comforting Liz as they walked back into the living room. Liz had known Jenny her whole life and now sat sobbing on the sofa in the living room. Silas sat next to his wife, staring blankly at the floor while sipping brandy. Fred was pacing the living room.

"Fred? What's wrong?" Ruth finally asked. The man oozed a confidence that most would be jealous of, but right now he was ringing his hands, a deep frown exposing his age around his eyes and crow's feet.

Fred sighed. "I've been waiting for the right time to tell you. Derek is gone."

"What?" Confusion settled on Ruth's face, and Tom froze.

"The phone rang a little while back, and he answered it. He wouldn't tell anyone who it was, but his expression told me it was Lou. He then left, saying he had no choice. I tried to stop him, but he said he needed to end this - said it was all his fault."

"Tom, we need to figure out where the fuck Lou is." The quiet desperation came from Ava.

Tom turned back to Ruth and Fred. "Is there anything you can think of that I should know about Lou and her family? Any clue where she may have taken Rebecca, a place Derek would know about?" He let them think, trying not to stare at them, trying not to put too much pressure on them.

Fred began pacing the room again. "I need to go out to my office," he stated suddenly and turned and walked from the room. Tom decided not to follow him; instead, he walked into Rebecca's room. He didn't know what he thought he'd find, but seeing her things comforted his soul. He stood near her bed, looking slowly at her things.

Ruth followed Tom. She stood in the doorway as he carefully began looking through her things. Tom glanced at her.

"Sorry," he said, "I just needed to look."

In the few weeks that she had come into their lives, she had settled firmly into the homestead, and her bedroom reflected that. Her bed was inviting with a tartan-patterned quilt cover in soft pastels and a couple of large throw pillows casually placed on top. There was a large rug under Tom's feet that covered the hardwood, softening the room and making it cosy. He opened her closet and searched through it quickly, not sure what he was expecting to find.

He was about to leave in frustration when Ruth spoke.

"Wait. That jacket is Lou's!" The urgency in her voice startled Tom. He looked where she was pointing and saw there was a denim jacket on the back of an old antique armchair that sat in the bedroom's corner. Rather though Rebecca had come into the room, shrugged it off and thrown it on the chair.

"How do you know?"

"When she came home from her night out with you all, she was wearing that jacket. She'd borrowed it from Lou when she got cold; forgot to give it back to her."

Tom remembered the night clearly. It was the evening Rebecca had her vision while playing pool. When they had come out of the pub, she'd been shivering, and Lou had given her a spare jacket to wear home.

Tom grabbed the jacket and studied it closely, not sure what he was looking for. He rummaged through the pockets and was about to give up in frustration when he found a piece of paper in the left-side pocket. He pulled it out and looked at it. It was a receipt from a petrol station Tom didn't recognise, and the print was already faded. The amount was eighteen dollars.

"Do you know where 'Nim's Petrol' is?"

Ruth's eyes widen in revelation. "Of course! How could I have been so stupid? It's Nimbin."

As she said these words, Fred appeared at the bedroom door.

"It's Nimbin! Lou's aunt owned a cabin there; Lou inherited it when the aunt died. I remember looking through all the paperwork with her. I signed a few things as her Justice of the Peace." Fred thrust the paperwork he'd found in his office at Tom. "I always keep copies of everything I sign," he shrugged, "force of habit."

"God bless you." Tom glanced at the paperwork and saw the address printed at the top of the page. "I'll grab Ava and Shane right now. You two need to sit tight. It's too dangerous for you to be anywhere but here."

They both nodded reluctantly and watched Tom race out the door. In the driveway, Mark was just climbing out of his truck.

"Did you hear from Rebecca?" Tom asked when he saw him.

"No, mate, sorry. But I've figured out where they might be. Lou owns a cabin near Nimbin. I remembered it while I sat at your place — you know, feeling helpless."

"Yep, we figured it out too. We are heading there right now. Thanks."

It would take about an hour to get to Nimbin. Tom radioed the station from his cruiser, organising backup to meet him there. Once done, he looked at Ava.

"Okay, let's collect Shane and head out there."

Ava nodded, while Mark collected his wallet from the console in his truck.

"Mark, mate, you can't come, sorry." Tom said sympathetically.

"Bullshit, Tom. I'm coming. These are my friends we are talking about. Derek is practically family."

Tom sighed in frustration. He had no time to argue, and Mark knew that. "Okay, whatever, just promise me, whatever happens, you stay in the damn car." He glanced at Ava, and she looked back at him defiantly. The woman had spunk.

The drive out to Nimbin was quiet, tense. Ava sat in the back seat next to Mark, and Tom could see her in his rear-view mirror. She stared out the window, biting her nails. Shane was in the front passenger seat. He was reading the file on Helen again, deep in thought, desperate for something to jump out at him he'd missed previously. He studied the photos of her autopsy, looking at every inch, reading every word the coroner had written. Had there been anything that could have led them to Lou before this? He kept seeing Jenny — her lifeless body stuffed inside a wardrobe — and the flame of anger ignited his senses. He took deep breaths, trying to control his emotions.

"Derek has been sleeping with Lou; she starts showing signs of obsession. She kills Helen to get her out of the way, thinking that's what needs to happen for her and Derek to be together.

Then Rebecca arrives; a 'replica' of Helen. That may have pushed her over the edge." Shane spoke his theory in a soft monotone as he looked at the country passing them by.

In the back seat, he heard Ava sigh sadly. Tom glanced at her in the rearview mirror.

"What are you thinking, Ava?"

She glanced at Tom in the mirror. "I'm just trying to figure out how Josh and Jenny ended up getting involved. And who put the photos on your car?"

Mark nodded. "Yeah, I've been thinking about that too. I mean, Lou could have used Josh to get Helen in the first place, then either paid him to leave town, or she's killed him. She then convinces Jenny to help her abduct Rebecca."

"Why would Jenny do something like that?" Shane spoke from the front seat again.

Mark shrugged. "She and Lou have been best friends forever. Maybe Lou convinced her by saying she wouldn't hurt Rebecca."

Tom added, "And it was probably Lou who put the photos on my car, put the lock box under the floorboards in the hostel — all to point to Josh."

"Yeah, but why would she then kill Jenny? Her best friend?" Ava whispered, shaking her head.

"Maybe she discovered Jenny had also slept with Derek and it triggered her," Mark said, before he added hopefully, "Maybe it was an accident?"

"It was no accident," said Tom grimly. "Viraj told me already. Jenny was shot in the back of the head."

Ava let out a soft sob in the back seat. Mark put his arm around her and pulled her close.

Derek arrived at the cabin within forty minutes. He and Lou had been there countless times over the years and could do the drive with his eyes closed.

He knew he shouldn't have left the homestead, but when the phone rang, and he heard Lou's voice, he knew he had to do what she said, or Rebecca would be dead. Just like his Helen.

He was standing by the phone when she rang.

He'd grabbed the handset and spoke into it urgently. "Rebecca?"

"Well, of course you're with Mummy and Daddy, desperately trying to find your precious Rebecca. Always doing what they say."

He froze when he heard her voice as it oozed hatred. He looked around the room and saw everyone staring at him expectantly. He shook his head and turned away from them and said quietly, "Why are you doing this, Lou?"

She laughed through the phone, and Derek detected more than a hint of hysteria. He realised he needed to tread carefully if he didn't want anyone else to die. "What do you want me to do?"

There was an abrupt pause. "I want you to get your arse over here. Now. You have an hour." Lou slammed the phone down in his ear, leaving him shaking. Before anyone could say a word, Derek grabbed his keys and stormed through the house and out the front door. He was getting into the car when his father caught up with him.

"Son, where are you going? You know Tom told everyone to stay put."

"I don't care, Dad. This is my fault. I'm the one who has to sort it out." Derek pulled the door shut, locking his father out, and had driven away before Fred could stop him, or even find out where he was going.

He drove towards Lou's cabin, breaking all the speed limits, and thought of Helen. She had been so beautiful. He knew he had been overly protective, yet he still never thought he had been abusive towards her. Whatever he'd dished out, she'd usually deserved. He sighed wearily. He should have stopped sleeping with Lou years ago, but she had been a hard habit to break. She allowed him to do nearly anything to her, and it was nice to have a woman as strong as Lou, adventurous in bed, who kept in the shadows and lived her own life. She had never been needy until he'd brought Helen home a few years ago. Derek had seen Lou's mental state decline slowly and had ignored it. He never believed she would hurt anyone, and he had made a point of never bringing Helen to their gatherings, knowing it might aggravate Lou. Helen always preferred being with his mother, anyway. He had to admit that as much as he loved Helen, she could be boring sometimes. Now, as he sped towards Lou, he would have swapped this shit to have his boring wife back by his side in a heartbeat.

***

Rebecca had actually dozed off when she heard the knocking on the front door. She listened as Lou opened the door, and she could hear muffled voices as they got closer to the bedroom. The door opened, and Derek stood there. He stared at her for a moment, with a mixture of fear and disbelief on his face. Lou was standing behind him, less than two feet away, and as he turned to Lou, she slowly raised a gun, pointing it directly into his stomach. Derek glanced down, and his eyes widened, fear overtaking every other emotion and settling in.

"I am going to give you one opportunity to tell me what is going on between you and her." She glanced towards Rebecca; a look of disgust hovered briefly on her face.

Derek's face changed from fear back to confusion. "Rebecca? Wait, what?"

He took his eyes briefly from Lou and glanced back at Rebecca, who remained handcuffed to the bed. He noticed her black eye; her nose was bent at a horrible angle, and dried blood covered most of her face. For a moment he forgot about the gun.

"Have you lost the plot, woman?" His head spun back to Lou and saw the look of rage cross her face.

"Have I lost the plot? Have I? You mean, as I watched you parade around with your stupid slut wife, who obviously hated you, and who I finally got out of the way, and now she comes along!" Lou flung her hand towards Rebecca, and Derek ducked, scared the gun would accidentally go off, blowing his head off.

A sob caught in Rebecca's throat as she listened to Lou rant. What the hell were they going to do? She closed her eyes and said a silent prayer, something she had never really done before, and something she knew probably wouldn't have any effect because it was something she had never really done before.

When she opened her eyes, Helen was standing at the foot of the bed. Her back was to Rebecca, and she faced the doorway, looking directly at her husband and his mistress. It seemed so real to Rebecca. Yet Helen was slightly transparent. Rebecca tried to stay focused on Lou and the gun, but a feeling of exhilaration came over her. Helen glanced back at her sister and then disappeared once again.

Lou pointed the gun at Derek once more. "I need you to uncuff her, and you both need to come out to the living room. It's about time we had a little chat." She threw the cuff's key at Derek, and he caught it with a shaky hand. As Lou watched closely, he moved around to the side of the bed, his mind racing furiously, and uncuffed Rebecca's sore, red wrists. He barely glanced at her, afraid of triggering Lou and her weapon.

"Hurry the fuck up!" Lou screeched.

Derek threw his hands in the air defensively. "Alright, alright!"

Rebecca hobbled slowly behind Derek, and Lou moved aside so they could both exit the bedroom while she watched them like a hawk. Lou moved behind Rebecca and pushed her into the living room. She lost her balance and almost fell, grabbing onto Derek's arm to steady herself.

"Don't you touch him!" Lou was so close to her, Rebecca worried her eardrums would burst. She tried to contain the anger rise from her gut and refrained from lashing out at the bitch. The gun at her back kept her in check.

As she passed the kitchen and moved towards the living room, she saw Helen was there again. Helen sat in the same dining chair where Rebecca had previously sat when she was psychically connected to her. She watched Lou now as she crossed the living room and motioned for Derek and Rebecca to sit opposite her on the worn sofa lounge. As Rebecca sat down carefully, she couldn't take her eyes off her twin. Still sitting in the dining room chair. Then, once again, she faded.

"Now, you two are going to tell me what I need to know."

Derek, sitting rigid on the couch next to Rebecca, afraid to speak, only nodded.

Rebecca spoke. "What if you don't like what you hear?"

Lou laughed spitefully. "Well, considering I know everything that's going on, nothing will surprise me."

"Then how come you need to hear it from us?"

Lou spat out her reply, "because I'm sick of everyone sneaking behind my back, pretending to care about me, pretending to give a damn about the poor little girl whose parents were slaves to the rich fuckers, who then continued to get fucked by their son. Jenny wouldn't tell me the truth either. I thought I could count on her. I thought she was my friend. But I was wrong."

"What's Jenny got to do with this?" Rebecca asked.

"Jenny is the one who took you, Rebecca," Derek said quietly, realising she hadn't the chance to see her attacker before being knocked unconscious.

Rebecca's eyes flew open. "Jenny? Sweet Jenny knocked me unconscious?" she said incredulously. "She would never do that," Rebecca said.

"I told her the truth. That you were sleeping with Derek and that I'd found evidence you were planning to kill me." Lou voice was smug.

Rebecca stared at Lou. "And she believed you?"

"Of course she believed me!" Lou screeched, standing and waving the gun around again.

Rebecca glanced at Derek, her eyes warning him to stop poking the beast. She looked around the room. "So, where is Jenny? Surely, she'd stick with you for moral support if she believes this theory."

Lou stared at her, and her eyes inexplicably filled with tears. "We had an argument" she stood and walked to the kitchen and stared out the window.

"About what?" Rebecca asked, trying to keep her talking so she could figure out what to do next.

Lou sighed and turned towards them again. "She told me that killing you wasn't worth it. That I should turn you into the police if you were really planning to kill me. She also said Derek wasn't worth the trouble. That she knew this from first-hand experience," she shrugged. "At first, I was confused. Until I realised what she meant; so, I killed her."

Derek and Rebecca sat unblinking at Lou. Neither of them could tell whether she was trying to scare them, or if she was telling them the truth. Rebecca felt nauseous when she saw a tear slip from Lou's eye.

"Did you kill Josh too?" Rebecca whispered, as Derek tried to come to terms with the casual way Lou had told them she had killed Jenny. Panic accosted his gut and felt bile rise in his throat.

Lou wiped a tear, annoyed at herself. Her brow crinkled for a moment. "Josh? Oh, right, yeah, the guy was an idiot. He had seen Helen around town and thought she was beautiful. I made up a bullshit story to convince him to grab her. Told him she loved fucking strange men. He fell for it, hook, line and sinker." She laughed now, feeling better. Why had she been upset?

Rebecca and Derek watched as Lou wandered back to the armchair opposite the couch. She sat and leaned forward; the gun pointed at Rebecca. She used it to push apart her knees while she stared at her. As she pushed the gun along her left thigh, she glanced at Derek.

"This must turn you on, lover. The idea of the two of us all to yourself," Lou grinned and leaned over, kissing Derek long and hard on the mouth. He tried to pull away, turning his face from her lips. Enraged, Lou growled, "So, it's just her you want?"

Rebecca was so scared that she didn't even see the butt of the gun as it came down swiftly, connecting with her left cheekbone. The pain was excruciating as her head slammed into Derek's shoulder. She kept her face buried against his shoulder, trying not to black out. Her eyes were closed, and the blackness behind them spun with stars. When she tried to open them, the room spun. She worried she would throw up in his lap.

Derek, terrified and helpless, rested his cheek on Rebecca's head.

"Don't move, Rebecca. Try to stay calm until the nausea passes," he whispered. His voice sounded calm, and she slowed her breathing. Derek said, "So, you want to hear that Rebecca, and I are sleeping together?"

Lou laughed, a high-pitched noise that pierced the air. "I know you are, Derek. But you need to say it. Once and for all." She stood up, aiming her gun at Rebecca, the barrel pointing directly at her face.

Lou took another step closer to Rebecca, ready to finally put a bullet in her head. She was about to fire when something knocked into her. Her whole body launched backwards. She flew over the armchair she had been sitting on only a moment before and crashed onto the dining table. The timber structure crumpled under her weight and velocity of impact. As the invisible force struck her, Lou let out a loud 'umph' as the wind left her gut.

Next to Rebecca, Derek cried out in fear as he watched Lou fly, and before he could even say anything, he saw Helen. Her apparition was transparent. She stood looking at him with sadness in her eyes.

Derek sobbed. She was there, his beautiful Helen. She had come back to him.

"Helen, baby?" he reached out his cuffed hands to her, but something pushed him from behind with such force he flew off the couch and knocked his head hard against the coffee table. He crumpled to the floor, out cold.

Staring in amazement, Rebecca was frozen by the power of Helen's spirit. She was feisty in death.

Her ghostly figure stood staring at Rebecca, and neither twin moved. The longer they stared into each other's eyes, the clearer Helen's apparition became. Within a minute, she stood before her sister in solid form.

"Helen?" Rebecca finally breathed.

"Rebecca, my love." Her voice sounded as though she was on a long-distance call. The connection to the real world was weak at best.

"I'm so sorry. Please forgive me." Helen's crackled voice broke, and she reached for Rebecca, desperate for more yet knowing her time in her old world was almost up. She needed the strength to protect her sister one more time.

Behind Helen, Lou stirred. As she tried to stand up, the timber snapped underneath her and she wobbled slightly. She saw Helen, then Rebecca, and confusion swept across her face. After which, a wild look emerged, and she laughed.

"She's lost it entirely," Rebecca thought as she glanced down at Derek, who remained unconscious. She understood her twin's desire to hurt her husband, but she wished she'd waited until after they subdued Lou. A ghost could not protect her from bullets. She had to act while Lou was distracted. And quickly.

A moan escaped Derek, yet he remained still. Rebecca slowly stood from the couch, moving an inch at a time, hoping Helen would keep Lou distracted. She needed distance between herself, and the gun still firmly gripped in Lou's white knuckles.

Moving away from Helen was all it took for their connection to begin fading, but Helen was not about to give up. She took a step towards Lou with a look of pure bemusement on her face.

Lou's laughter died off.

Wait. She had already killed Helen. She looked around and saw the empty couch. Rebecca was standing a few feet away. Confused, Lou took a step away from Helen; or whatever she was now. But her body was paralysed. A whimper of confusion escaped her lips as Helen stretched her pale hands towards Lou, who finally squeezed the trigger.

***

Rebecca watched the moment unfold as though in slow motion - and when Lou fired her weapon - threw herself to the floor, terrified of copping the bullet that was meant for a ghost.

The bullet flew through Helen as though she were air, and past where Rebecca had been standing. It lodged in the front door of the cabin. Lou tried to squeeze another round off but had no time before Helen grabbed Lou's head with both hands. She squeezed with all her might.

{ **38** }

Lou opened her eyes slowly with confusion. The cabin was gone, and she was alone in the night. She spun around, filled with terror. Then she heard a voice. It was Josh.

"Please get in the car."

"Wait, what?" she tried to speak, but no words escaped. She looked down and saw herself in running shoes, a Walkman clipped to her yoga pants. As if in a dream, Lou had no control over her motions, over her own voice. When she spoke, she sounded like someone else. She blinked and was sitting in a car. Josh was next to her, murmuring. She glanced in the rearview mirror and saw Helen staring back at her. Wide eyed Helen. She hated Helen. Helen was dead. Lou shook her head, realising she must be dreaming. Realising she must have knocked herself out when she landed on the table.

Wait, did that happen? What had shoved her so hard she had literally flown into the table? She closed her eyes and counted to five.

When she opened them, the car was gone, and she was back at the cabin. She breathed a sigh of relief and tried to stand up but couldn't. Then she noticed her arms were bound behind her, and her feet bound to the legs of the chair. Lou worried she was going crazy; she was dressed like Helen, and everything seemed real. She tried to protest; but something punched her so hard in the face she cried out in pain. Her head whipped back, and she felt her nose snap. She kept her eyes closed, waiting for the dizziness to stop. When she opened them again, she saw who was assaulting her.

It was herself. Standing in front of her, wearing her constable uniform, staring with pure unadulterated hatred.

"I will kill you tonight," she whispered to herself.

Lou, trapped in Helen's body, smirked. Helen was bemused that her demise would be because of a boy.

"Go ahead, kill me, Lou. Do you really think I care? I'm trapped in this stupid town with a man who controls my every move. Kill me, and have him for yourself," she paused, "he'll never love you though. He'll just keep using you."

Whack! Once again Lou hit her so fiercely, she began to lose consciousness.

"Hey, Lou, maybe take it easy?" Josh stood nervously in the kitchen, just out of earshot, watching the scenario unfold, regretting terribly his decision to help his new friend. He had been told Helen was a willing participant in the kidnapping scenario. Lou had made such a song and dance about what fun it would be to role-play. She had convinced him that Helen led a secret life and enjoyed fucking strangers. What an idiot he was.

"This is not what I signed up for, Lou." He reminded her.

Lou turned to him and smiled. "It's all part of the role-play, but you're right, I'll ease off. Do you want to get her a glass of water?" She said calmly, sweetly.

Josh smiled, relieved. "Of course." He turned towards the sink, and as he did, Lou strode over and shot him point-blank in the back of the head. He crumbled to the floor, completely unaware that he had died.

Helen stared at the dead man on the floor. He was her only way out. For the first time since Josh had snatched her while running a few hours before, fear and sadness welled up inside her. She closed her eyes, bowed her head, and prayed.

***

When Lou opened her eyes, she was lying on the floor of her cabin, with the broken table next to her.

She blinked nervously, trying to gauge whether she was back in reality or if she was still in some alternate reality. She had just watched herself kill Josh, hit Helen, threaten to kill her. Yet, as she relived all these moments, she had felt what Helen had felt. She did not like it. When Helen prayed, she had prayed for Lou.

Glancing around at her surroundings, she saw Derek still slumped over unconscious in front of the couch, and Lou realised only a few minutes had passed since her weird out-of-body experience, or time warp, or whatever it was.

What she knew was that enough time had passed for Rebecca to slip away. Where the hell was she? She needed them both here, sitting next to each other, to admit their little affair to her. Then she could kill Rebeca and finally keep Derek all to herself. Steadying herself, she walked over and sat on the couch, Derek at her feet. Gingerly she stroked his hair, trying to help him regain consciousness. Didn't he realise she had done all of this just to protect him?

"Derek? Sweetheart?" Lou ran her fingers through his hair, feeling the softness of his skin, and the dampness in his pores. Finally, he stirred, his eyes opening with disorientation. Registering on Lou's face as she peered above him, a look of love and concern edged in her face. It was a stark contrast to the pure rage he had seen only moments before.

"What happened?"

"Rebecca hurt you; she's gotten away."

"Wait, what? Rebecca? What do you mean? Why are we here? What's going on? Where's Helen?"

Lou sighed and stroked his cheek lovingly. "Oh, babe, she must have hit you hard." She smiled sympathetically at him. "Helen's dead, baby." She breathed.

Derek became irritable. "I know she's dead, Lou. You killed her." His voice hardened and he ducked away as her hand stroked his head. "Why did you kill her? She did nothing to hurt you. Ever."

Lou's expression changed, and she stood quickly. A frantic insanity filled the air, and she began pacing. Desperate to explain.

"Don't you realise? She was always taking you for granted. She never loved you. After everything you did for her, she just didn't care. You always chose her over me. I was okay with that — well, I would have been if she had been a good wife. But she was never good to you, Derek. You know yourself how much trouble you had keeping her in line. She was always so shy and pathetic. Always with your mum. She would never go out with you. She was just not right for you." Lou finally paused. Derek was staring at her, unblinking.

"So, you killed her?"

"So, we could finally be together! Don't you see?!" She knelt down in front of him on the floor, grabbing his knees, staring up at him, desperate for him to finally see her after all these years. "I love you."

Derek sighed, thinking slowly about how he could get himself out of this mess.

He had no idea where Rebecca had gone, and for all he knew, Lou had already killed her. He must have dreamt the entire scene with Helen. It must have been a struggle between Rebecca and Lou, not Helen and Lou. Rebecca had knocked him out, and he must just be confused. And now he needed to defuse this situation before she killed him too.

"Okay, babe, you're right. And I love you too. I'm so sorry I hurt you. I see it now. All you've ever done was try to help me." He stared at Lou as she gazed at him. He had known her since they were kids. Had always known she was slightly crazy. She'd had a pretty poor upbringing and had always hung around him wanting to be a part of his life. When he finally started sleeping with her, it was just for fun, and when she became a cop, it also made his life easier.

She was an excellent distraction whenever Helen was annoyed at him, or he got bored, or he needed to release some energy, and besides, Lou was always willing to do what he wanted, and his libido demanded it.

He was a man after all.

He had just never realised Lou had become so obsessed with him. She was always just there to accommodate him. Always complacent, seething with resentment.

{ 39 }

Rebecca was hiding behind the couch, only a metre from Lou and Derek while she listened to Lou's ranting and Derek's desperation. She clamped her left hand firmly over her mouth, and squeezed her eyes shut, and silently begged Helen to help her one more time. A tear slipped down her cheek, but she was too afraid to wipe it away. Her brain was going crazy as she listened to Lou's ranting. All she wanted to do was lash out, kill Lou for taking her twin away from her forever. Her rage also filtered through to Derek.

If only she had stopped Helen all those years ago when she first met him. If only she hadn't stayed out of it, fearing the worst and hoping for the best. So, most of all, she was screaming at herself. The self-hatred bubbled to the surface, and she worried it would erupt. Closing her eyes, Rebecca counted to five, knowing she needed to get control of herself and get out of this alive.

She glanced around, looking for a weapon of any kind. Her hands remained cuffed and clanked with even the slightest move. Any moment she would glance up and see Lou's face looming over her. To her right was a dresser that sat under one window. It held a lamp and a few stacked blankets for cold winter nights. To her left was the front door. If Lou walked a few feet to the front door, it would expose her hiding place. She would only need to glance down, and it would be game over. Closing her eyes, she implored her brain to settle down. She needed a moment to think.

When she opened her eyes a moment later, Helen was sitting in front of her.

Sitting cross - legged on the floor, the two women were almost knee to knee.

Helen smiled.

Too shocked to even breathe, Rebecca stared, unblinking.

Helen's outfit was directly from their 'grungy' years. She wore a pair of ripped jeans and a 'Use Your Illusion' Guns and Roses t-shirt. Each of them had purchased one when they had seen them live in the early nineties. Helen's hair was shorter, a relaxed, shaggy quality from her youth, when she had spent way too much time every morning ensuring the 'casual' style stayed in place.

So close, Rebecca was sure that if she were to reach her hand out she would be able to touch her twin's soft, delicate skin beneath the tips of her fingers. The idea terrified her, and she kept her hands locked together in her lap. Helen continued to smile.

But a change had begun. The grunge shaggy hair grew longer, and her clothes faded, only to be replaced by a pair of culottes. Rebecca's culottes. Helen's nose blurred, as a crooked, blood-caked one appeared in its place, a gash on her forehead encroached her smooth pale skin and a swollen left eye, puffy, black, and half closed, replaced the emerald sparkle.

The twins were now identical in every way.

***

Positive she was going mad, just like Lou, Rebecca blinked rapidly.

Helen grinned at her, and without warning, stood upright. The perfect distraction to allow Rebecca a chance to survive. This was Helen's one shot and she was determined not to screw it up.

Lou jumped back in surprise when she saw Helen emerge from behind the couch. Fury swelled inside her gut. Of course she was behind the bloody couch. People don't just disappear.

Wishing for a chance to sneak a peek, Rebecca restrained herself, pressed against the back of the worn-out sofa, out of sight.

Derek saw Lou's expression and followed her glance. Rebecca was back! What a stupid woman. Before even considering the consequence, he yelled, "Get out of here, Rebecca, run!"

Helen just smiled and sauntered casually towards the woman who had killed her, never allowing her gaze to falter.

Perplexed at Rebecca's behaviour, Derek worried she'd received one too many blows to the head. Until the most remarkable thing happened: her appearance transformed. She became translucent, and her clothes morphed into her running gear. Her smile faded, and she stared at the man she had once loved. She shook her head, and Derek could see the grief coming off her in waves.

"Helen?" he whispered. His voice wavered in denial as he stared at his wife.

"No, it's not possible," Lou muttered to herself. "This is not real. This is not real. I killed her." She looked at Derek with desperation, and then back to Helen.

"I fucking killed her!" With one smooth sweep of her arm, she gestured towards Helen, and her gun fired. The bullet moved so smoothly and quickly through Helen's apparition, it lodged itself in the bedroom door behind her.

Derek and Lou stared in awe; and Helen began to laugh. No sound escaped her lungs, and she shook her head in pity. Spinning on her heel she glided through the living wall and into the bedroom.

Doors be damned.

Lou forgot all about Rebecca. In untapped rage, a howl of outrage and fury escaped her lungs. She ran after Helen, flinging the bedroom door open so hard it hit the wall and splintered the plaster, lodging the doorknob in place.

Rebecca could hear the commotion but stayed in place until she was sure Lou was no longer in the room. Finally, she peeked over the couch to see her brother-in-law still sitting, dumbfounded, as he stared after Lou.

"Derek," she whispered, so close to his ear, he yelped in fright.

"Shut up unless you want her to come back in here", she hissed. "We need to get out of here while she's distracted."

Derek turned to see the real Rebecca behind him. The poor girl looked awful, and Derek felt a pang of guilt. Just a pang. If she'd stayed in New York, none of this would have happened.

"She's gone. You should run for help. I don't think she plans to kill me," he whispered without confidence.

"Unless she realises, I'm gone, and Helen disappears again," Rebecca whispered back, already manoeuvring into an upright position. She backed towards the front door of the cabin, keeping her eyes firmly on the doorway into the bedroom, anticipating Lou to reappear and begin blindly shooting again. Fear oozed from every pore of her skin and dripped off her in beads of sweat.

Derek nodded in encouragement, so she spun around, using both cuffed hands to grab the doorknob and twist. In terror, she kept her head swivelled, her eyes firmly planted on the bedroom doorway. Yanking the front doorknob, it groaned away from the frame, and gave way. Rebecca bolted.

Right into something hard and large. Firm hands grabbed her upper arms, and she thought, "I'm done for."

Sobbing, she looked up and saw Tom holding her, his face full of relief and fear and absolute love.

{ 40 }

Tom, Ava, Mark and Shane had arrived at the cottage ten minutes before Lou had fired the first round. They had parked a few hundred metres back from the driveway entrance and scrambled out of the car in silence, securing their vests and ensuring their weapons were ready. Mark sat in the backseat, sulking only slightly.

The three had then spread out, each with their hands on their holsters, stealthily moving alongside the thick shrub and foliage that adorned the dirt driveway.

* * *

Mark stared out the window. He felt helpless, worrying his fiancée was walking towards certain death.

Tom had no idea what to expect, but decided not to wait for backup, which was still an hour away. It was early dawn, and time was of the absolute essence.

Tom listened to the morning songs of birds while he walked in silence towards the cabin. He cursed the universe and its antics as he closed in on Lou. How could birds be singing when the woman he loved was being held hostage?

He then heard the loud, clear gunshot ring out through the woods, validating his feelings. His knees almost buckled, and the overpowering urge to yell Rebecca's name and scramble without rhyme or reason towards the cabin almost seized control of him.

He glanced at Ava, who was about fifteen feet to his right, slightly in front of him. She was already at the left side of the cabin. Everyone froze, and Ava and Shane kept their eyes on Tom, waiting for his signal.

Ava silently begged Mark to stay in the car.

***

Mark jumped out of the car when he heard the shot ring out. It was so loud he jumped, causing the car to shake, which interrupted a wallaby as it searched for breakfast. It bolted in fright, disappearing into the thick bush.

Mark glanced around, unsure of what to do, but terrified Ava was about to die. She was his life. He could not lose her. Suddenly he didn't care that she was doing her job, worried her newfound strong, unwavering friendship with Rebecca, would lead her to make poor decisions. He felt bad for not trusting her, but only for a moment.

He looked around the ground, found a large, thick, broken tree branch, studied its usefulness as a weapon, and headed towards the cabin.

***

Shane trembled slightly when he heard the gunfire. His field training and prior army experience ensured he would not waver in times of war; however, he had worked alongside Lou since his first day as a junior constable and was still unable to reconcile the woman he trusted and served with, and the potential crazy woman she might be.

Shane suspected it was Derek who had killed Helen. He always thought the guy was shady. He once watched him drink a Midori Splice at a party. Intentionally. Anyone who could stomach that shit surely had a few screws loose. Shane steadied his hand that held his weapon and said a silent prayer for everyone in the house, as he crept towards the cabin in the woods.

He reached the right-side of the cabin a moment later, and Tom motioned for he and Ava to continue flanking either side of the house, which would bring them into the backyard, surrounding anyone who might be ready to go out the back door.

The cabin was smaller than Tom had imagined, which relieved him. The idea of clearing a house with multiple rooms, of a floor plan he had no knowledge of, was not his idea of a good day at the office.

He watched as his two constables disappeared on either side of the house and silently asked the universe to watch out for them.

An unstable porch was a few feet in front of him, and he moved silently up the three steps, closing in on the front door, prepared for anything.

What he was not prepared for was the door to fling open, and Rebecca literally fall into his arms.

But the door flung open, and Rebecca literally fell into his arms. They stared at one another, dumbfounded, and he was about to said something like "Thank god you're okay!" or "Holy shit you scared me!" but her eyes widened with fear, and she whispered hoarsely, "we need to run. *Now!*"

Tom's years of training kicked in automatically, and he grabbed her firmly, turned on his heel and hurried out of the opening of the doorway, more than aware of the danger.

From inside the cabin, he heard a loud, frustrated scream. It was not a scream he had ever heard before. The visceral sound sent chills down his spine as he frantically looked for a spot to hide Rebecca, so afraid of losing her, just as he had hold of her again.

Whatever Banshee was inside the house would not stay inside for long, especially if Rebecca was what it was hunting.

He half carried, half dragged Rebecca around the side of the cabin. As they reached the backyard, they found Ava, who was crouched down, hiding out of sight below the back porch. She glanced at Tom and then saw her friend. Ava's breathing eased, and her heart was freed from the vice in her chest. She motioned for them to get down.

Rebecca marvelled at Ava's professional stance as she crouched, her weapon drawn, her eyes furrowed in concentration. And fear. And relief. Rebecca held back the tears, worried they would actually hurt her skin if released. She felt safe with Tom and Ava, and now realised she hurt, a lot. Everywhere. She tried to focus on the task at hand. Stay still and quiet until Tom got Lou into custody.

Shane still hovered on the other side of the house. His back flanked by timber, his gun faced toward the ground, its muzzle waiting patiently to fire. He listened carefully, hoping to hear something coming from inside the house, but it stood silent at his back. The longer he waited, the more nervous he became.

Finally, he took three side steps — like a lanky, terrified crab slinking into open waters — and tripped over a large branch that protruded from underneath the house. He landed daintily because he had learned ballet when he was a kid and managed not to fire his weapon into his own kneecap.

He stayed still for a moment, face to the dirt, expecting Lou or Derek to charge at him from a secret location, but all stayed quiet. He rolled over to confront the branch.

But it was not a branch. It was a leg. Shane stared uncomprehendingly. He glanced to his left, lowering his head to peer underneath the cabin, which sat precariously on mounds of bricks. Ironically, he was relieved to see the leg attached to a body.

It was unfortunate, however, to see that the body was badly decomposed and buried in a shallow grave. He scuttled on his arse to move closer and realised his assessment of 'buried' was premature. The man was so carelessly buried one might believe a toddler had used a bucket and spade to do the job.

Shane sat for a moment. He continued to stare at the leg. It was almost too much.

First Jenny, and now a leg? How much was one guy supposed to handle in a day? He sighed into the silence and carefully picked himself up, dusting himself off and collecting his pistol, resuming his alert stance and trying to ignore the pungent smell of mouldy cheese that wafted from the body. He continued past the house and into the backyard.

It was deserted, the clearing only small, with a mass of tall grass and weeds growing out of control until it reached the line of the property and morphed into thick native bush-land. Shane hoped to God that whatever was happening in the house, it wouldn't move to the outside of the house, right as he stood exposed in the backyard. He thought of being shoved under a house, or pretzelled in a wardrobe, and shivered.

In his periphery he saw movement and twisted his body, bringing his gun up to attention. But it was Tom and Ava, and they had Rebecca with them. His eyes widened, and he held his hand up flat to show peace and quickly lowered his gun. Tom motioned for Shane to take Rebecca to safety so he and Ava could move into the house.

Tom looked at Shane oddly when he moved towards them and took Rebecca by the arm, leading her back to where they had just emerged from. There was no way Shane was planning on subjecting her to what he'd just seen on the 'leg' side.

Within moments, Rebecca was ushered to the safety of the house with the fewest windows and decomposing bodies. The two of them crouched down together and waited.

$$\{\ 41\ \}$$

When Lou stormed back into the living room, irate that Helen had disappeared again, she stopped short, blinking rapidly. The room was empty. She was feeling very confused, and as her head continued to pound; a weird tingling sensation crept behind her eyes. She turned slowly, peering steadily through the confusion. They couldn't have gone far. A guttural sound escaped from deep within her, resulting in a scream. She raised her gun and began firing blindly as she turned in a circle. If she couldn't yell at them to come back, she could remind them of just how serious she was.

Derek almost made it to the front door when he heard Lou coming back. He threw himself behind the couch a moment before she emerged and squeezed his eyes closed when Lou started firing her gun like a lunatic. The couch was no comfort to him, and he knew that if she fired into it, he was a dead man. He needed to get out of there but was out of ideas.

He opened his eyes, expecting to see Lou standing over him smugly, but his hiding place was safe. The back of the couch was close to the front window, with only a couple of feet in between. He glanced out and saw a figure crouching just below the broken balustrade of the old porch. He could see only a dark head of hair. Derek breathed a sigh of relief. Thank

Christ someone had arrived, silently praying the person wasn't alone. He had the urge to pull back the old lace curtain and tap on the window but restrained himself. He then saw the person move. A pair of eyes emerged, peering over the porch and into the living room. It was Mark. Derek broke into a stupid grin, ecstatic to see his mate outside.

Lou stopped firing when she needed to reload, and at the back of the house, Tom chose that moment to open the back door. He had seen her through the back kitchen window, firing aimlessly, enraged by something Tom was not privy to see or understand. He saw her growl in fury at her empty chamber, rush into another room, and slam the door closed behind her. It was his moment to make entry. Silent, with his gun raised and in firing position he entered the cabin.

Ava had moved around to the front of the house. And spotted Mark crouching in the dead garden bed below the porch. She threw him a scolding glance, like that of a mother with a toddler, before she mounted the stairs, and waited for Tom to open the front door and let her in.

Within a moment she was greeted by Tom, who opened the front door, deciding to leave it wide open so as not to hinder a quick exit. They both surveilled the living room, looking for movement.

Tom spotted Derek crouching a couple of feet from where they stood. Their eyes locked, and Derek almost cried with relief. Tom motioned for him to get outside and Derek nodded, indicating to where Lou was, before bolting out the front door.

Tom and Ava stood motionless, flanking either side of the bedroom door. Waiting for Lou to emerge.

***

Lou stood alone in the bedroom. She had not slammed the door shut, had she? Why would she do that? She stared at the door, her gun resting against her right thigh. A heavy tiredness settled over her, and she closed her eyes, wishing she could curl up on her bed, and sleep. Her body was lethargic, and her brain was like fog as she tried to think about what to do next. "Where the hell was her cartridge?"

She opened her eyes again and blinked at her bedroom. The bed was in disarray, and she remembered the times she and Derek had made love. Sighing, she allowed her mind to drift back to those days, and her vision blurred. A tear escaped, and she wiped it away, determined to get herself together.

Her satchel was by the bed, and elated again, pushed the memories aside, and reached for the remaining cartridge, smacking it into the gun, and locking it in place.

Outside the bedroom door, Tom heard Lou reload her weapon. He quickly announced his presence before she had the time to exit and become startled, forcing him to make a lethal decision.

"Don't shoot, Lou. It's Tom." His voice was soft, strong and commanding.

Silence.

Tom glanced at Ava and saw her furrowed brow. She stared intently at the bedroom door, wishing for it all to be over, praying everything could go back to normal.

Behind the door, Lou froze. 'How had it come to this?' She looked down at her gun, wondering why she was holding it.

To her left, the wardrobe door opened. Its old hinges whined at the movement, as it revealed the contents. Lou stared at the open cupboard. "Who's there?" she whispered.

Outside the bedroom door, Tom could hear Lou whispering, but he couldn't make out her words. He leaned in closer, trying to understand. The whispering stopped. And a scratching noise started. It was on the wall separating the bedroom and living room. It sounded like mice behind the plaster, scurrying around, chewing wires. On cue, the lights flickered.

Ava's furrowed brow became a deep scowl as she took her eyes off the door and glanced around the room behind her. She felt a breeze on her back before the lights flickered off completely. Natural light filtered through the windows from the sheltered woods outside, now bathing the cabin.

Dawn was in full bloom, and she could hear the wildlife enjoying their morning activity. Her heart fluttered, and she turned toward the window, expecting to see it open. However, all the windows were closed.

Another shiver ran down her spine and her eyes met Tom's, who stood staring at her, totally spooked. His expression almost made her laugh. Gone was the tough, authoritative exterior. Now he just looked scared shitless.

From inside the bedroom, Lou began whispering again in gibberish. Ava listened, desperate to understand what she was saying, yet unable to distinguish anything clearly.

She shook her head at Tom, who shrugged, as though trying to shrug off his fear. "Suck it up, big fella," he said to himself.

He took a deep breath and said again, "Lou? We know you are there, and we are here to help. Please open the door so we can help you."

Lou was beyond help. She could hear Tom outside the door, but she knew he wasn't there to help her. He would shoot her in the heart as soon as he had the chance. She supposed it didn't really matter. Her heart was already broken.

The whispering intensified from behind the wardrobe door. Still afraid, but determined to figure out who was there, she leaned in closer. It was two people whispering. But it wasn't Tom. Whoever was in her great-aunt's antique wardrobe - like freaking Nania -continued their relentless chatter. She became infuriated that two people were sitting in her wardrobe. It must be Derek and Helen. No wait. Rebecca. The bitch was trying to confuse her again. It was the only explanation.

"It's no use!" she screeched. "I know you're both in there! He doesn't love you anymore, Helen." They needed to realise they were trapped.

The whispering stopped.

Tom and Ava jumped in unison when Lou yelled. He looked at Ava, puzzled, and mouthed, "Helen?"

Ava shrugged and couldn't help rolling her eyes. How come no one had noticed how crazy this woman was?

Tom sighed. He was exhausted and now, annoyed.

"Lou?" he tried again. "Derek's not here; it's just me and Ava. We are here to help you."

Inside the bedroom, Lou paused. "Ava was there too?" She didn't understand. Why were they all at her secret cabin? Her head pounded again, and she drew up her gun, knocking the side of her skull with the butt of the weapon. The whispering from the wardrobe increased.

"Just stop talking!" she screeched.

Tom fell silent, but from inside the wardrobe, the whispering intensified. Lou still couldn't understand what they were talking about, but she knew it was about her. She heard Helen giggle, and it infuriated her. Or was it, Rebecca? That's it. She drew her weapon, pointed it directly at the wardrobe and fired.

On the other side of the wall, Ava dove onto the floor for cover. She landed with an "oomph" on her stomach as a bullet flew through the wardrobe and wall, passing her head and lodging into the load-bearing post behind her.

Tom moved fast when he saw Ava launch out of harm's way. He flung open the bedroom door with such stealth that by the time Ava rolled onto her back, her weapon aimed in front of her, Tom was no longer in position, and the bedroom door stood open.

"Shit," she cursed under her breath. Her ears were ringing from the gunfire, and her breathing was heavy. She waited only a moment before shimmying to her right so she could get a glimpse of the bedroom beyond and be ready for action when Tom needed her.

There was nowhere to take cover when Tom entered the bedroom. Lou stood to his left facing a wardrobe.

His favourite senior constable no longer had a look of quiet confidence and brazen determination to succeed. Someone unrecognisable had replaced her, and he berated himself for missing the slippery slope Lou had been on over the last months, or even years.

He had never picked up on chemistry between Lou and Derek, never even contemplated they might know each other more than casual group friends. He wondered for a moment if his sixth sense was slipping before shrugging off the idea. He raised his weapon and aimed it at Lou.

"Lou, honey. It's over."

His voice interrupted Lou's obsession with the wardrobe and she stumbled back in shock, spinning around to see Tom. Lou stared blankly at him. Why was he here?

"Do you know where Helen is? And Derek? I've been looking for them" Lou's voice sounded soft and in control, but Tom could see she was completely disassociated from reality.

"Why are you looking for them? Tom's calm voice was a stark juxtaposition to the gun trained on her.

Lou blinked and glanced around the bedroom. "Tom?" she said.

"Yeah, Lou, it's me."

Lou nervously looked around, and then back at her boss. "I don't understand what's happening." Her voice quivered, and she shook.

Tom took a tentative step closer. "I'm here to help you."

Lou nodded and repeated, "Yes, good. I'm looking for Derek. Have you seen him?"

"He's outside," Tom smiled reassuringly, and Lou nodded, relieved.

"I'll need you to put the gun down, though. No here wants to hurt you."

"Helen's hiding somewhere here," she stated, glancing nervously at the cupboard again.

"No, Lou, Helen's dead, honey." He studied her closely as the realisation settled over her.

Nodding, she turned and walked towards the window. Tense, still ready to fire, Tom watched as she stared out to the bushland beyond, her back towards him.

"I have been in love with him since I was a kid," she shrugged, a smile playing on her lips. "I realise now though. He never loved me." She raised her gun, wedging it firmly under her chin. "Sorry, Tom. I never wanted to disappoint you."

Lou closed her eyes and within a second felt the bullet enter her body.

However, her brain remained intact.

Lou's eyes flew open in shock as the bullet entered her shoulder, forcing her into a delicate spin. The gun flew from her hand and landed with a thud on the floor next to the bed.

The bullet whizzed by Tom's head, causing him to yelp. Ava was few feet from him; her weapon still trained on Lou.

Ava's shot was made with exact precision and timing, passing Tom, and entering Lou's right shoulder, forcing the gun from her hand before she could pull the trigger and take her own life.

There was no way Ava was going to let her off the hook that easily.

Lou cried out in pain, her eyes wide with surprise as she stared at her colleagues.

Tom sagged with relief and looked at Ava who whispered, "No more death, Lou. Enough is enough."

{ **42** }

Tom handcuffed Lou, mindful of her injury, and guided her to the bed. She was awake, but subdued, confused and uncommunicative. He found a shirt in the dresser next to the wardrobe and wrapped her shoulder wound as best he could.

Ava secured the rest of the house and headed outside. The others sat on the driveway, away from the house. Shane had grabbed the first-aid kits from the car, and Mark was tending to Derek's face. Shane was talking to Rebecca, making sure she stayed back from the house while tending to her wounds. It was a hard job. When they had heard all the gunfire, the three men almost had to tackle her to the ground to stop her from racing inside.

The group looked at Ava anxiously when she appeared on the porch, and she stated, "Everyone's okay, but Shane, can you please run to the car and radio for an ambulance? I subdued Lou with a shoulder shot. She'll be fine."

Rebecca sagged with relief. "Am I allowed inside?"

"It's safer if we all stay out here. Lou is confused, and even though she's docile at the moment; seeing you may spark another episode."

Rebecca nodded. "Yeah, okay." She turned to her brother-in-law and said, "Let's wait on the front steps," and walked away without waiting for his reply.

All five of them ended up sitting on the porch while waiting for the cavalry to arrive. Ava returned to the house and made them all coffee. Each stared into the bushland, lost in their own thoughts, drinking lukewarm instant International Roast as the sun rose higher into the sky. It was another perfect day.

***

Lou lay handcuffed to the bed dosed with morphine Tom found the medical kit. She was asleep and comfortable.

He wanted to secure the house and take photos of poor Josh half buried under the house, but he was beyond exhausted. Shane had driven to the nearest service station, spoken to their superior in Lismore, who instructed them all to stay put. Another detective would arrive to take over the investigation. Tom was under strict instructions to stay away from the evidence as best possible. The fact one of his own constables had murdered three people; well, it would not look great on his resume.

As he sipped his coffee, he wondered if it was time to consider a new line of work. He honestly didn't care, as long as he had Rebecca by his side. He looked over at her as she gripped her coffee mug, occasionally gulping the warm brown liquid, and stared into the void, thinking of Helen; of what had unfolded. Still shocked she had survived; she knew her sister had saved her. Her heart felt full yet ached at the same time.

Tom put his arm around her, pulling her in, and she rested her head in his shoulder. He considered telling her about the interference they had experienced in the house but knew there'd be time for that.

Derek sat by himself on the steps. Sipping coffee, he thought of his relationship with Lou. How had he not seen how unstable she was? Deep down he knew he should never have used her the way he did, but he was not ready to face those demons.

He thought of Helen. Never having taken religion or the afterlife seriously, the last few hours felt surreal. She had saved him, but not without communicating how disappointed in him she was. He'd seen it in her eyes. Had felt it when she projected him off the couch, he thought it was done in anger, but he realised it had been to protect him. She had died because of him, and she still saved him. He put his head down and sobbed, succumbing to the guilt.

***

Within an hour, the police and ambulance arrived, and not far behind them were Ruth and Fred. Derek saw his parents driving towards the cabin in their truck, their heads bouncing with the truck's suspension on the dirt road.

His eyes crinkled with worry. They would never forgive him. Hell, they were probably here for Rebecca. He lowered his head in shame and stared into his empty coffee cup.

When he looked up again, Ruth was rushing towards him, her arms outstretched, a look of fear and relief painted on her aging face.

"Oh, my son, you're alive." She sobbed, throwing herself into his unprepared embrace.

Derek crumbled into his mother's arms, and they clung to one another. Fred stood back for a moment, allowing his heartbeat to slow down, tears freely escaping down his cheeks. He watched his wife and son reunite for a moment, wiped his eyes and thanked the Lord, before moving into his family's waiting embrace.

Rebecca watched the Cox's reunion from the back of the open ambulance. She was unconvinced their reconciliation would be a lasting one, unless Derek's brush with death scared the narcissism out of him. She prayed for Ruth and Fred's sake that they could look forward to some semblance of a healthy relationship.

Ava sat next to her in the ambulance, her head resting on Rebecca's shoulder, their hands entwined. She was tired, yet completely wide awake. Unsure she'd ever be able to close her eyes without seeing Jenny's blank, empty eyes staring back at her, an involuntary shudder escaped her. Thank God the department offered counselling.

Rebecca would always have Helen, but as Ava squeezed her hand reassuringly while the paramedic applied some god-awful liquid to her broken face, she felt blessed to have found Ava. She glanced at Tom and Mark as they spoke to the other cops who'd arrived. Both men would glance up every few moments to make sure the women were okay. She smiled reassuringly at Tom, and he grinned at her and winked.

The paramedic interrupted her thoughts by telling her she needed to have her nose reset at the hospital and asked her if she'd like some pain relief.

"Hell, yes," she answered so quickly it made Ava giggle.

"Not a problem, ma'am. Are you allergic to anything?"

Rebecca shook her head, and within moments felt the morphine surge through her veins. She lay back on the stretcher bed and closed her eyes. The tears finally arrived. And once they began, they wouldn't quit.

"Oh, honey," Ava began stroking her hair with one hand, and beckoning Tom over with the other. "It'll be okay. You're safe now."

Rebecca cried harder. A moment later, Tom swapped with Ava as she climbed out of the ambulance and made her way back to Mark.

***

Josh's body was bagged. Both Viraj and Jerry's teams had arrived without Ava even realising. She watched as Josh was loaded into the coroner's van, and watched Lou get wheeled out on a stretcher, ready to be loaded into the second ambulance. Everyone was relieved that she was cuffed to the bed, for when she passed the first ambulance and saw Rebecca, she started screaming like a banshee.

It was when Lou began screeching that Helen was a witch and was going to kill everyone, that Rebecca finally stopped crying. If she had not just almost died, she may have even laughed.

By the time the paramedics were ready to take Rebecca to the hospital it was mid-morning. She called out to Ruth, who climbed into the ambulance, passing Tom as he climbed out, like a baton team on the track field. The two women hugged fiercely, and Ruth smothered Rebecca with kisses any little girl would dream of from a doting mother.

Rebecca sighed with contentment. "Will you come to the hospital?" she asked.

"I don't plan on leaving your side darling."

Rebecca nodded, refusing to cry again. She smiled at Ruth and said goodbye, offering an exhausted wave to both Fred and Derek.

Tom handed his car keys to Ava, "Can you get Shane home safely?"

Ava nodded, and watched as he climbed in next to Rebecca, eager to get out of the woods and the creepy-arse cabin once and for all.

They hugged fiercely, afraid to contemplate what life could have been like if they had lost one another so soon after meeting. Tom pulled back to study Rebecca's swollen face, the black and blue bruising, and her nose bent and swollen. Her wounds of war showcased just how much she had survived.

"I love you. So much" was all he could muster.

Smiling gently, Rebecca leaned in to kiss him. "I love you too. Thanks for coming to rescue me."

Chuckling, Tom pulled away from her and buckled his seatbelt as the paramedic driver started the engine. Slowly, it drove down the dirt driveway, away from the cabin. Rebecca stared out the back window, watching the cabin grow smaller.

As the ambulance paused before turning onto the bitumen, Rebecca's heart quickened. Helen emerged from the cabin. She stood on the front porch. Her auburn hair shone brightly and hung simply to her breasts. Gone was the blood-soaked running gear; she now glowed in a long yellow sundress. Her skin shimmered with a summer tan, and her emerald eyes sparkled.

She looked at the ambulance as it transported her sister to a new life. She smiled one last time at Rebecca and raised her hand in a wave, as her other hand pulled the cabin door shut behind her, closing the door to her violent death.

Rebecca stretched out her arm, her fingers spread wide, wishing she could reach Helen one last time. Instead, she watched in silence as her twin glided gracefully away from the cabin and slowly vanished before her eyes.

The End

The End